E D I N B U R G H

EDINBURGH

For Julie —
With best of luck for
your novel —
It's been a pleasure
to meet you.

ALEXANDER CHEE

PICADOR

NEW YORK

www.picadorusa.com

Picador ® is a U.S. registered trademark and is used by St. Martin's Press under license from Pan Books Limited.

For information on Picador Reading Group Guides, as well as ordering, please contact the Trade Marketing department at St. Martin's Press.
Phone: 1-800-221-7945 extension 763
Fax: 212-677-7456
E-mail: trademarketing@stmartins.com

Library of Congress Cataloging-in-Publication Data

Chee, Alexander
    Edinburgh / Alexander Chee.
       p. cm.
    ISBN 0-312-30503-6
    1. Adult child sexual abuse victims—Fiction. 2. Korean Americans—Fiction.
3. Gay youth—Fiction. 4. Choirboys—Fiction. 5. Maine—Fiction. I. Title.

PS3603.H44 E35 2001
813'.6—dc21   2001045539

First published by Welcome Rain Publishers LLC, New York

First Picador Edition: November 2002

D 10 9 8 7 6

P R O L O G U E

AFTER HE DIES, missing Peter for me is like swimming in the cold spot of the lake: everyone else laughing in the warm water under some too-close summer sun. This is the answer to the question no one asks me.

The time that I think will be the last time I see Peter, isn't, as it happens. There'd be one more to come.

My grandfather lost his six older sisters to the Japanese during World War II. Gone and never heard from again. Comfort women was what the Japanese called those they stole for their soldiers. They were girls, though.

My grandfather tells me the first stories I hear about what a great animal the fox is when I am a child. Foxes rescuing children in danger, foxes with magic rings. *Korean name, Yowu.* Years later when I read in college about how the fox is a demon in Japan, I think of him. I ask him about it when I come home and see him next.

Anything kill Japanese, my friend, he says. Fox, bomb, Chinese. Anything. My friend. He's a gaunt now, hollowed, a silver-haired hat rack, beautiful in the way of anything missing something else. He has a picture of his mother and sisters on his wall, beautiful women almost identical to each other in the manner of old families. Of his sisters my grandfather has one left, born after the others had been stolen. He'll die still missing these sisters who used to run along the beach tossing him back and forth between them.

After his sisters were taken away, the Japanese occupying force sent my grandfather to Imperial Schools. My first language is Japanese, he tells me. English far away. But, okay. Be like a fox, he says. Okay. Sometimes, right after he told me, I would look at him and wonder what it felt like, to have the print of your enemy all the way inside you, right into the way you shaped your thoughts. But I know now.

The fox-demon often takes the shape of a beautiful girl. You fall in love with her and she leaves and you live for thirty days more afterward and die of missing her. She can breathe a fireball, a will-o'-the-wisp of electric air. When she marries another fox the sun shines and rain falls, at the same time, for one day. It's considered good luck, days like this, for the fox trouble ends for that day. Fox-demons can change their shapes at will, assuming the forms of lost loves long dead. There are stories of how noblemen and their wives in ancient Japan had picnics and watched the foxes change shape on the hillside, transforming from armies to castles and back again in ritual battles. When possessed by a fox-demon you can fly and walk through walls. You can hear the demon speak through you in a second voice.

The Lady Tammamo was a fox who fell in love with a man and took the shape of a woman in order to marry him. Her hair remained red and so she was feared, for at that time in Korea the only people with red hair were said to be demons. She was very beautiful, in the way of fox-demons, and her husband loved her. And she loved him.

She bore her husband children, all sons. After some trouble in their village, for which she was blamed, they left and moved to a tiny island between Korea and Japan where they settled and were accepted by the fishermen there, who had seen many things and were not afraid of her. I'll be safe here, she told her husband. And she was. Rumored to be from Mongolia, she told people, when they asked her where her clan was from, that it was a place where the sky bent the earth.

When her husband died and his family came to burn his body, she stood by him and stoked the fire under him. Her husband's family watched her, afraid. Would she turn back into a fox, now that her husband was dead, and kill them all? Make their skulls into helmets and hunt the fishermen? She smiled at them, pressed her hand to her husband's cold face, and stepped up onto the fire, which then rose until the family could not see them. The fox can breathe a fireball, if she likes, and so she did, and it burned husband and wife both to ashes.

Her children, now without their mother, never learned to be foxes and so her descendants have lived as ordinary men and women since. The village sometimes wondered why Lady Tammamo fled into the fire when fox-demons can live to be hundreds of years old. Some felt they'd been wrong, and that perhaps she hadn't been a demon after all. The children, seen sometimes selling their fish in the markets, were so beautiful and kind to everyone. You couldn't see the red in their hair unless the sun shone right on it, and then you'd see it, red threads among the black.

My father tells me the story of her when I find a red hair on his head, growing from his left temple. This is all that remains of her, my father tells me, when he tells me the story. And he pulls the red hair out of his head and hands it to me.

When I show the red hair to my blond mother, she laughs. He always pulls that hair out, she says. I had a red-haired great-grandfather, you know.

My hair is brown. But in my beard, the red threads grow. I shave them. My name is Aphias Zhe. Aphias was the name of a schoolteacher in Scotland five generations back on my mother's side. Zhe is the name every man in my father's family has been called by since that first day we fished the sea between Korea and Japan, five hundred years ago. Aphias became Fee in the mouth of my friend Peter, and Fee became Fiji in college. But Fee is the name that stuck, because Peter gave it to me.

This is a fox story. Of how a fox can be a boy. And so it is also the story of a fire.

SONGS OF THE

FIREFLIES

Fee

I

I AUDITION FOR the Pine State Boys Chorus on an afternoon at
the end of November in the year I am twelve years old. The audition, I recall, is my own idea. In a gray-stone cathedral's practice
room, somewhere near Longfellow Square in Portland, Maine, I
sing, for a square-headed, owlish man, a series of scales that he
plunks out on the piano, his pink fingers playful over the black
and white keys.

It's good, he says. Your voice. You've got a terrific range.

On a clipboard next to him, a list of names. Some have been
checked off. The afternoon sunlight in the room lights stained-
glass windows of Bible scenes I can't recognize, due to inatten-
tiveness in church. The light casts them as brilliant colors on the
bare wall opposite me.

When I sing, I feel that I am like the wall is now. This is why I
have come.

Do you know any songs, he asks. He looks down toward me as
if I might run from the room.

Christmas songs, I say.

He unfolds some music and hands it to me.

I sing Silent Night. O Come Let Us Adore Him. Good King
Wenceslas. Angels We Have Heard on High. That one's my
favorite, I say, when I am done. I've never heard my voice alone
with a piano before. The quiet that follows, when I stop singing,
seems new, too.

Rhythm, too, he says.

My science class has taught me that breathing turns the air inside you to a carbon, a little different from smoke, but a little like it. We have this in common with flames. We are just slower. I take a breath, waiting. Impatient.

I am looking for boys just like you, he says, finally, and checks my name off the list.

I leave with the folder of sheet music for the first rehearsal, given a seat in the choir right away. In the car on the way home I can't wait to start. I remember the director's odd soft handshake. I'm Eric, he'd said. But there's another Eric in the choir. So I am Big Eric, and he's the little one.

Did you hear me, my mother says right then, as she drives through the early-evening traffic on the bridge between Portland and Cape Elizabeth.

No, I tell her. I didn't.

In Korea, my grandfather tells me when we get home, everyone knows all the songs. Sometimes, like in a musical, everyone starts singing. He makes Korea sound like a place made from happy families and wisdom, and it makes me wonder why he's here, in Maine.

The next day the Korean American Friendship Association of Maine arrives for a kimchee-making party. Here in Cape Elizabeth, a town still half full of farms, we live on several acres that overlook the marsh at the town's edge. Thirteen families arrive and fill the yard with their cars. Their dark-haired children coming running and yelling for me. Aphi-as, Aphi-as, they yell. Their parents divide, the mothers into my grandmother's kitchen, the fathers into the garage. The mothers chop cabbage in the kitchen, mince peppers and fish. The fathers take beers and shovels and head to dig the hole where the giant barrels of kimchee will sit.

My grandfather and grandmother live in what was once a barn, converted for them into an apartment and connected to our house by a breezeway, where my father stores firewood. I've hidden here. My grandparents moved here from Korea a few years before.

There was some turmoil, my father says of it, when people ask. He redid the farmhouse for them himself with these men who are headed to shovel the hole. My mother needs her own kitchen, my father had told my mother, who laughed. No, really.

Korea is in trouble, my grandfather will say. Every now and then, he will follow it by saying, Maine, Maine is okay. Many fat people. But okay. My grandmother will say only, I am here for my grandchildren.

The other children frighten me a little. I can't speak Korean, my father's decision, and so I can't understand them much of the time. How you like funny-funny, round-eyes, they ask me and my brother and sister, whenever they play a joke on me. My brother Ted and sister Sam, both younger, find them funny. While they distract themselves with my Monopoly games, I slip out the back to where the men are digging.

Look, my grandfather says, chuckling. Here's fox. And he picks me up. His strength surprises me, and he sets me down. Fox dig hole, look.

The other men talk in Korean around us, including my father, and I can tell they haven't heard him. English falls off their ears. I sit and watch them and wait for the hole to appear.

I meet Peter in the first rehearsal I attend. The other boys and I do not talk to each other beforehand, but we set our voices side by side as if it were no matter at all. In this practice chapel, the twenty of us sit in metal chairs that ring as we sing through the first part of an early-December night. Some boys I recognize from my town, the others are unfamiliar. The one beside me looks up at me now and then as we sing, making little faces. His white-blond hair is like candle flame.

Almost all of these boys are blond. Which is to say, I am the one who isn't.

Boys, Big Eric, the director, says. Please say hello to our newest members. Aphias Zhe, Peter O'Hanlon. And at his name, the blond boy next to me looks up at me and says, You're new too?

Are you Chinese? another boy asks.

No, I say. Korean. Half. Saying it always makes me feel split down the middle. Like a cow diagrammed for her sides of beef.

I'm part Indian, Peter offers.

The rehearsal continues. At the end we wait on the curb for our parents to come and pick us up. Do you want some, Peter says, and holds out a can of chewing tobacco.

No, thanks, I say. He burps red spit into the street.

Come over and ride bikes, he says.

Okay, I say.

He walks and I feel the air come off him toward me, wherever we are. His sounds reach me wherever I am, not the only sounds I can hear, but the first ones: they trample all the others. My mother calls him a towhead blond, the word, apparently, for that kind of hair, so pale, so bright, it seems to be what sunshine reminds you of.

What do you want of him, I ask myself. I tell myself, to walk inside him and never leave. For him to be the house of me. Below, a list from my notebook at school:

Likes smoking and chew
Find out: What is New Model Army, Gang of Four, DOA
Peter, Peter, Fire-eater, kissed the girls, felt like a heater
Hates his sister, loves mine
Wants to never go home again, always: Why?

To save time for reading, I've taught myself to walk and read at the same time. My father doesn't want me to learn Korean, English only, he says, and so at school I walk the halls reading from the *Webster's Dictionary* for several weeks. Around me the other kids pass in a rush of winking colors and pillowed sounds. I can't hear anything they say to me when I read. I can only hear inside me, a voice, reading to me from the book, lower than my own. This voice hints at directions, possibilities, even as it presses forward, inexorable, to the next word in line. Defect, Defection, Defective. Define. Definition. Definitive. On the next page, I peek. Demon.

What the hell is that, Zach asks, when he sees me in the cafeteria at lunch. He is a choir member in my same class, a lacrosse player with a deer's walk who stayed back a year. He is my class but older, and he likes me for reasons I don't yet understand.

I'm preparing for a spelling bee, I lie.

Tow, it turns out, is what is beaten off the harvested flax. Transparent. Light passes through it, barely. Tow, Towhead. Peter.

By the time the spring comes five months later, I am the section leader of the first sopranos. When I am given this job, Big Eric tells me how my voice is to lead the others. Now he watches me in rehearsals as I watch him. I sing and follow Big Eric's hand as it bobs in the air, showing us the silent percussion to our songs. If I have to look at his eyes, I look at the reflections in the little rims of his gold-framed glasses. I do not think he is completely fooled by this. I feel as if he can see into my throat, to the place just below where my voice starts, where, as he says, the breath resides.

As my voice follows the scales while we warm up and we align our voices around the piano's tone like muscles on a bone, I feel larger. As if the room belonged to the voices that filled it in the way my throat belongs to my voice. The top notes remain for only me and Peter. All the other boys cannot go up this high, high A over high C. Big Eric looks first at Peter and then at me as we hold this note. The sound wavers only when we alternate taking breaths, and then only faintly. Peter barely contains a smile at me that might distort the vowel coming out of him. He seems too small to generate the force he does. His body barely fits around his voice, his mouth a gate to another dimension made up of these pure notes.

Eric touches the next key up. B. We rise together.

Afterward, as the boys prepare to leave rehearsal, running and yelling as they put on their coats, Big Eric approaches Peter and I where we stand. You should have a solo, I think, he says to Peter, at which Peter laughs. A descant, he says.

The descant is a melody sung by a soloist in counterpoint to the melody sung by the sopranos. A single voice above all the others, stepping its way through by means of lyric and syncopation, one part song, one part refrain. The chorus sings at the same time as the descant singer. I want the descant. I know I am good enough. My voice, my range. I learn faster. But I see immediately then, what Big Eric wants. The blond hair at the top of the riser, imagine him singing. You would want to touch what you heard, hold it to your face.

In the car pool with Peter, on our way back from choir rehearsal, I try to read and not look only at him. The other boys in the car cluck and shove at each other, ask loud questions about things that have just happened at school. The mother driving us regards the traffic ahead. On the pages in front of me, the words dissolve a bit, the letters thinning until I can see, on the other side of them, like spying through a wire fence, the pictures of Peter I have collected inside me: Peter laughing as he falls on the ice at Lake Sebago, Peter walking through his dark house, his dog fluttering at his leg, Peter asleep in my basement, gripping the edge of his sleeping bag as if he were, in his dream, trying to escape it. Occasionally I look up, and the real Peter flares beside me. I try to place the smell of him. He smells of carnations and, very faintly, cigarette smoke. Like a corsage someone left in a bar. I am in love with you, I think then. That's what this is.

Too bad you didn't get the descant, he says.

It's yours, I say. You're better for it. There isn't anyone else.

I don't care if I have it. Big deal. Extra rehearsals.

I don't mind, I say. And I won't. There's probably something for me later.

A book I had with me for one week was about Russian psychics spontaneously combusting into flame. The author thought it mysterious, the sudden acceleration of the body's heat to a temperature that would sear bone. This did not mystify me then. The person writing had never met Peter.

2

THE SUN ON the first day of the section-leader camping trip with Big Eric is a shiny white smear in the center of a white sky.

There's four of us: me, Zach from the altos, Little Eric from the second sopranos, and Big Eric. We hike for hours that first day and then find a rock pool to swim in at some distance from the trail. We decide to camp here and pitch our tent, first. Then we take off our clothes, Big Eric first, and he removes all of his and stands, looking at us, waiting. Swimming nude, he says, is one of God's greatest gifts to us.

Zach shrugs. I like it. His clothes come off, then Little Eric, then me.

Big Eric takes out his camera then.

Krick. The camera shutter flicks open–shut.

Little Eric perches on the edge of the rock pool, sylphlike, naked. His blond wavy hair frames his profile, an elegant twelve-year-old Swede. Big Eric holds his camera across his broad hairy chest. He aims at Little Eric and shoots. Krick. Slower, that time, his finger lingers at the sight in the frame. Zach and I stand to the side, crouch occasionally in a pool here at the stream, naked also, the summer air like a wet towel on my back.

That's great, he says to Little Eric. You look like a faun.

I sink myself under the water and expel the air from my lungs to make myself heavy, to fall quickly to the bottom of the deep pool. It's a diver's trick my oceanographer father taught me. I keep enough air so I can lie flat on the smooth stones of the bottom and look up, through the glossy, pearled surface of the water, to the sky.

The currents spill softly around me. The water has the milky freshwater taste of having come through granite, which is why it is so clear here. The sun above turns flat and silver like a dropped coin.

I stand and shove and a dolphin kick brings me to the surface, where I gasp. Little Eric and Big Eric continue. Click. I dive down again, drifting.

Zach punctures the pool in a jackknife and water careens in sheets. I lift my head from the water to see the Erics disturbed. Little Eric is laughing, and Big Eric says, Don't you worry, You're next.

Later, we build a fire and cook dinners wrapped in tinfoil: hot dogs, potatoes, corn on the cob. I am sunburned again and Zach rubs a lotion on my back for me. There is a quiet in which I pretend I don't know what all of this means, Big Eric's talks on the drive up here about libertarianism, nudism, child rights. And then I don't pretend. The mosquito-screen zipper sizzles shut.

In the tent at night his body is huge. Covered in hair. His penis looks comical, enormous, a cartoon. His age renders him like another gender, or a species apart from us. Our bodies are small, bones are small. Of the three of us boys, I am the only one with a little bit of hair swirled at the base of my penis. I feel half him, half them. Zach and Little Eric reach out fingers toward me, and touch the hair.

In the morning the sky lights an hour before the sun shows and we wash in the pool with Dr. Bronner's, check our food for raccoon assaults, make a fast breakfast. Big Eric makes coffee and I ask for some. At some point I remember: the Erics huddled in a sleeping bag, like hideously mismatched twins. Zach and I. And then a switch, Little Eric slipping inside with me, Zach gone over. I didn't think I would like kissing so much, Little Eric giggles.

And then the trees, the prismatic air presses on everything that needs it here on the earth, the sun fires itself on the stream and spreads light through the underbrush where we are camped, spangling our faces. Vertigo. The night before scatters away. I press the hot coffee to my face. I look at my face in his shaving mirror and don't recognize myself. My hair is streaking from the sun. My pupils are huge. I want to say, Take me apart. Leave me here for dead, if you can.

Zach gets out of the tent and stands in front of me and when I meet his eyes he winks. He puts a finger on my lips and smiles. Hey, he says. Nice tan.

Too bad we can't hike nude, Big Eric says to me, as he stands, his camera in hand. Zrrick. The hideous slide forward of film. He slides into his shorts and shirt reluctantly.

3

JULY. TWO WEEKS before camp, I am at Peter's house watching television. His mother and father are gone to work. He lives in South Portland, next door to my town, Cape Elizabeth, the town of a rival swim team. We rode our bikes to the beach this morning and ran in the ocean with his dog, Peg, for hours. Now we are sunburned. I am brown and red like a rose cane and when I pull down my shorts I see a band of white skin that sits there around my hips like reflected light. Peter is red all over and now lies on the couch, covered in Milk of Magnesia that his mother applied before leaving. We are watching television now. I want to tell him, to warn him not to be alone with Big Eric. What that means. But I don't.

Later, the sun sets. We wrestle on the couch. My mother is coming to pick me up, as I can't ride my bicycle home in the dark. I have Peter trapped on the couch, my elbow across his chest, as he jabs his knees into my ribs repeatedly. His mother is in the kitchen, his father is still not home. I want to kiss him. I want to not want to kiss him. His face is red from laughing and his sunburn. As I pound his chest a last time, I tell myself, Not possible. When I finally let him up I move to the other side of the couch and we catch our breaths. You suck, he says, laughing. You suck so bad. I slap his hot face and he laughs harder and I pin him back to the couch again.

I leave without telling him, afraid all the way back home in my mother's car that it leaks out of me, this desire I have, like the fungi that grow in Peter's yard, puffing out little clouds when you crunch them with your feet.

You have freckles, my mother says at home. Angel kisses. They sure love you a lot.

In the bathroom I kick off my swimsuit from where I lie on my sunburned back against the cool tiles of the floor, One, two, three. The door is closed and locked and after a while my mother knocks. Aphias. Open the door.

I say nothing because that is what nothing says. I am nothing, a o, an outline around a hole.

Aphias. You are worrying me. Dinner's going to be ready soon. If you aren't downstairs for it, I'm going to call your grandfather and father to come and get you.

Time passes. Eventually, something passes through me and I get up and pull on my suit. I close the bathroom door behind me.

It's still daylight and I find my mother in the yard. Hey there, she says. She is squatting over a plant. Poppies, she says. After they bloom, they die back. You can't see them. I run a finger over the fuzzy leaves, the yard-long stems. Now I know what I want to be when I grow up.

The difference between a remainder and a reminder is an *A*, which stands for Aphias, my name, and the letter slips in and out like a cartridge in a rifle.

4

CAMP BEGINS. FOR two weeks we rehearse twice a day, before and after lunch. Immediately after lunch is a play period of ninety minutes, including a supervised swim. The morning rehearsals are for memorization and pronunciation, lectures on the meanings of the words. The afternoon is run-throughs and music. Our fall program is in the majority sung in Latin and Italian.

I am the designated cabin leader of Cabin 2, bed checker, referee. The first night arrives damply. We unroll sleeping bags across skinny mattresses and change into long T-shirts down to our knees. I move through the cabin, touching each mattress with my finger, saying each boy's name as I go. Across the yard, down the hill, the other cabin glows, light pours out of it, and the moths and mosquitoes that dive in it are like fairies, holding long glowing trains. Through the tall grass, fireflies flash and in the distance, the lights of far-off cabins ring the lake's edge. Big Eric is down in the first cabin, and even though it is minutes past lights-out, the boys sit in a group in the main area, naked or in their underwear. Big Eric, whenever possible, preaches to us the virtues of nudism. Our swim hour is clothing-optional. Today, the first day, I wore a T-shirt in the water, like the two fat boys, Jim and Paul.

The bed check done, I turn off the lights. Around me in the dark the other boys turn in their beds. A few are instantly asleep. I haul myself up into my bunk. In the bunk beneath me is yet another Eric, Eric B., as he is called, for further clarity, with all the Erics around. He whispers, Fee?

I stick my head over the edge to see him. Where Little Eric is pretty, this one is handsome. You can see the man coming on in him, like the change of a werewolf, except better. What are they doing, he asks.

Telling stories, it looks like, I say. First cabin is like a cabin of brothers, blond, Scandinavian, mild, clean-limbed. Peter is down there and I have not been able to concentrate since finding out. I want to pretend to Eric B. below me that we are just in the woods at a normal summer camp, but as I make out the trace of his eyes in the dark, I can see this will not happen.

Down the hill, the light stays on. When it goes off, I slip out of my bunk, pull on a pair of shorts, and shrug out the door. I have in my mind the idea that I need to make this end, that there should never be another place like this. I sit down on the dock instead, watch the lake heave in the dark. The waves there seem like a mockery of the ocean. The stars look fake. I sit like this until Peter finds me.

He sits down beside me. He leans against my shoulder, and I can feel the sunburn off his cheek. I make room and he slips against me. I don't ask him why he is crying and when he stops, why he's stopped.

He pulls his head off my shoulder and spits into the water. He lights a cigarette he has had hidden in his hand, and drops the match into the lake, where it sizzles when it lands. We watch the match float in the faint dark together.

5

YOU WERE THERE, he says. The night it happened you were there.

I was on the dock, I say. You came and found me.

You were there.

Wood-plank floors, dark like molasses, cool to the touch like a lake rock passed to you by someone who held it briefly. Screened windows run the length of this cabin. The low dark ceiling, almost invisible, registers on the mind more as a color and a shade both, than as a roof.

Rehearsals here go long. In the stillness between phrases, we save our voices. Some young sopranos, drunk on high notes, shrill and squeal when away from the room, or sing recklessly their favorite songs. I have practiced writing on my sheet music without looking at it, so as to communicate with Peter, who sits next to me. His pale hair blows up off his head, as if his real mother were a dandelion gone to seed. A few times, at night in my bunk, I find one of his hairs in my bed, left from him sitting there, and I run it through my teeth.

How do you mean, I write.

You were there. He points his pen to it again, what he just wrote. The gesture raises an eye from Big Eric, in the front. I look away.

You need a break, Eric says from the front. I won't keep you here when you all want to be outside right now. Go and take a forty-minute break and be back here to finish. I want full attention for the Kyrie.

The music we are singing has been sung for hundreds of years by boys. I wonder if God expects to hear it rising off the earth, like the bloom of a perennial flower. Or if it is a standing challenge, for us to come together and sing it for Him. Eric tells us, in the old days, of the castrati, the elite Italian choristers who gelded themselves to keep their high clear voices. Some boys hold their crotches when the story is told, but I understand. I could want it that badly, to keep a voice.

Peter walks out at the break first and heads to a large rock out in the center of a field between the rehearsal hall and the canteen. At night the fireflies fill this field with sparks, as if it were ready to burn. Now, during the day, the thick grass is full of Queen Anne's lace and daisies and a little red flower like a cut knot of red thread that my mother calls wild-fire. The rock is enormous, left behind thousands of years ago by a glacier, and a slim white seam runs diagonally through the porous gray granite. Smooth dents in a row lead to the top and Peter climbs them quickly. Sitting up there, Peter looks off to the forest that begins on the eastern edge of the field.

Peter, tell me what you mean, I say.

Go away, please.

I was on the dock. You came and found me.

You knew. How did you know.

He's done it to me, too.

I stand beside the rock. Underneath it, moss crawls up the side. I couldn't believe what I had just said. It wasn't exactly right, though. I had never had a solo. I was not like the others. When Big Eric spoke to me, he knew I knew what he was. That I had always known. And then I remember, the pictures. Try to remember if any were of me.

A shadow, tossed on me, wears a halo made by sun-colored filaments. I look up. Hello, Peter.

He comes down and jumps up on my back, his chin digs between my shoulders, his legs kicked around my waist. Giddy-up, he says. I carry him toward the rehearsal room. Across the way, in the room, I feel what I am sure are the eyes of Big Eric.

This horse sure is slow, Peter says.

In my head I pray. There is a saying in Korea that you know who your God is when you think you are about to die. Hello, God. I pray to be able to carry Peter, to carry him off to where he belongs, way above this earth. Well above what could ever touch him. But wherever that is, I instead set him down at the entrance to the dining hall, where we go inside and sneak a soda from the fountain.

In rehearsal again the altos falter, unsure. Most are newly altos, and slip into their old soprano or second-soprano parts, thinking no one can hear them sing falsetto for head tone. Eric calls the rehearsal to a halt then.

A head tone's quality, he says, cannot be duplicated. There is almost nothing like it except the clarinet, for sound. Is that clear? Falsetto, falsetto sounds like this, and then he trills a terrible, reedy impression, screwing up his features. His beard bobs. The new altos are almost in tears.

Do not, I repeat, do not ever use falsetto. If your voice is changing, you will be moved to the altos, so that you may sing with us until you develop into a tenor, bass, baritone, et cetera. I will not tolerate it. At all. Don't think I can't hear it, because I can. I can hear it. Is that clear?

Clear, we say, in unison, as if it were another piece we would be rehearsing throughout the afternoon.

After a dinner of meat loaf and peas and soggy boiled potatoes we go into town in the van for a movie. They are showing *Xanadu,* starring Olivia Newton-John and Gene Kelly. Gene Kelly plays a clarinet. Olivia Newton-John sings in a clear high voice and roller-skates through a tepid plot, something involving love. There is laughter in the audience when several of us sopranos, including me, sing along. The songs are easy for us to pick up. Olivia plays one of several muses who descend to earth, arrayed in beautiful mortal bodies that cover their true selves, beams of colored heaven-made light. We sing the songs afterward, in the van on the way home, softly, as we have already sung all day. Some of us boys sleep as we pass through the dark quiet towns along the main road back. We are on the other side of the equation of light and sound. When we sing, we try on the robe of a muse. We wear a color of light.

6

IN THE NUMBER 2 Cabin bathroom Zach and I are pressed up against each other, Zach sitting on the sink as I push toward him. I am trying to get used to his tongue in my mouth. The first time it happened he said, This is how you French kiss, and then licked my lips with his tongue.

At the time, I wondered who it was that taught him.

I get down on my knees. I take him in my mouth. I have read that this is something that men like. It makes me nervous when Zach does it to me, but I feel in control when I do it to him, and this much I know I like. I don't like doing it for itself.

Jesus, he whispers, and I pinch him. The other kids in the cabin are supposed to be asleep. I had finished my bed check when I heard the door open, not even the sound of the door itself but the whisper of the air moved by its opening. Days ago I had greased the hinges and oiled the spring. For him.

He jumps against me when I pinch him, knees knocking my chest. He smells like warm bread down here, if you rubbed it with salt. I take advantage of my swimming lessons, I breathe through my nose and take him in my throat. He squeezes my shoulders, starts pounding lightly and then harder. His legs shake.

What's that on your shoulder, Eric B. asks me the next morning on my way back from the shower. I look back to see, on my skin, five purple dots in a row. I got punched, I say.

Eric B. grins. Yeah.

7

WHEN YOU SAY Excelsis, you need to land hard on all three syllables. Egg. Shell. Cease. Got it? Egg—Shell—Cease. Excelsis. Put it together. Now, Do-ho Na-ha No-beese, In-Egg-Shell-Cease Day-Oh. Ready?

The baton flicks up. And then down.

We have been working on this piece for three days. We rehearse two hours in the morning and two in the afternoon. This is my first summer camp. Usually, *camp* means a cottage my family rents, where we drive up and swim more or less continuously. Zach's family has one on Lake Sebago, a log cabin with a screened-in porch and a dock, built by his architect family. Here, we have the rehearsal building, the canteen where the food is served, the two cabins, with another half cabin for Eric's wife, Leanne, and her new baby, a big-headed round ball of a boy who is so quiet he makes me afraid. Ralph, Eric's foster son, stays in Cabin 1 with Big Eric.

Leanne is a giantess, taller than Eric, who is tall. Each of her breasts right now seems as big around as my head. She is the camp nurse, a title that fits as she is always breast-feeding her new baby. The half cabin, her tiny domain, is the last one in the row of buildings going down to the dock and the lakefront. There are no near neighbors. Watching her come and go, it seems there should be hidden compartments to accommodate her bulk.

Dona Nobis. This whole phrase, it means thank you lord for your gift. It is sung to celebrate Jesus. Thank you Lord for your gift, all thanks be to God. Noble gift, all thanks be to God above all others. Big Eric tells us the meanings of the words, because he insists it will help us sing. I like it better when I don't know the meanings. When the word is empty and I fill it like a glass. Knowing what they mean takes away some of my courage.

We sing for a half hour past the rehearsal end. The altos have finally adapted, the sopranos are holding themselves back, the second sopranos support us both through the gap left for them now. Big Eric sets his wand down after the end is reached for the fifth time that afternoon. He wipes sweat off his forehead and smiles at us and says, You're done. Come back for dinner, at six.

Back in my cabin my sweat dries in the cool air coming off the lake. I think about writing to my family. I wouldn't know what to say. Last night, Big Eric broke up a Dungeons & Dragons game I'd been leading for the Cabin 2 boys, so they wouldn't feel so left out by the nightly naked story hour. But then Peter and Zach had wanted to play, and so Big Eric came up and shut it down and took them back to Cabin 1. I look over the interrupted game story, and then put it away. I take out a book of Greek mythology I stole from the town library. The myths are occasionally checked by a pencil, as if this were a catalog, and someone had gone along marking what they wished to buy. I read until the dinner bell, dreading what Big Eric will say. When I go to dinner with my book, Big Eric looks at it. Greeks, he says. Wise men, the Greeks. He smiles and I shut the book, slip it under my thigh on the bench. At dinner, Big Eric announces that cliques are forbidden in the choir, and that, until further notice, the D&D games would be suspended. I wonder about naked story hour.

After dinner, I take my sketch pad down to the edge of the water, where I can look at the late-summer sun still afternoon-bright at six-thirty in the evening. I draw two eyes there on the page. I can never decide easily whether to draw the eyes as white eyes or Asian ones. My eyes are white eyes, though slanted slightly, but with the white-boy eyelids. The irises have green centers and brown edges. Split through the middle.

I look at my two eyes there on the page. I begin to draw hair, then fill in the face shape, put in lines for the neck. I taught myself to draw by tracing comics, so I draw smooth-lined broad-shouldered men and women of enormous cleavage, supported by powerful, tiny waists and long, muscled legs. I always wait for the eyes to tell me who they are, so I can know who I am drawing. I decide I am drawing my favorite character from D&D, a sorcer-ess I've named Tammamo, for my long-ago great-grandmother. I draw a heart-shaped face atop a long beautiful body, with flowing red hair past her waist that rises behind her like fire in a storm wind. I try to make her look like one of my grandfather's missing sisters.

Who are you drawing? Behind me stands Big Eric.

A character of mine, from D&D. As I say this, I feel a change come over me, like a direction change in the wind. All my air is now coming from another direction.

You're very good. She looks scary.

She's not supposed to. I guess I'm not that good.

I look up at him. He is a tall man, he does carpentry. His round-rimmed gold-framed glasses gives him an owlish demeanor, though not the wise owl but the startled one. When the owl blinks around trying to see.

I'm not targeting you, he says.

All right. If you say so.

They tell me you are the Dungeon Master. What does that mean?

It means I am in charge of the game rules. I have the maps, I tell them who the enemies are, and I monitor the plays, to make sure the dice are rolled and everyone gets a turn. And I make up the stories.

I turn back to my drawing. I draw Tammamo wearing a white buckskin fringe bikini and her power gem rests on a headdress that rides atop her hair. Her boots are thigh-high.

I say, Adam's a dungeon master too. A good one. Zach hates it. Merle or Luke can be good if they don't get bored. It's not just me.

Big Eric bends down. All right then, he says. Just remember, some of these boys are not as sophisticated as you. I don't want them feeling left out, and I don't want them complaining to their parents. If someone wants to play I want you to find them a way. All right?

Yep.

When I finish my drawing, the light is nearly gone, and Tammamo's hands each hold a ball of fire-lightning. I see her leap into the wind's wide arms, her hair a torch, see her laugh as she rides the night. Before she fell in love, I think, she would have been mad with grief, wanting love. How would she have fallen in love with her husband? Was she preparing to destroy him and fell for him instead?

Back in my bunk, later, I read some of a comic book a cousin sent me from Korea. He is learning English and has translated it for me, his careful, squared-off handwriting, all in capitals, tells me the story. FOX-DEMON MUST EAT THOUSAND LIVERS, YOUNG MEN VIRGINS, TO BECOME HUMAN. This fox has been drawn ugly, but she wears a beautiful mask, made from the face of a victim, to hide her ugliness. She is Korea's most famous fox-demon.

I write him a letter. Dear Paul, Thank you so much. The comic book is very good. At the bottom of my drawing I write FOX-DEMON, and mail it to him.

8

THE NEXT NIGHT storm clouds come up quickly after lights-out. We slip from our beds, drop tarps from the eaves and tie them to the sills, to seal the cabin windows, which have no glass. The rain falls hard and lightning lights the tarps occasionally, followed quickly by thunder. I lie on my bunk, reading myths by flashlight, comforted, thinking that I am perhaps like Lady Tammamo, that I have managed to conjure a storm. I compare her to the Greek gods and goddesses. Tonight I read about Atalanta, who wanted to outrun every man. I read about Europa, carried off to sea by Zeus. I read about Ganymede. How Zeus turned into an eagle in order to carry him off. Because he was so beautiful.

Tammamo, I decide, is mightier. For the man she loves lived to die a natural death, and the Greeks always kill the mortals they love, through design or accident. None of these gods would renounce their godhood.

Do we have lightning rods on the roofs, asks Eric B.

I didn't know he was still awake. Now wouldn't be the time to find out, I say.

I like walking in a thunderstorm. Do you?

I do.

We walk into the front room of the cabin. Rainwater sweeps in a stream down the hill to the lake, revealing steps made from the roots of the trees. I swing the door open.

If we stay out in the open, and wear rubber shoes, we're fine, he says.

I think of the lightning swarming over me, unable to grasp the interior circuitry of nerve because of rubber soles on my feet. I want to wear a bolt. I say, All right then, and he and I step out.

The night is the lighter for the storm, the clouds reflect light back to us. Somewhere in Cape Elizabeth, my mother's porch light sends out a ray of light and part of it bounces off this cloud and arrows into my eye. I know my mother will keep her light on all night.

Do you believe in the Loch Ness Monster, Eric B. asks.

Sure, a little.

Do you think this lake has a monster?

I think it might, I say.

Really?

I look at him in the dark. We are now in the woods. The rain reaches us here in little waterfalls collected off the roof of leaves and falling in through small openings. Eric B. will never be one of Big Eric's chosen. He really doesn't know, either. Some of these boys would never know. I say, Let's go to the lake.

9

HE HAD HIDDEN inside one of the boats. No one knew he was there. When the storm began, he pushed out and the normally corpulent tides of the lake, now turgid with rain and wind, took him quickly out into the center, where Eric B. and I did not see him. What I remember is almost thinking there weren't enough boats, that one was missing. I remember something about them called my eye to them, but I couldn't have said what it was, and I said nothing at the time to Eric B. And so it wouldn't be until the morning that Ralph, Big Eric's eleven-year-old foster-child, was discovered to have drowned. The storm capsized the rowboat in the lake.

Breakfast is an untidy half hour of silence and gulped oatmeal, and then gradually the speculations begin, in whispers. The screen door slaps open then, and Big Eric enters.

Boys, he says. Ralph has been found. He drowned sometime last night, evidently from taking a boat out alone in the storm. I would just say that for today, Fee and Eric are in charge of rehearsal. I will excuse myself from your midst. Thank you.

And then he leaves.

The silence creases after the door closes, and then splits. Zach, sitting next to me, says, All right, Mr. Director.

I look across to Little Eric, who smiles at me. He gets up from his table of chattering sopranos and heads toward me. As he stands in front of me and Zach, I consider how we are the original three. Everything began with us. Even this.

Something feels wrong here, I say.

What do you mean, they ask at the same time.

Jinx, I say.

And so the rehearsal. A brief conference beforehand decided that Little Eric would sit at the piano and I would direct, as he had the piano skills and I was adept at the pronunciations and rhythms. As their gazes arrow in, I understand. If my baton had been a candle it would have lit on its own.

As the warm-up scales begin and the summer sun whitens the sky outside, the morning haze fills with light. I feel, in the cool dark of the rehearsal room, the boat. The oarlocks would have been about the level of his chin. For him to get there on his own reflected a terrible determination. Ralph had been a slip of a child, large unhappy dark eyes, curly dark hair that reminded me of an elf. He was as pale as a mushroom.

The key changes. The boys' voices thunder through the scales, as if to call to Big Eric, wherever he was, in town with the small cold blue body. I sing alongside, use my voice as I use the baton, to guide.

I let myself know. It's no mystery why Ralph took a boat alone into the center of the lake during a storm. My eyes fill up, as if I had walked out into a rain and turned my face to the sky. It comes to me, something covered up in what Big Eric had said about the songs. *Kyrie eleison means, Lord have mercy.*

10

THE DAYS AFTERWARD filled with parents calling the camp. A few insisted on a weekend visit. What they found was a more or less placid group of boys, as unrippled as the lake. The camp was not called off because technically, Ralph was not one of us. He was Eric's foster son. The police determined the cause of death accidental, death by drowning, the state sent Ralph's caseworker to interview Eric and his wife, and all agreed that Ralph's had been a short life of hardship and that it was possible he had killed himself. I overheard the interview, as it was conducted inside the Nurse cabin. I stood outside, my ear up against a crack in the wood frame. I wanted to know.

. . . the whole time, asking repeatedly at nighttime if it was going to be soon. Returning to his mother.

Does she know? Isn't she in prison?

She does know. She had to be sedated, actually, after she was told. Very sorry situation, for which she blames herself. But, I must ask, how was it he was able to push the rowboat out by himself?

I don't think he was trying to row anywhere. I think he went out and fell asleep inside the rowboat, and that the storm tides of the lake took it off the beach and that he awoke too late.

He was always saying how warm it was here. Even with the fan. And the boats are cool. Like a cave.

How is your baby?

He's fine, poor thing won't remember. A blessing I suppose.

I switch bunks with another boy so that my bed faces the field instead of the farther cabin and the lake. I am grateful the body was found, also grateful that we will not be asked to swim today. In the afternoon I write to my mother and father and grandparents a quick postcard: Dear Folks, The rehearsals are good and the other day I was chosen to lead one with Eric. Not too bad with mosquitoes here, and I am getting a tan. I am the best swimmer, of course. Everyone is very sad about Ralph. Please tell Grandfather and Grandmother that I love them and I have some pressed flowers for their book.

I walk out to post the letter in the mailbox at the edge of the road and then walk back. The field has sprouted sunflowers, on the cabin side, and already they dwarf me. Their golden heads tower on slender green stalks rising as high as ten feet. Cleis was a girl who fell in love with Phoebus Apollo, the sun. To take pity on her the gods turned her into this flower, so that she might watch him all her life. I mistrust the myth, though certainly it seems a plausible story. All of it except for the part where the gods do this out of mercy. They do it for fun, it seems to me. In Greek mythology, loving Apollo seems to be among the most dangerous of the heart's choices: the fields and gardens are full of his lovers, multiplied by time into millions. I think of Peter. How much more I could love him, if there was another of me. If there were millions. If I had been scattered. I go back to my bunk and flop down.

What are you writing, Peter says, coming into the cabin. He throws himself onto my bunk. The sun is shining, he says. We should be outside.

Outside, we head into the woods to find a birch tree to ride. My mother's cousins taught me birch riding. You take a tree and bend it slowly until it touches the ground. You tie it so you can climb on and then you cut the rope. The rope we took from the cabin, and the knife, Peter brought: a child-sized deer knife. In the woods, it doesn't take long to find a tree for us. You first, he says. We wind the rope around the tree and then under the edge of a stone for leverage and the tree lowers. I sit down across the papery trunk, dry against my thighs.

Cut, I say. And the tree swings me up harder than I expect. I go up and then as I come down, the tree bobbles and I fall. I hit the ground hard. I put my left hand out to stop the fall and when I pull it up the forearm is crooked, like a tree branch, and they hear my scream across the camp.

On the phone later, my mother is circumspect. Honey, these things happen. You always were a troublemaker and this is what comes of it. But I hear the arm is well set.

It is, I say. The camp phone is located in the mudroom of the rehearsal building. I stretch out flat on my back, my new cast a solid weight on my side.

Terrible thing, about Ralph, she says.

Yep.

But you know, this is why we always insisted you kids be good swimmers.

What?

So you could swim to shore. So in case the boat you were on was going down, you could swim to shore.

The lake has a monster.

How do you know, I ask.

I can feel it. It watches me.

My arm cast glows in the moonlight here on the dock. Under the plaster, the doctor said the arm would lose its hair and skin, that for a little while after the cast's removal, it might even be smaller. Peter sits beside me, wet from a night swim. The night air feels as thick as the cast. Even the crickets sound tired.

Why didn't it take Ralph, I ask.

Nobody wanted Ralph, Peter says, after a long quiet.

11

AS MY VOICE may change soon, I have finally been given a solo, in an a cappella song.

Well, that's one way of keeping you out of trouble, Zach says.

What do you mean by that? I ask Zach. We have gone out of sight of the camp, and we stand now, naked, in the lake, pressed against each other lightly, face to face. I hold my cast just above the water, resting it against his back.

He laughs and looks up. Extra rehearsal time. Less time for D&D. Plus more time spent with him. He co-opts you. A very smart tactical move.

We aren't at war, I say.

Sure. If you can't see that, I can. I can see that easy. He wants Peter.

The trees lean out over the lakeshore above us, a green scrim hung across heaven's summer face. The birch trees are a pale fire running slow through the summer woods and there isn't a thing wrong. Kissing Zach now spins me, makes me feel like I want to run myself all the way through him. I understand, why people like this.

I have to go back, I say then. I have to go ride bikes with Peter.

Where are we.

We took a bad turn there. We need to think about going back, I guess.

Above, thunder clouds. Peter and I are on bikes the camp lets us use, having ridden down dirt roads that line the forested countryside. Above the firs that toss the air around them I can see boiling clouds, dark like duck wings and glossy from carrying their rain. The air fills with dust, pollen, twigs, and torn leaves as the winds conduct playful raids. I can smell my sweat, which alarms me. I consider that my odor has caught up to me, now that we are stopped.

How many turns, Peter asks. How many did we take. Seven, right?

I run through my memory. I have a serial memory, I remember sequences, patterns, numbers. I am finding it applies equally to sentences and mathematics, spelling words or building numbers. Seven turns, I say. A left, two rights, two lefts, two more rights.

Peter climbs up on his bike, rising out of the seat. Because of my arm cast, I lag behind, sweating until wet spots slick my shirt; a dull ache radiates from under the cast. We are now shadowed completely by clouds. Peter seems about to lift up like the pieces of the road and field lifting around him. And then he comes down again. He says, We shouldn't ride until the storm is over. You aren't supposed to get your cast wet.

I think of all the sweat on it. Huh. But we aren't supposed to stay under trees during storms. Lightning.

Peter hoists himself up again. To the field then, he says, and he bobs up and down through the grass that almost covers him. I push my bike, following his new trail, my nose itching already from the grass broken by his passing.

We sit down in the middle of a field under a roof we make from our bikes and windbreakers. I guess that we are at least a mile and a half from the camp. Heat lightning passes from cloud to cloud without visible impact. The trees roll their branches around and around as the wind passes through them like a running line to some giant, lost sail. Until now, it had been a clear if sticky day.

Are you psyched, Peter says. You have a solo.

Yeah, I say. Our two coats, tied together, burp up, a wind having snuck underneath. We hold the bikes. I want this wind to continue, for us to lift into the sky, holding on. To go far away, just me and Peter.

Did you ever tell anyone, Peter asks.

I didn't. Guys like Eric can be dangerous, for one. And then my parents would have to know, which I couldn't bear it. I couldn't.

Dangerous how.

Violent. I read about it in the paper.

I had actually gone to the library and looked up everything I could find on pedophilia and homosexuality. I knew that Eric was a pedophile. I remember sitting in the aisle with the book, sure the librarian would find me. There in the card catalog were two neatly printed, plain-faced titles: *Greek Homosexuality*, *Homosexuality in Ancient Greece*. And then one day I opened the paper to a news feature that told of how sometimes, a pedophile, fearing discovery, will turn to murder. Little girls and boys turned into silent, bloody bits.

The grass around us rises and falls, rippling like waves coming in off an ocean that won't move, won't spray, and the coats pop up and down.

I want him dead, Peter says. I want it to end.

And then I feel the beginning of rain, raindrops pulverized by winds near the ground. I imagine the drops coming behind them taking the pieces in, welcoming these pieces as they make themselves heavier to speed their passage to the earth.

Don't tell anyone, Peter, I say. Please.

He watches me as I say this. His mouth a hard flat line, he says, Okay. For now.

The field flattens in the rain, but I know by tomorrow the grass might be even three inches taller. Things grow so fast, it is amazing we don't all lie awake at night, listening to it all happen.

Eric's demeanor is nearing normal again, now that Ralph has been properly buried at a service in Lewiston. He is now intent on resuming the camp's routine. And so after dinner, after dark, it is another naked story hour in Cabin 1.

Eric B., in the bunk beneath me, asks, Do you ever want to be down there?

Sometimes, I say.

Me too. Sometimes. I mean I like those guys. But I don't get it.

Mm. I slide off to the floor and pad softly to the door. I am tempted to go right in and sit down. Now that I have a solo. When Eric passed out the sheet music today, I looked over the notes and lines. The solo began each section of the four sections with a complete phrase alone, and then the choir joined him: the sopranos for the next first two stanzas and then the full choir. The choir echoed him and answered him. You had to hit your notes quickly and surely and get off them to the next ones or get tangled in the verses of the others. The song was from Shakespeare's *The Tempest,* set to music by Ralphe Vaughn Williams, and arranged by Big Eric to create a solo for me. The song frightens me. Still, I like the way it fits my voice like a sleeve of words.

I stare at the dark distance between the cabins, the golden light filled with golden boys behind mosquito screens, like a lamp made from fireflies. I turn and get back in my bunk.

What were you going to do, Eric B. asks me.

Shhh.

Zach in the dark. All smooth dryness, salty. I am like a deer at a salt lick. He giggles. I am stern, and he likes it.

One, two, three, fou—

Full fathom five thy father lies;
of his bones are coral made;
these are pearls that were his eyes;
Nothing of him that doth fade,
but doth suffer a sea change
into something rich and strange.
Sea-nymphs hourly ring his knell.

Lies, Eric pauses here. Lu-Hies. Enunciate. Or you'll sound like a Chinese laundryman saying Rice. Those soft consonants need to fire out.

Chinese laundryman, I say.

Quiet oils the room. The other boys know I am quick to avenge insults to my race and wait for a reaction.

Fee, he says, head cocked.

Chinese laundryman, I say.

Are you ready to start again?

Yeah.

Full Fathom Five my father lies, of his bones are coral made, these are pearls that were his eyes, nothing of him that doth fade, but doth suffer a sea change into something rich and strange. Sea-nymphs hourly ring his knell.

And the choir joins me. A tear pushes out. Peter points to his sheet music. In the margin he has written, DICK.

—Full Fathom Five my fah-th-her lies, of his bu-hones are co-rhal mayd—

And the baton comes up and flat, Eric's fingers scissoring against his neck.

What do I have to do, he says, to have your full attention? Do I have to wear a clown hat? Do I have to beg? Do I have to come around, and with that he proceeds to walk toward us, and then circle from behind. Peter turns his page.

That's not the page, Eric says, from above him. No wonder it sounded so awful. Let me turn your page for you. His finger drops low, toward Peter's lap.

I can turn my page, I was just looking back. Peter meets his gaze.

The finger hovers. Have I made my point? he says. And the finger hooks the paper, peels it over slightly, and then pushes it flat to the other side. Mmhmm. Love notes.

The other boys giggle, lightly.

I don't want to separate you but I will. Am I understood? Am I?

Yes, we both say, a sigh.

All righty, then. Five minutes for water and then where we were.

The boys slip from their chairs. The late-summer heat exhausts

us more than usual, and even the cool hall today stifles. By unspoken agreement, Peter and I wait with Big Eric.

When does it stop, Eric says, softly. As if I don't have enough
to deal with. Is it that you don't feel I'm giving you enough
attention? You are forcing my hand here, boys. I like both of you
more than I like the rest, but you are antagonizing me now. You
really are. You will have to show me your pages when I ask to see
them, at any time. And they should be eminently readable.

He sweats as he says this. He reaches in his back pocket for a
linen handkerchief, and wipes energetically his shiny forehead,
his red cheeks. And then he grabs Peter's music sheets, hands
him a clean copy, and throws the other away.

Who's Ariel and who's Caliban, I ask, when he tells me this is
Ariel and Caliban's song.

Ariel's a magical servant, he says. A wizard's helper. Shape
changer. Could ride lightning, stand at the bottom of the sea, or
impersonate a storm.

A girl, I say. Inside, I think of the fox. How Ariel was perhaps
a fox, far away from home and lost.

A boy, he says. He's a boy. Funny, isn't it, how Ariel is this
girl's name now. But it was a boy, for the play. Caliban's a monster. They are both Prospero's servants.

12

TONIGHT, AFTER THE lights are out, I remember. Or is it
remembering?

The pale screen. A golden head, resting against a larger, darker
one. The sound of pages turning. My heart pounding so hard I
am sure it can be heard over the crickets and frogs. A large furry
hand touches tentatively, to check to see if the golden one is
asleep. And strokes down the leg.

The smaller head turns up. No.

The hand comes back the way it has gone. And Peter rolls out
of his lap, turns, facing him. No.

Eric stands, a wall of pink skin. He makes no move. Peter
turns his head.

Were you there, I ask myself. Around me: the damp night floats through the screen, the boys smell bitter in their sleep, as if as they slept, nightmares made them sweat. I turn my face into the pillow, the familiar scent of me still warm there. Pull the cover up higher. Were you there, did you watch that night? Had you snuck down, and watched. And done nothing. Or are you making this up.

Outside the cricket hum embroiders the lake hum and here and there, a boy sighs. I hear Luke start to mumble in his sleep and decide to watch, crawl from my covers and slip past Eric B. to the floor. Down the hill I can see that Cabin 1 is asleep, all the gold laid out on pillows, all the lights off.

I don't know what I remember or what it is I imagine right now. I don't know why that is. I go back to my cabin, lie down, sleep takes me in a swipe.

Light and thunder. I wake up and open my eyes. Above me, in the air, a ball of lightning. So this is what it looks like, I think. I apparently had been asleep in a storm and now the light and then the thunderclap follows so quick behind, the cabin shudders, is engulfed. I half expect to shatter, the bunk bed to fly up. My hair stands up. I don't dare breathe, as if I could somehow inhale it. As if, without thinking it, I exhaled it.

And then it goes, winks out against the wall above my head. The dark falls in where it used to be.

I stand slowly, in my bed, to peer out the window. The storm lightning falls to the ground. I climb down and begin waking the boys to go out and unroll the tarps again. The rain soaks everything. The trees look cast in gunmetal and oiled. The lake, I can see in the distance, rises and the boats, tied to their mooring, tilt nose-down, end-up, the mooring now well under water. Soon they will turn over in the wind.

13

THE FALL IS almost here. We go back to our towns, to our families.

There are stories in Cape Elizabeth of seeing someone fly through the air at night. I think of them as Zach and Peter and I tie the birch trees down to ride them. We are out on a hill, across the road from a graveyard and the marsh. I wonder if one of them is out in the woods late doing this by himself. Peter and Zach tie me on, because of my cast.

You shouldn't be out here, Zach says.

There's always a moment when it seems like it won't work out. Like the whole thing's a fake. And then the tree rises up and you head for the sky. Scream as you go. And then the tree sets you down again, and then brings you back up. I scream as I go up. This time, I do not fall.

Peter leaves to go home on his bike. Bye, he says. Are you leaving, he asks Zach.

In a bit, Zach says. See you later.

Zach stays. We wander around my dark house. My parents are watching the evening news with my grandparents and my younger brother and sister. How long before dinner, I ask.

You have half an hour, my mother says.

We slip out the back door and head down the road.

The greenhouse has been deserted for years with the exception of Zach and I using it as a kind of clubhouse. Overlooking the marsh, through its many broken panes, we can see my house in the far distance, above which clouds parade, today, toward the sea. Zach and I ride our bikes out here on Route 77 and drop them in the tall grass just outside the door. We stand now, facing each other under the patchwork of light coming through the smashed roof. The floor under our feet has cracks and saplings have pushed through.

What's wrong with you, Zach says. I have said nothing since arriving.

Above us gigantic clouds careen through the deep sky and the summer sunset bleaches the long marsh grass. The nearby sea colors the air, preparing to send us a fog later, and in my hand I hold a sea rose I have pulled off a hedge along the road.

This is for you, I say, and hand Zach the rose.

He holds the bloom lightly, the stem between his fingers.

Did you know, before? Zach twirls the flower and then puts it behind his ear. Ouch.

I did know. A wind change brings a sea wind passing through, a memory of something better. I thought I knew what Big Eric was. I thought I knew because I thought it was the same as me. We are both in love with boys. I know what Big Eric watches, now, though, in me. He sees that I know, we are not the same. I did not know before and now I do, and so he watches this knowledge in me, a light moving closer slowly through some faint dark.

I lean in and Zach does not close his eyes, even when I kiss him lightly on the mouth. The space between his lips is wet.

Back at home, after dinner, my quiet parents are now watching television comedies with my grandparents and my siblings are in bed. From where I sit on the floor, I can see, they think I am still here. They can't see that I have a secret as big as me. A secret replaces me.

My solo rehearsals with Big Eric take place on Fridays. Today is the day before my birthday, and so after the rehearsal, the boys from the choir will be over for cake. My mother drives me over to his sad downstairs house on Munjoy Hill and as his wife plays outside in the yard with their big-headed baby, Baby Eddy, we sit at the upright piano. I practice my solo. My voice stays strong, clear, cooperative. The solo is the harder for being a cappella: no guide except the memory of the music in my mind. No piano music to surround me. Just me.

Full Fathom Five my father lies, of his bones are coral made, these are pearls that were his eyes, nothing of him that doth fade but doth suffer a sea change, into something rich and strange . . .

In the yard, the baby is trying to learn to walk. He bounces up and sits down, up and then sits down again, his knees not quite strong enough.

. . . Sea nymphs hourly ring his knell . . .

In the yard, the baby suddenly stands, as if tethered to the sky by a sunbeam. And then falls, as if tugging the light down with him.

Fee, Big Eric says, and turns the pages back to the beginning.

Yes, I say. On my chest now, a weight, like Big Eric standing there. His two feet, pressing into me from above.

Fee, your mother tells me she's worried about you. She called to ask me some questions. He turns and looks at me as he says this. In his eyeglasses, my grim reflections.

My heart hammers, a frog under my ribs. I'm fine, I say.

But your mom doesn't seem to know this. And neither do your teachers at school. They don't know you're fine. And if your behavior becomes more disruptive, or strange, then there will be not only questions, but people will do things. Like, for instance, you won't be able to be a part of the choir anymore. And I know we both would regret that.

Yes, I say.

So you're fine. He rests forward on the piano, on the lip above the keys.

I'm fine.

I'd hate to lose you, he says, setting his fingers back out, spread over the chords.

I understand, I say. I do. Outside the baby plays on peekaboo sunbeams, up and down. Clouds rush over on their way out to sea. Baby Eddy laughs. He presses a key, to give me a note to start on, and I sing again.

After the lesson concludes, Baby Eddy is returned to the crib for a nap. Leanne leaves, the screen door clapping as she goes. Big Eric takes me into a sort of music room, with books. Let me play you this, he says. It's Holst's *The Planets*. We sit there listening, and so I forget what happens to boys who have solos, up until he slides a book, hardbound, from the shelf. He sets it out in front of me. I look at it sideways, not turning in my seat. The book falls open into the middle, shiny pages of boys sliding around naked on carpets with dark-haired, bearded men who look so much like Big Eric that I can't believe it isn't him. It almost looks like they are helping each other to exercise, do sit-ups, leg-raises. It looks like certain athletic manuals I have seen.

I raise my head and we exchange a glance, and whether it is the deadness in me that he can see, or whether I have somehow raised the strength to repel him, I don't know. But he pauses, unsure. The music surges. This is Saturn, he says. Do you like it.

I recall a painting I saw printed once, in a book, called *Saturn Eats His Children*. To prevent the new race of gods from overtaking him, Saturn ate his children whole. They cut themselves out of his stomach, and went on to rule the world. These boys on the carpet look like they are trying to escape being eaten.

I love it, I say. It's beautiful. We both know I mean the music.

What about these, he asks.

Where are they from, I ask.

Sweden, he says. Much more liberal there. They care about human life and feeling there. I met my wife there, while hiking one summer.

And so the afternoon walks away from us, and then the other boys arrive, driven by their mothers. The book has been put back for an hour by then, all the Planets have played, and I am ready to leave, but now is my birthday party. I feel a shield around me, like the gods did for their favored ones, and so I walk to meet Peter's mother's car pretending I am a favorite of the sun, with a possible future as a flower, and that Apollo himself is glaring at Big Eric. The other boys arrive in groups of four and five, piled into a few cars. Hey, says Peter. Loser. Who says you're special?

I laugh. I want to say, Get out of here. But I don't. All the shouting in me hides in my smile.

We go into the house for cake. The birthday song is tightly sung, harmonized, even, and too loud. The boys laugh as we slip discordantly into harmony. Here I am. Thirteen at last. Someone should kill me now, I think, as I blow out the candles. Before the damage spreads. You are fools not to, you will all regret that I lived. All the boys sign HAPPY BIRTHDAY FEE on my cast.

Did you make a wish, Zach asks.

Yes, I say.

Afterward, I go into a room I don't recognize. A rug askew here, boxes repacked in some rough manner, as if whoever searched them was not done. A quick review places the room as having been Ralph's. His death still providing disorder.

14

THE MORNING OF my birthday my father comes and wakes me up, early. The sky outside my window is a dark door with light peeping under the crack. Son, he says. Wake up. We have dolphins in Falmouth, beaching. He is dressed in his wet suit, a snorkel against his neck.

An hour later, I eat a cheese sandwich, peeling the crusts off and dropping them in the water as our Boston Whaler skids over wave crests that slap the bottom of our boat, my father driving us across the waves at an angle, his hand firm on the outboard engine. He smiles at me as I chew. How you doing there, he asks, as spray fans in bursts behind him. He knows he looks silly there and is waiting for me to laugh. I know I don't have to answer if everything is fine. I hold my arm cast so it doesn't shake. Behind my father blue sky burns pink at the bottom, where the sun floats, red-orange, clearing the horizon. The waves are glassy and long, brown-blue like kelp. The wind is a cold hand against our heads. We wave at the other boats that pass, my father speaking occasionally into his portable marine radio to the other dolphin rescue members.

They're headed this way, my father says. And he pulls us up short around to a cove where he has taken me on occasion to see seals. We wait. I shiver.

There are three dolphins here. They hang just under the water's surface, as if they were frozen in a leap. Two more arrive and the four push the sick one to the surface again and again, where its blowhole plucks at the air. Occasionally, a belly flashes white through the dark water.

How do they know it's sick, I ask my father.

Because she tells them, my father says.

We return home for lunch, replaced on our watch by a lobster-man and his son, a salvage diver who has worked with my father. You'll have cake and ice cream at home later, my mother says to me as I eat a fast bagel pizza. When we return in the early evening, we go by car, because now the dolphins are trying to beach themselves. We are going to have to try to get them back in the water.

There are seven other rescuers there, including a veterinarian with a stethoscope. The four healthy ones are rolled back into the water. My father, in his wet suit, swims dolphin-style out at the edge of the cove, trying to get the dolphins to imitate him. He splashes as he breaks the surface. The other men wait in the water, in case the dolphins try to turn back.

I am on the beach, with the dying one. She is covered in wet towels and I pour seawater on her with a cup from a pail beside me, my cast wrapped in a plastic bag. Her eyes roll under her double lids, and inside, her heart beats a soft tatter. She is warm still. I turn at the sound of my father in the distance, to see his orange snorkel blow water as he clears it before going under again. No one is saying anything.

Her heart starts to beat faster, as if her blood were tightening. It amazes me how fast the seawater dries. I pour more water onto the towel. Away from the rest of the sea, the seawater joins the air, instead. How does the ocean stay together, I wonder.

You'd better come over here, I say to the vet. I think she's going to go.

Off in the distant water her friends try to learn to swim without her, following my father's lead.

Why does she want to die, I asked my father, after he returned from his successful swimming lesson. We stood over her cooling body.

I think it's like getting buried, Aphias, my father said to me then. We put our dead underground. They lay their dead above-sea. She wanted simply the right rest for her race.

But we don't bury ourselves, I said.

I had watched the water on the way home in the car, the sunset across every wave.

I lie awake, thinking of her, under the guard of the printed Jacks and Jills linked in repeating patterns on my bedroom wallpaper. I watch as the passing lights of cars sweep through my room, the teenagers on my road coming home from dates, businessmen returning to their families, mothers driving car pools for theater, or speech and debate. The light swings across the room in bars, shaped by passing through my window frame. Light splatters, I know, on the outside of the house. I can almost hear the impact. I watch the hall light come in under the door. Light is a force, a wave and a particle. Light can touch me, and has to, actually, in order for anyone to see me.

15

SCHOOL BEGINS IN August this year. I live nearby, and so I walk and skip the bus. I read while I walk to school up the two hills, one sidewalk, a more or less straight line. I pretend the streets I pass through are empty. I have been reading about the Neutron Bomb. I want to be like that, radiant and deadly, a ghost of an impact, to pass through walls, to kill everyone, in flight among the empty houses, punching through molecules like a knife through a paper bag. See me. I am five feet and two inches tall. I am still thin, freckled, large eyes, small nose. My hair waves and grows long, to my neck. I pick flowers for my mother as I walk. The neighborhood kids call me Nature Boy. I want to die.

Help with my roses today, my mother says. We have to deadhead. She hands me a glove and the shears; this is something I can do one-handed. While she walks around the house watering, I snip off the faded blooms, spotty leaves. It is the final day of August, the sun already has its mind on its vacation, distant skies. I pause, hold up my arm cast and the shears: Look, Mom, I'm a crab.

She laughs. Blond and tan, a faint sheen from the hose gives her a glow. She squirts a pip of water my way and I yelp, dodging. You sure are, she says.

Later, inside, over lemonade and peanut butter and jelly, she tells me that Eric has called to say we have been asked to be a part of an opera this fall. A production of *Tosca,* she says. He's calling the boys he wants in advance, to clear it with their parents. You're supposed to act surprised when he announces it, because there is some small pay involved, the part is small.

Oh-kay, I say. Surprise. No problem. I push my hair out of my face. My hand as it goes by smells like the inside of the glove.

I guess he doesn't hold grudges, huh, she says. She begins putting away the lemonade, sets the jars of jelly and nut butter away.

I guess not, I say. Not until I go up to my room to get a book do I realize, I have no idea what she means.

In my gifted-and-talented speed-reading class seven of us sit in a dark room with a projector that prints lines on the walls. We read stories in this way and then are tested for comprehension.

Today we begin Boccaccio's *Decameron.* Jay, one of the more aggressive students, turns the machine on.

The story flashes by. The teacher opens the door, glances in. Oh, he says. All right then. And he goes back out. We sit, the story beaming on, punctuated by the projector's loud fan.

And it pleased Him that this love of mine, whose warmth
exceeded all others, and which had stood firm and unyielding
against all the pressures of good intention, helpful advice and
the risk of danger and open scandal, should in the course of time
diminish in its own accord. So that now, all that is left of it in my
mind is the delectable feeling which Love habitually reserves for
those who refrain from venturing too far upon its deepest waters.
And thus what was once a source of pain has now become, having
shed all discomfort, an abiding sensation of pleasure.

The *Decameron* was a collection of love stories told by ten people running from Florence during the time of the Black Plague. They told the stories to pass the time rather than playing games, at the direction of the Queen, traveling with them. Seven women, three men. Everywhere they looked, people dying. What a pleasure it must have been, I think, as the story flies up the screen in front of me in sections. To survive.

Afterward, the comprehension quiz asks, what were the afflictions of the Black Plague? And I write, bloody noses in the East, but in Florence, egg-shaped swelling in the groin.

How many people does the narrator describe dying?

Several hundred thousand in Florence, many more through the countryside.

Rehearsals in the fall are tighter: the camp has done its magic. We sit in ordered rows, we sing that way as well, chords offered like gleaming chains. Cathedral ceilings are references to Noah's ark, I have just learned. The idea being that he founded his church by upturning the boat: when we look up, it's supposed to be like looking at the prow of a boat above us. I think of this often, as I look at the bowed ceiling. This boat, I say to myself, is turning over.

Today is warm, and our rehearsal is going well. The choir has recently auditioned new members, and now we sit, forty, in broken arcs around our director. New money has provided music stands, nice folding chairs with padded seats. You're real pros now, Big Eric announces in one break. In another, he points to Little Eric and says, Now, and Little Eric gets up and leaves the room. I have a surprise, Big Eric says. Eric is helping me with it.

Little Eric returns, a miniature monk. Muslin tunic, burgundy overtunic. Rope belt. The shoes are obscured by the hem, which falls to the floor. He smiles at us and raises his hands palm-up in mock propriety. Big Eric walks around to stand beside my seat. If he were Friar Tuck, Big Eric says to me, Robin Hood would not be so busy rescuing Maid Marian.

This, Big Eric says to the room, gesturing to Little Eric, is the way we will dress for the Italian pieces. I'm having the costumes ordered, and you will all be fitted for them afterward. Also, please welcome Freddy Moran, a new soprano. Freddy stands from where he is seated in the row in front of me.

Unable to join us for the summer, he is a new soprano with a clear light voice and all the other details of Big Eric's favorites:

long blond hair, straight, cut in a Viking mop, with a short sturdy frame and then the surprise, brown eyes, long lashes. The sort mascara means to replicate. He doesn't look particularly Irish except perhaps this last part, the eyelashes. Zach's mother, Mrs. Guietz, calls them sooty eyes. Merle and Peter have them also.

Big Eric then makes his announcement about *Tosca* and reads off the boys to be included. Little Eric and Zach are a bit old for this and so weren't included, Big Eric concludes, and he laughs as he says this and puts his hand on Little Eric's shoulder.

Little Eric, mouth firm, continues to stand in the tunic beside him.

In the rehearsals that follow, we learn to wear the robes. How to stand for hours without fainting under the hot lights, and sing: breathe from the diaphragm, tilt the head forward slightly to project sound from the throat out through the forehead, keep the knees bent slightly; feet under the shoulders, and the fingers of your hands rest on your thighs, your pointer finger pointed at your foot, along the seam of your slacks. We go to Biddeford to meet the opera cast where the director tells us stories of past Toscas, past choruses: one director told the boys to follow her wherever she went on the stage, and so when she dives to her death, the boys followed her, jumping also, all landing in the orchestra pit trampoline installed for the stunt. In another, the diva dove and bounced back up. In another, she missed the pad, crashing into orchestra members and breaking a collarbone.

I combine the stories gradually over the rehearsals, until in my mind I see us all following Tosca, jumping with her and bouncing back up, all of us in the air together, broken.

My mother picks me up today from rehearsal. She has come after a teacher conference at school, where my teacher team, Mrs. Strauss and Mr. Christie, ask if everything is all right at home. My mother assures them everything is.

They say you don't have friends, she says to me. She drives the slow rush-hour traffic across the bridge back to Cape Elizabeth, the brake lights of the cars ahead of us flashing between bright and dull red in the early night. This week my father is in Sweden. I imagine him surrounded by blond people, the overwhelming numbers, him a shiny black-haired speck at the center. My blond mother. Sweden looks like a country of my mother. When he told me he was going, I thought of Big Eric's books. If my father had ever seen anything like them.

They parent me in a team, these two, my mother teaches me about people, my father about science. These subjects each teach me patience about the other. My mother and I sit quietly in the car as we consider this evaluation of me. All of my friends are in the choir, I say to her, finally, and she nods as she takes me home.

16

THE PLASTER SAW takes the cast off in a minute. Beneath, my arm is a scaly white thing, the dark hairs stand out starkly. How's that feel, the doctor says. Smiling. Rose-colored fat man, big black-framed glasses.

Fine, I say. I stretch it forward. Fine. And this is not a lie. The hand looks like it belongs to a monster. I think of my mother's rose cuttings, covered up for a month, until the branch, in desperation, grows new roots to live. This hand, it looks like it is ready to grow a whole new boy off itself.

Out in the waiting room, my mother stands as I come out the door. There's my little tree climber, she says. In the car, on the way home, the sunlight yawns through the trees, more faraway fire. Soon the clocks will go forward, the nights shrink close like turtleneck collars.

17

YOU, AS THE chorus, Big Eric tells the opera choir, are supposed to be innocent choirboys, and yet you all are supposed to act as if you are passionately in love with Floria Tosca. And you are both.

Saturday mornings belong to Opera now: the eight of us meet in the church room alone to rehearse, and soon, we will rehearse with the rest of the cast and orchestra. While my little brother and sister watch the Smurfs, I learn songs about vengeance, love, and slow death. Today Big Eric is explaining to us the role we have in the opera. The coffee he has brought bitters the room's air while we all drink hot tea with lemon to clear and tone our throats. Again, it reassures me less to know the history here. The story, though, is a good one: Tosca, the lover of a handsome painter, Cavaradossi, betrays him in order to protect him from his torturer. Tosca can save her lover by giving herself to the torturer, and she says she will in exchange for a mock execution. He comes to her and she instead, impulsively, stabs him to death with his dinner knife, in his chambers. She then visits her lover in prison, assures him of his safety, rushes to his side after the firing squad, only to find he really is dead. The torturer's murder is discovered, and his police come for Tosca, who then flings herself from a parapet to her death.

Operas, Big Eric announces, as he walks the room in long paces, are mainly about betrayals in love. Squalid light surrounds him from the stained-glass windows as he says this. His round bald head gleams, recently polished, he tells us, and from above the ears, the remaining hair, vigorous, grows long, to meet his mustache and beard.

After, he comes up to me. How did you like *Fire from Heaven*, he asks me. He twists his hands over each other in a way I've never seen before and only read about. He's the only person I know who rubs his hands.

It's fine, I say. I liked it. Big Eric had urged me to go read this novel, and I checked it out from the library. When I got home with it, I realized why he wanted me to read it. The novel is about Alexander the Great, who has an affair with his older, adult teacher, when he is still a teenager.

He smiles. Beautiful, right? You should read the *The Persian Boy*, next. About his eunuch lover.

I will, I say.

Every now and then, I think of Ralph, dead Ralph. He wings in, hovers over the rehearsal chapel, paler than ever before because he is slowly fading away. I know it is not a proper haunting because no one else sees him. We sang for him at a memorial service, held for him in a country church up by the camp. It was a choral service, which is to say, we sang a selection of things, and then there were remembrances and a sung prayer.

Occasionally, I imagine that the ball-lightning of that night at camp was him, finally emerging from the lake, the part of him that really was lost to the depths now running loose, looking for its small body lying in its small grave. That he is now a Will-o'-the-Wisp.

Now that we wear these rope belts, I think of him often as I knot it. The boat rope, too thick for a child to loosen easily. Think of the boats, the oarlocks above him. When he turned his face in the rain to the bottom of the boat, I wonder, looking up at the cathedral ceiling, did he think of God? Did he think of Noah? What did he pray for?

And then Big Eric swings back into view. And I mutter, Father, Son, Holy Ghost, inside, in the mouth I keep in my mind, as opposed to the beautiful mouth, the real mouth, the slave that sings beautiful things. Or kisses.

18

AT SCHOOL NOW, as it has been decided that I need friends, my mother has mentioned I must go out for a sport. I am a good swimmer, so these parents of mine decide that I must join the swim team. I am somewhat angry at my parents for being duped by my teachers this way but consent, because what else am I going to do?

The Cape Elizabeth High School swimming pool: Long thin windows band the walls reaching up to triple-height ceilings. The starting blocks at the shallow end remind me of altars. The pool has six lanes, is twenty-five yards long and is forever aquamarine, stinking of the chlorine acid poured in to clean the water. Now the time that I spent in the library between class and choir is spent here, doing laps. All those words, obliterated by this: I look to the pool bottom through goggles, where there is a single stripe at the bottom of each lane in the shape of the letter *I*.

We do drills for distance and speed. We separate out the elements of the stroke: first, just the arms, then just the legs, then the whole stroke, reassembled. We stretch, led in visualizations: Visualize yourself winning, my coach says, a young man watching his tiny potbelly, named Dan. See yourself ahead of everyone else. Do you see what that looks like?

I do. I see myself, having outdistanced them all. I begin to win races. I give the ribbons to my grandmother, who kisses them and then kisses me. My champion, she says. My grandfather laughs and rubs them in his fingers and he says, Fox is fast swimmer too.

I see Zach occasionally in the gym, when I have to do weight training. He is filling out from lacrosse. He shrugs. Says, Hey. We see each other less now, but my knowledge of him runs through these school rooms between us, so that some days, I feel like I know where he is no matter where he is. Other days, it feels like he doesn't even exist.

Come over, he says sometimes. Sometimes I do.

In Zach's room, we kiss. Like in a movie, long slow kisses, I count his teeth, he bites my lips. Today we haven't seen each other this way in over a month. When Little Eric's mom's car pulls up for choir car pool and honks, we separate and lie still for a moment, regarding each other: disheveled, our lips swollen. I need to put on jeans, he says. Go out and stall them. I wait a minute for him to pull off his shorts and then I get up, and pulling his penis toward me, give it a quick kiss, before heading out the door to tell Mrs. Johannsen that Zach will be right out.

Late October.

The concert where Peter is to sing the descant is held in St. Andrew's Cathedral. Zach and his parents come here. Stained-glass depictions of the lives of saints. A few angels on a mission. For the occasion we wear the robes and rope belts as we stand on the choir risers, a priory-in-miniature. The audience watches. We are halfway through the program and each pair of eyes in the audience, it seems, emits a force like a breeze—we stand before a gale of attention. The organ starts and we sing. I wait. Peter is to begin his descant. As I sing, it feels suddenly airless, as if in taking his breath, Peter has swept the atmosphere clean away. We hit the air repeatedly with the chords in our throats and bellies, making our devotions.

Peter opens his mouth. The first note pierces, the next goes inside the choir's airborne array, and then he is there, a part of us, all our tangling voices skein the air and Peter slips up, born aloft. My jealousy scrapes off as he keeps breathing, keeps sending more air through himself. Slow fire.

Love melts all our murder. As much as it makes it. Love melted me. Peter, it could only have been you.

Later, it is my turn in the program. I'd forgotten, in some bizarre way: the piece forced from my mind entirely. As we tuck the pages of our scores into place, Big Eric's eyes find mine. I sweat. All the colors around me leave. I don't remember more than the first three words. The people in the audience come into sharp focus, and I see small hats, wrinkles, tired eyes tired for years. Big Eric's eyes have the look of the owl now, but this time it's the owl descending. The owl who can see you from some-where in the night sky, where the flying hides it.

Right inside my chest, a space opens. He brings to his mouth a mouth harp, and he whistles a tone for me to begin on. The tone opens in my chest, rolls over in language, opens my mouth. All along, I thought I was the one singing. I am not. He sings through me. He opens his mouth and I sing. My mouth is his.

Full Fathom Five my father lies . . .

At the entrance of the choir, as they surround me, I feel myself return. For the moment I was alone, I was gone. I vanished. I keep singing, though, for here I am, a song again.

Afterward, as we stand around, receiving our parents and friends, I want to walk away from here with Peter. I want the doors to St. Andrew's to fly open at heaven's bidding and on a plank of sunshine to walk right up to heaven with Peter, where, looking at God's face, we explode into flame, as all mortals do, looking on His countenance.

Instead, we return to the dressing room where we change in

the smell of sweat socks and old dust, hang our robes, coil the ropes around the neck of the hanger. We climb into our clothes. We look at each other.

He knows.

All this singing seals something in. And so Peter says, You were really great.

In the dark gothic closet, dust spins around us. You were great, I say. In the only way. You were the only great thing.

No, you were, he says. You were.

I hug him to me and suddenly, I kiss him. On the mouth. Briefly. When I pull back, he's frozen in place. Looking off to the side.

Like a tap I feel Zach watching us from the door.

You both were great, he says. Now let's go.

Outside, my grandparents stand on the sidewalk, smiling hugely. Somehow, they seem stiller and stronger than the other people around them. As if gravity hugged them a little closer. Koreans very good singer, my grandmother says.

Yes, grandfather says. Very good singer. You have good Korean voice. Very strong.

My grandfather tells me again about how in Korea, everyone knows all the Korean songs, and sometimes, they start singing. On the bus, in the street. Everyone just singing, like in a musical. And for a second it seems like maybe I only wanted to sing because I am Korean, and not over there, with all the rest of them.

My grandparents haven't come to my concerts before now. They don't, in fact, often leave the property. My grandmother likes her garden. My grandfather likes our kitchen. But here they are, and at the sight of them everything evil in me seems to blow away, like dust from the top of a book. They hug me between them. Around us on the cold sidewalk the people my grandfather calls the potato people walk the streets, headed home.

BACKSTAGE. BIDDEFORD OPERA House, opening night. We sit
in our costumes, playing cards in our dressing room. Our faces
are made up.

The diva slips into our dressing room, a beautiful young
soprano by the name of Mare Winslow. Her hair is dyed red for
the part. Her low-cut dress reveals a very full chest. She smiles at
us. You're so beautiful, she says. All of you. Your voices, so beautiful.

She doesn't quite say it. That it's a pity, the voice won't stay.
Some of us might end up with a contra-tenor, but that seems to
me to be, at my childish vantage, wildly, unreasonably effemi-
nate. A boy's voice is a masculine voice not in pitch but because it
does not waver. I remember a rehearsal warm-up she attended,
where my voice and Peter's remained, scaling up and up, and she
said afterward, even I don't have that note. Envious then, she was
a little like a child looking at monkeys climbing and wanting a
tail.

Later, on stage, in the lights, her face slick with sweat, she
radiates sound out to the audience in passionate bolts and rays.
Tosca is demanding her lover repaint the eyes of the Mary Mag-
dalene to match hers, that he blot out the eyes of the Marchese
Attavanti, whose portrait he has incorporated into the picture
there in the church.

I see as I watch, her comparison of our voices is a false one: a
woman's voice *is* different, so very different, and hers, ridged by
vibrato, cuts like a serrated blade, where we boys stab like
swords—our voices tremble not at all. In this way, musically,
innocence is represented. Knowledge, specifically knowledge of
passion, makes you shake, apparently. As you answer for it before
God, singing for your short, beautiful life to inch forward even
by another minute. Even in the agony of loss is passion, is love,
and measured against death this sort of pain is a feast, also, and
requires a knife to carve it. Or so it seems, watching her run back
and forth across the stage.

We have one other scene, apart from singing in the first act. In the second one, while Tosca rehearses, offstage, for her royal command performance at the Farnese Palace, we sing with her. We sing softly, to represent distance, and the composer has arranged Scarpia's interrogation in counterpoint to what we sing. And even later, at the beginning of the third act, as the prisoners wander the yard, Freddy Moran has a brief solo offstage, where he sings, I send you as many sighs as leaves rustle in the wind.

And then later, in the prison, Tosca sings with Cavaradossi, Our love will glow like a blazing rainbow over the sea. She says good-bye to him, before his execution, I'll close your eyes with a thousand kisses, I'll call you by a thousand names.

Peter, somehow, shining there in the dark, all the light manages to find an excuse to go his way, to leave him the gifts of their colors. In his choirboy robes, bored by the passage of the opera, waiting for the ride home, the tucking into bed.

Peter sees me looking at him, finally. He smiles and waves, silent. I wave back. I tell myself, Not even the light should dare to love you.

After, as I sit, waiting for my mother to come and pick me up, Mare walks the empty stage, sits down beside me, adjusts the skirts in her costume, and sighs. Her powdery breasts push tightly together, like grapes pinched by fingers. I wanted to laugh tonight, she says.

I can feel the days ahead pulling her away, into other songs.

Me too, I say. Why is that?

Because love like this looks funny. People yelling for each other, shouting their jealousy, killing. Singing the whole time.

I think it's beautiful, I say.

Of course it's beautiful, she says. And there's really nothing like it, when you are climbing the notes and you realize suddenly, there, right there, this, and the music opens to you. You see how you aren't there, something else is there that belongs . . . to the music. It doesn't belong to you at all.

No rehearsal that Monday. My father returns from Sweden. He has begun a consulting business. As far as I can tell, that means he gets paid to tell people how to do things and how much it will cost them. Each time he returns from a business trip he has presents for all of us, my brother, sister, and I. Teddy gets skates. Sam gets a stuffed Laplander reindeer. I get a ski sweater, of some wool from an animal so vigorous, knitted by people so powerful, I feel like I am wearing a force field and not a gray sweater. The yarn seems to add muscle to me. In the mirror, I look powerfully built, like a boy-hero. When I remember the sweater is from Sweden I never wear it again.

While Big Eric runs the newer altos through his spiel about head tone and falsetto, I write about How to Fill a Heart with Hate, a poem, which I title that way. I write, The Heart to become Hate removes the R, which is Rue / a witches' brew of regret, separates the A which is Art from the E which is Eros by the T, / which was together and is now Terror. Or Time. But never loses / the H, which is Heaven, which is the way back. To the Heart.

Peter has cut all his hair off in what he calls a fade haircut. A blond frost covers his bare head. The altos finally learn, but now we are out of time. I close my music folder and cover my poem. Big Eric announces, at the rehearsal's close, a tour for the winter. Schools and churches, throughout Maine.

After the rehearsal, I watch Freddy walk in a slow circle as he waits for his mom. Peter waits beside me, pulls out a jar of black fingernail polish and begins to paint every fingernail. My sister, he says to me, dared me to do it. Fifty bucks if I did every finger.

Really, I say. Can you do that at a Catholic school?

Mmm, no. Clashes with the uniform, he says, and giggles. But the hair is fine. I'll just walk around with my hands in my pockets, like the rest of them do anyway. He casts a green eye my way. You want, he says, offering the bottle.

Just the pinkies, I say, thinking of a boy I saw downtown the other day, hair spiked red, black pinkies.

Tomorrow night, Peter asks, do you want to go to a hardcore all-ages show? Seven bands. My sister and I are going, and she's driving.

Yes, I say.

On the way home, I feel like I have Peter on my fingers. I curl my hands inside my pockets, and no one sees until swim practice the next day, where the other boys only wrinkle their noses, swimmers being mild-mannered. After practice, I ride my bike over to the barbershop around the corner from the bank near the school and sit down for a five-dollar fade. Fade. Something going away slowly. Pomade? the barber asks, and I ask what is it, and after he tells me, I leave, my hair shining, straight up, like the cut end of a paintbrush. I buy the pomade. I walk out stepping on my own hair, like feathers there on the floor where someone killed a bird.

The next day, when I go over to Peter's house, he says, It's good, and traces my fade with his finger for a moment.

What's this group's name, I ask Peter.

We're in his room, the door closed, his big old ugly stereo's volume turned way up. New Order, he says. He's smoking a Marlboro, blowing smoke into the sunbeam crossing his room. We are waiting to go into Portland with his older sister, Elizabeth. She's in the bathroom spraying her hair straight up with Aquanet and drawing lines of eyeliner out to her hairline. Punk-rock pharaoh, she says when I ask her about her look. Liz Taylor Bad Hair Day.

I like Elizabeth. She and Peter say they hate each other. She steals my butts, Peter says. He's a twerp, she says. Elizabeth is pretty, her blue mohawk cheers me up, like a sail or a blade, the crest of a lizard. Today we are going shopping at Goodwill and then from there to the show.

At the Goodwill, everything Peter finds he grabs one of for me, and there are patch-elbow sweaters, brand-new indigo jeans rolled high, T-shirts from rival high schools or faraway ones, their letters faded off, and then the precious black overcoats. Ten dollars. Good deals, Elizabeth says, who has found an old beaded black dress. I want to wear it now, Elizabeth says, and hops in the car. Play lookout, she orders, and starts to pull her clothes off. Peter and I sit on the sidewalk and paint our thumbs silver, because, we decide, we walk around with our thumbs in our pockets anyway. From far away, sitting down, it looks like we have a nickel out, ready to call, heads or tails.

Later, Peter and I stand together at the back of the all-ages hardcore show. Elizabeth is drunk and hitting on skinheads. The band starts to lean into their guitars and the lights blink. Everywhere around us, kids are throwing themselves into each other, banging and falling. A few, like me, pretend that nothing is happening and light cigarettes. Peter takes a straight razor from his pants and runs the razor up his forearm. A bright bead of blood follows. He does it again. And again.

Peter, I say. What the hell.

Don't worry, he says. You cut across, so you don't slice a vein. He begins on his other arm. And then he hands the razor to me. His arms a red crisscross. He winds himself up with a kick and throws himself into the boys.

Blood starts to come off on the other slam-dancers. I look at my arm, the skin there starts to look like it could be anything. I test the blade there but I can't press down. Peter returns, winded. Splashed 'em, he says. God, that's good. And he jumps back.

I try to imagine myself at swim practice, my arms marked. I wouldn't be able to swim with open cuts. I take out a cigarette and light it. The smoke takes the image away.

Dick-face, Peter says, reappearing in front of me. Blood now dried dark on his arms, across his white T-shirt. Give me that. And he takes my Zippo. He runs fluid over his hands and closes the tank, and flicks it across one hand and then the other. His hands on fire now, blue-white, he raises them over his head and spins back into the bodies. Ha! he shouts, and goes down to the floor, and then up again, and with his hands still burning he leaps from the edge of the stage and lands across a tangle of boys. His fire-hands go out.

I am watching Elizabeth. She has been drinking, talking all night to a cute skinhead boy about four inches shorter than she is. I find myself wondering if he will grow those four inches this year. He looks almost our age.

My sister is such a slut, Peter says, as if he can see what I am watching. He sits down. She's had every skin between here and Portsmouth between her legs, he says, and he lights a cigarette. He just moved here from Boston and he's heard of her, I bet. He spits on the floor behind us.

According to my mother, I'm over at Peter's. According to Peter's mom, Elizabeth has taken us to a late movie. Somehow after the show we go to an apartment building up off Congress Street, where loud music sprays the sidewalk and seventy-odd skinheads and punk kids drink beer and try to have sex. Peter and I are hiding outside the house, in a shadow now, trying to avoid the mean skins, our coats wrapped around us. They are threatening to shave our heads. Make you a proper skin, they say. Crewcuts are for hippies. We went outside when one of them asked me what I was.

What do you mean, I said.

Are you a gook or what? Eh, Charlie? Eh?

She's passed out for sure, Peter says, looking down the dark street. Street lamps post bleary light in rows away to either side. Lucky for us all those skins want a piece of her more than they want to shave our heads. I'm sure they're upstairs on her. His breath clouds on the winter air, a personal weather.

Peter takes my Zippo out of his pocket, twists and pours lighter fluid onto his thumb. He closes it and running it along his jeans, lights the lighter and then his thumb. A blue candle of his hand in the dark. He holds the thumb against the trash in the can next to us and the cartons and paper in there catch. If a cop comes, he says, we can pretend we're vagrants. He walks over to the side of the house. Wait here, he says. I need to go get my sister.

The fire gets larger. A peaceful warmth, some light for this dark corner, a bit of bitter smoke. I take a cigarette out and light it. For no reason I can account for, I am calm, searching myself for panic and not finding it. The cold is like a hand at my back, pushing me forward toward this burning can. I see Elizabeth's car, and go over to sit on the hood, where I wait until Peter comes out, his sister and another girl with him. They are helping Elizabeth walk but it looks actually like she's floating, carrying them with her as she flies. Wait, she says, and turns her head to the side, and dull amber vomit chokes out of her in a spurt. Steam rises where it hits the ground. Her head looks like it's bleeding, but closer I see it's actually an A for anarchy, painted there, shiny. Like it was done in lipstick. Fuck, she says. Oh, fuck me. She drops, cross-legged, onto the ground beside her vomit.

Peter fishes through his coat and comes up with his pack. He holds a cigarette out to his sister. Here, he says.

Thanks, she says. He lights it for her.

She looks into the trash fire and starts laughing.

Oh, fucking A, she says. A camp-out.

Peter taps on the shoulder of the other girl, a broad-shouldered swimmer I recognize now from meets. She swims for Falmouth, Butterfly. Her hair is cut short, almost like mine and Peter's. She leans in and says, Yeah. I'll drive. Peter hoists his sister up and loads her into the backseat, and I climb into the shot-gun seat.

Hang on, he says, as the girl settles behind the wheel. He runs back to the trash fire and for a second, I think he's going to put it out, but instead he kicks it against the side of the building, where it falls over the snowy ground. He picks up a stone and hucks it through the window. FIRE, he yells after the broken glass, and he hoofs it to the car, tossing himself into my lap. The door shuts with a bang, the flames splash the other trash cans, which start to roar, and the girl beside us is cursing, quietly, flooring the pedal as the wheels grind and then catch. Soon we are on the road out to Cape Elizabeth.

Peter says, Fee. Look back. Is she passed out?

I peek back to see her staring, wide-eyed, her hands crossed in front of her, laid across the seat. One hand cradles nothing, and then on the floor, I see the cigarette, which I pluck and hand to Peter. She dropped this, I say. He raises his eyebrow and then pushes down the car-lighter. As he relights her cigarette, the orange ring lights his face. He inhales hugely and smoke pours out of his nostrils.

Why'd you do that, the girl driving us asks.

It's one way to make sure she can't go back, he says, and he laughs. I fucking hate those pricks, he says, and finally leans into me, and I do not move for the rest of the ride.

•

I get home late. My mother waits, a single light in the kitchen, reading a book she puts down the moment I walk through the door.

Is it rebellion, my mother asks, my hand between her hands as she rubs off the polish with a cloth, the acetone on it making me dizzy. I sit on the shut toilet seat. I want to scratch my neck.

Just tell me you aren't sniffing it, she says, and I say, Oh, I hadn't thought of that.

Oh great. Honey, listen. Please remember that people at school are worried about you and that this reflects on me. It'll be hard for you to be friendly with the boys on the swim team if you do stuff like this.

Good, I say. They're ridiculous and I hate them.

She lets my hands go and pats my hair. That word. Will this shampoo out, she asks.

I don't know, I say, hoping that it doesn't.

A regular little iconoclast, aren't you. I guess I'll stop while I'm ahead. Is this blood? She looks me over, as if I were someone else's child, and I try to stay calm. Don't say I didn't try, she says.

I don't want her to wash the blood off. It's not like I got a mohawk, I say.

The next day, when Peter and I walk into rehearsal together, identical hair, identical Goodwill clothes, Big Eric asks, Are you cadets or sopranos?

Soprano cadets, I say.

We'll learn Britten's *War Requiem* someday then, he says. We'll all get crew cuts. He taps the music stand. Tck tck tck. His promise to remove me, if I showed bizarre behavior, broken.

20

DID YOU SEE his arms, Zach asks me.

We are in his beige room, naked. The afternoon on Sunday. His parents are out, his brothers are out, and in an odd way, it feels as if this is our house. I get up to get a glass of water, and look at myself naked, with my short hair. I have a premonition then, of my future. That this is the start of what it looks like. I go back, and settle next to Zach. He has been asking me questions about Peter.

I didn't, I say. What did they look like?

Like cigarette burns. Round, red scabs, blistered. James Dean used to do it, apparently.

I think of James Dean. Peter has the same look, at certain angles. The raised eyebrows, the beautiful eyes, the way the whole face seems to lean forward to get your confidence, and, having it, whispers something just for you. I say, He's going to pierce his ear.

Big deal. Does he burn himself? Zach rubs my head. I like it, he said the first day. Soft.

I haven't seen anything of it. But I'll look for it, I say. And I have a memory of pale arms in the dark, hands burning.

I look down to see my hand on Zach's penis, the silver nail. Soon we will get dressed, leave, we will speak as if none of this is happening. I'll find out, I say, and unspoken in the air is, to tell you next time.

Zach turns over my forearm. Plain skin, he says.

21

FREDDY MORAN'S HOUSE takes up most of the plot it sits on, a narrow stripe of yard barely surrounds it. He lives in Cape Elizabeth not far from me, in one of the town's newer houses, on Old Ocean House Road. This house is newly made, the carpeting new, and Freddy has an enormous upstairs room, a sunroof he can climb through to the roof deck, furnished by his telescope, on a steel tripod mounted by bolts into the wood.

Some days I feel like a perfectly normal boy, and this is one of those. Freddy and I eat pizza his mom made and watch television. We wait for the sky to be dark enough to see stars.

Do you like the X-Men, Freddy asks, during another commercial break.

I do, I say. Who's your favorite character?

Charles Xavier, he says. I like that he can go into people's minds and see what they're thinking.

Phoenix is mine, I say. She can blow a hole through the world if she's not careful.

Christmas is near and Mrs. Moran comes into the room suddenly with a box that turns out to be full of decorations: pine boughs, modeled birds with real feathers and wire feet to twine around branches, twinkling lights. She begins to put the string lights up around the edge of the ceiling. Hi boys, she asks. How's everything?

Good, I say.

Are you excited to get away at the end of January, she asks.

I am, I say. I really am.

I thought your solo was wonderful, Fee. You have a remarkable voice.

I think of my mom, hear her say, accept all compliments with thank yous. Thank you, I say.

She taps tacks into place with a tiny ball-peen hammer. Freddy tells us he's getting a solo soon, for the Benjamin Britten concert in April, at Easter. We're looking forward to him singing for us.

The television chatters away, merciless. I hadn't heard that Freddy was getting this, but it makes sense. I want to say, Take your son out of harm's way. I want to say, Run, go on, get out of here. I want it to be like in the movies, where the dangers are ridiculous disasters no one faces regularly, like nurses who deliberately shoot air into your veins, or villains from Russia who want to fake international incidents. If a robber were to knock at the door, I would know how to respond.

We go upstairs to look at stars. There's worlds above this one, a night sky full of separate infernos so far away they look to us like they are only tiny lights, and easily extinguished. Freddy and I try to make out the rings of Saturn and Jupiter, but the sky, clear as it looks, won't allow it.

February.

I remember that this night is very dark. I remember the tour as long dark nights and short days, and starchy, sleepy food. I remember families looking at us, trying to decide what we are.

The motel we have in Bar Harbor is dark, every window shut against a cold night. Beside me, Peter smokes, the only light besides the security light comes from the tip of his cigarette, getting brighter and darker. We sit together in the oily parking lot, on a snowbank. Peter's crying and I'm pretending not to notice, even though it is the single reason I'm keeping him company.

I'm not, he says. Fuck him. I'm not.

The school concerts had finished to uniform applause, everyone clapping thirty times, more or less. I'd started to count, to know the time it takes for your hands to get sick of each other. The church concerts were bizarre, little pale white-haired men and women emerging slowly from the pews to escort each other home, as if we were visiting a country where only the elderly prayed. We arrived in Bar Harbor, and went to the spitting rock, where the tide shoots up through a throat-shaped tunnel from an entrance just below the water, to blow a spume, accompanied by a basso whump, like a merman clearing his throat. Other such attractions followed, ending in a fish-and-chips dinner eaten in an early, unwelcome dark. After unpacking and watching television for an indeterminate period of time, Peter came to our door, knocking, and drew me out. Zach's eyes as I left indicated he didn't want to wait up long for me. The whole trip long, Adam and Merle fell asleep quickly and deeply, snoring loudly together and not waking each other, and so we had been having what felt to me like a busman's honeymoon. For two busmen.

I'll be right back, I'd said to Zach. That had been some hours ago.

Now we sit in the parking lot surrounded by what seems a slow nighttime convulsion of darkened houses and bright streets and air that tastes like cold metal between breaths of a cigarette. I'll tell this time, Peter says to me. Fucking unbelievable.

Was anyone else there, I ask, as if it makes all the difference. As if there are details that will order what is currently resisting order. Peter came back to the room, and Big Eric had emerged from the bathroom with his fly open, partly aroused. Nothing had happened like that since the tour began, and we had all begun to pretend again that nothing happened ever, of that sort.

It comes to me that there was a time when we could have said something, but I can't think of what that time was. As if I have been sleepwalking all these years, singing through a dream, waking only occasionally. And this time out here will end and the dream pick up again.

Our breath looks like smoke. As Peter twists his cigarette, looking at it, I think of what Zach told me about cigarette burns. I turn, meet his eyes. He sees what is there a moment too late, as I lunge, knocking him into the snowbank. His cigarette bounces to wink a few feet away, and he makes a crying groan underneath me. What the fuck, he says, sobbing. What.

With my teeth, so I don't let go of his wrists, I pull back the sleeve of his sweater, to see his wrists, crisscrossed with pale red lines, some purple, raised circles. Almost a tic-tac-toe. Knife sketches.

What are those, I ask.

What do they look like, faggot, he says. Just leave me alone. Fuck off me. Get the fuck off me. He pushes, unable to move against me, and then he manages, rolling us over so that he pops up and off. Dick, he says, kicking snow across the top of me. Dick. The snow on my face begins to melt.

Peter, I say. I love you. I sit up, to see his face, dark and wet.

What. Is. This. He yells each word. What. Shut. Up.

A light comes on in a room next to the lot. I jump up and run, hear Peter following me. As I head for the corner, and begin climbing the far snowbank there, I hear Peter's feet dig into the crunchy snow, and it is like he is climbing my heart. In the lot on the other side of the snowbank, I head for a space between two parked cars and we sit, each facing over the other's shoulder, assuming the automatic position that allows us to look out, each way. We are panting, and Peter pulls his pack of cigarettes out, and as he holds it up to light it, he notices that the filters were smashed off when I rolled him over. You fuck, he says, holding the pack up for me to inspect. He flicks the filter off and lights the cigarette, spitting out tobacco shreds as he exhales.

I wanted to kill you, he says, chuckling.

Peter, I say.

Shut up. Just . . . you're my fucking best friend, okay? But be a friend. Just, uh . . .

Okay, I say, and reach for his cigarette.

We do not finish the tour.

According to the police report filed by Freddy Moran and his parents, Freddy returned to his room after watching television in my room with Zach and Adam and Merle, at around 9 P.M. on the night of January 27. He walked in to find Big Eric lying in bed, naked and erect and fondling himself. He appeared to be alone. Big Eric began talking to him in a casual manner, as if nothing was different, and asked if he had seen Peter. Freddy could only reply that he had been in my room, and that Peter and I had left together and not returned. At which point Big Eric, referred to in the report as Mr. Gorendt, became agitated.

Dungeons & Dragons, eh? Is that it? he apparently asked.

Freddy reported that there had been, to his knowledge, no game planned for tonight, as tomorrow was to be an early day. At which point, Freddy asked after the whereabouts of Little Eric, in the report known as Eric Johannsen. He had advanced into the room only a little.

He's right here, Mr. Gorendt replied, and pointed to the floor by his bed. Freddy Moran approached to confirm this, to see what appeared to be either an asleep or unconscious Eric Johannsen, he couldn't be sure. Eric Johannsen was later confirmed to have been asleep, as the result of a sleeping pill dosed to him by Mr. Gorendt so that he would not interfere with the seduction of either Peter or Freddy.

Eric Johannsen was naked. Freddy waited to see a rise in his chest, to confirm that he was still alive, and then he looked at Mr. Gorendt, sitting calmly, now pulling a sheet over himself, as if he were cold. He's sound asleep, Mr. Gorendt said, and dropped a towel over him. Freddy Moran drew back.

I know that if Big Eric had been photographed in that hour he wouldn't have recognized himself at all. Freddy pretended to be looking for something, and then at the door, he bolted, running, full speed. He knew Big Eric wouldn't chase him naked. He pounded on the door for Zach to let him in, who did, and he called his mother. I'm okay, he said. I'm not injured or in pain, just scared. At this point, Big Eric was pounding the door, now locked against him, bellowing various threats. Freddy's mother called the police, who were there in minutes, already having been called by the owners of the hotel, frightened into thinking Big Eric was a stranger. They didn't, they said, recognize him as being the kind man who had checked in.

The police found Peter and I in the parking lot, where we had fallen asleep, beside each other, between the cars. They had feared on first seeing us that we were dead. Like Freddy thought of Little Eric.

22

I HAD ALWAYS wondered exactly how many, had tried to figure it out, but the twelve counts surprised me. Me and almost every friend I had in the choir, except for Merle and Eric B. Adam had been a surprise. He had brown hair, was stocky, was not his type as I had come to know it. He resembled me. Until recently twelve boys represented half the choir. I saw us then in a dim procession, Big Eric *was* Saturn, he had swallowed us, out of fear and gluttony, and now we marched out of him as out of a cave, and overhead, a now-happy Ralph, winged not like angels but with the tiny brown wings of a sparrow or a phoebe. He would perch, hold the walls tight, as if he didn't trust his wings to hold him up. When nothing else had.

23

IT'S NOT YOUR fault, my dad tells me.

I can tell, he doesn't understand. He can't understand. How it really is all my fault. We are out in back of the house. I can see my grandmother, slicing at her cutting board. I can't see what she's cutting, but I can tell she's cooking something for me. When the first news of the scandal came out in the papers, and Mom and Dad told her, she stayed quiet. She sighed, and it sounded like a sigh that had been learned under a different sorrow. Her face had deepened for a moment then, in a way I had never seen but would see again, many times.

It is my fault, I say.

He draws a deep breath. We love you, Aphias. And we feel terrible, that all of this happened and we weren't able to protect you. He kneels as he says this, and now our eyes are even.

His eyes dark like the color the Atlantic takes, when there's no land in sight.

I say it again. It is my fault. It really is all my fault. My face is running wet now. It is all my fault.

And here my grandmother comes running across the lawn. I have never seen her run. She is crying also. And she pulls me into her skirt. Aphias, she says. Aphias. Come in and see what Granmi has made for you. Come in and see.

Peter and I, next to the sea. On a beach in Falmouth, a sand spit. The far water ripples like smoke. It's over, he says. He's in jail.

He's in prison, I say.

Peter had to change schools when the kids found out. He goes to Waynefleet Academy now, a private school in Portland. He helps pay for it by bar backing at his father's bar. His angel-face now a study in waiting. A man coming on in him, too, there's added sturdiness now, every month a soft edge loses to a harder one. What do you do, when the criminal goes away? Where's the rest of the story?

The criminal is still here. Story, here.

The sheet music told us, what you are trying to do, boys have tried to do for five centuries. They used to castrate the boys with the most beautiful voices. We were afraid to find this out, but also, excited. This seemed, if not reasonable, understandable. To always be able to sing like this. Five hundred years of beauty.

When I was a boy and I sang, my voice felt to me like a leak sprung from a small and secret star hidden somewhere in my chest and whatever there was about me that was fragile disappeared when my mouth opened and I let the voice out. We learned, we were prisons for our voices. You could want to try and make sure the door was always open. Be like a bell, Big Eric would say. But he didn't know. We weren't something struck to make a tone. We were strike and instrument both. If you can hold the air and shake it to make something, you learn, maybe you can make anything. Maybe you can walk out of here on this thin, thin air.

Fifteen. I lose my voice. My new voice sounds like a burned string rubbing. Singing is touching, you bang the air and the air moves something inside you and the thing moved registers, says, That is a sound. When we sing to each other we are touching each other through this sleeve of air between us. When my voice changes I know this new creature is capable of no significant touch, no transformations. This voice cannot erase me, take me over and set me aside. This new voice has no light. It can barely push enough air aside to tell people, Hello, Good Morning, Good Night. I stop talking as much.

I hear my recorded new voice in a tape my school music teacher makes, and it sounds like a stranger. If I called after myself in the street, with this voice, I wouldn't hear me. I would keep walking, away.

The memory I have of my old voice, the soprano of my childhood, is a memory of desire. For the voice to unstring itself. To rise free of the vocal cords, shed the body like a cormorant sheds the sea after plucking its catch. Not to fly but to be flight, not to carry but to be the carrying.

I go to classes, swim. Swimming is good, shucks me off of me. In the water, nothing. No harm anywhere, and the repetition excites me. Everything, when I feel it, feels bad. The swim team avoids me, even when I win. Zach and I continue to see each other. Peter and I go out with his sister sometimes to "straight-edge" shows where no one drinks or does drugs or smokes. Peter lights up only on the way home. He has to change schools now again. Sometimes I wonder if he knew why I always asked him to never tell. Why I helped Big Eric hide in plain sight. I didn't have an answer for Peter then but he never asked. I have an answer, now.

Hiding him hid me.

January's
Cathedral

F e e

I

THE CHURCH-CHOIR director's daughter is the only person who
saw him. He had walked to the far edge of the field, burning,
unrecognizable, unable to make any sound as the fire took the air
out of his lungs. He had set himself on fire and then, perhaps
unable to bear the pain while seated, walked, and while walking,
Melinda, poor thing, saw him. She was at home, eating some
cereal, a few minutes left to her before she was to go down and
catch the bus. That morning as he fell to the ground, she left the
house to get help, her mother already at the school.

It would have been around seven in the morning on a morning
at the end of August, perhaps the last day of the month. Peter
had planned his death for two years. In letters sent to his friends,
he talked of how he had tried to kill himself for the first time
when he was eleven. He had failed and in such a way that no one
suspected he had even tried. He resolved then to keep it a secret,
and to plan well for the next time. He threw a Dungeons & Dragons game that lasted until late and then we left to go home, as it
was the first school night of the summer. He stopped me to take a
picture of us together, a Polaroid. Here, he said, and gave it to
me, and then laughed. I said, It's not as much fun to play anymore, is it. And he said, Yeah. It's not.

At the end of the night he went to bed for a few hours, waking
up in the early morning to go and buy the gasoline he would use
to burn himself to death.

I remember Melinda, the choir director's daughter, going away for a season and not knowing why, and how, when she returned, the curiosity I'd always seen in her eyes was gone. Mildly retarded, with glasses as thick as a bottle, it seemed like her glasses let you see more of what was going on inside her rather than showing her anything at all.

When she returns, I see her first again at church. She has grown over the winter, and her eyes no longer meet mine; she no longer seems like she is pressing up against her glasses to escape, like before. She seems like she hides now. As if she feels someone blames her for seeing the burning boy, and so now, she has no particular interest in seeing something else that will get her sent away again.

I wonder, if it would be like being with him forever, to see him like that. I think it is. I want to ask him what it was he thought he was going to burn when he set his fire. And if what burned, if that is what is really gone now. In the picture, he is a white glare, his face there the shape of a fist, his hair a gold outline. His blue eyes alight with what looks like real cheer. That is what burned, I tell myself. Not the thing he hated. Because that is with me.

At Peter's funeral service, his mother approaches me. Fee, she says. Come by after for the wake. We'll drive you home if your mom can drop you off. It'll just be some family, mostly, but you were a good friend to Peter. We'd like to see you.

During the service I had stared at the dark brown mound, pale flowers in a pile where the head should be, some six feet below. No one said, I wish he was still here. No one seemed to rage that he was gone. For all that we were surprised, I saw, as I looked around at the mourners, we also accepted it. Boys and girls from the private school he attended filed past me in twos and threes. This whole time Peter's mother hadn't asked to see the letter I had received from Peter. I'd not offered to show it. And until then, it didn't occur to me, that it might belong, in a way, to her. But then she breathed, hugged me to her and moved on.

I stayed until everyone was gone. I think I was waiting to cry. I think I was waiting to fall apart, and to find him standing there at the center of the pieces of me, alive again.

In his room after the ceremony the sunlight, the last of the day, makes a bright patch on the carpet and I watch it as it moves, slowly, across the floor, which I later realize means I have been there for over an hour. I throw myself onto his bed, briefly, to smell cigarette ash and tobacco, old beer, the salty carnation smell of him underneath that.

I pass by his father downstairs, who nods at me, saying nothing. He shakes the ice in his glass gently, as if he is thinking about pouring the Scotch on the floor. His mother moves about the kitchen as she always did, except she is dressed in widow's black. I go out the door to find his blue-haired sister, Elizabeth, outside. She had braided her mohawk for the ceremony, tucked it under a hat, and the whole effect had been, actually, quite elegant. It's the end of the summer, and the heat is just bearable. She smokes, her right arm holding the cigarette with the support of her left, crossed under her, holding herself.

Do you want one, she asks, and holds out a pack of Marlboros. Peter's brand. And then I notice his handwriting on the pack. POH.

She sees me read it. He always did that, she says. You never saw it before? He always did it so I wouldn't take his cigarettes. I always did, though.

I take one, light it. There's a half carton upstairs, she adds. Go take some before you leave.

Peter's dog slips through the hedge, back from a hunt at the yard's edge. Odd, she says, exhaling as she spoke. To buy a carton before your suicide.

For a few weeks after, I keep seeing her around town. Elizabeth everywhere, it seems. She smiles, nods, chewing gum and smoking or talking and smoking, seven safety pins now in her left ear and her boot buckles rattling every time she steps forward. I think, when I see her, about his initials tucked somewhere in her clothes. From the attention I give her I know she thinks I'm strange, but I also know I'm on her list of boys people think are gay, because we don't go skinhead. Peter told me about the list, because she had showed him. In order to show him our names together on the list. I see her with a new boyfriend. I see her smoke Marlboros, and then not, and then I know, when I see the white filter in her fingers instead of the yellow, the carton is gone. I think of the initialed packs, tossed out in different cans wherever she was, a Dumpster here, a riverbank there. Of how I wanted to follow her, and pick up every one.

2

HERE WE GO a car-oling among the leaves so green, Here we . . .

Christmas Eve. On the street where I live, we carol to our neighbors regularly every year. At the end, one family has everyone inside for eggnog. This year is suddenly cold, where before it had been mild, and snow upon snow arrives on the days before Christmas. Cape Elizabeth is going from being one kind of town to another, everyone says. And when they say it they mean there is nothing good to this, and they say it always to the new arrivals, who accept this as a kind of hazing, even as they assume it doesn't mean them. Here in the Masrichs' house, on a kidney-shaped downturn off our street, Brentwood, these pronouncements are meaningless at the party. We are all new on this street. All our houses are not quite ten years old. During the caroling I had finally put together what another child from down the road had said, about how he could find the bathroom in my house even if he had never been there, because it was just the same as his. There were, I could see now, four or five different plans, used in rotation, so that no matches were visible each to the other. At the Masrichs', also a Frontier Colonial, like ours, I sat on the stairs to the side as adults trooped up and down past me, glow-bright cups of eggnog in their hands. Let me give you the tour, Mrs. Masrich said to each newcomer to the house, and so they would go, up and down and around. This is the sewing room, and the bathroom is over here, I hear from the upstairs hall. You can put your coats there.

I have grown two inches in the last year. I have big legs. I look at them a fair amount, amazed at them. My thighs are as big as heads. I think of when I was on vacation last summer with my Grandfather Zhe, to the man who wanted to massage them for me. I'm a soccer coach back home, you know, he said. You look like a nice husky boy. The hotel where we were staying had a faux-desert landscape, around the pool area, and so we were hidden by a peach-brown dune of cement from the view of my dozing grandfather and siblings. I told him, I don't think so. But thanks. He told me his room number, just in case I felt "sore." Later that night, in my hotel room, I thought of how I could kill him.

My mother appears in front of me at the bottom of the stairs. She has dressed in a foam-green crew-neck sweater under a loden coat she wears on her shoulders, her blond hair arranged there, pulled back with one barrette to her nape, making her look much younger than most of the other mothers. Why are you here on the stairs, she asks. She settles a hand on my leg.

She asks me something I don't hear over my own thoughts. I'm sorry, Mom? I ask.

You were looking right at me, I'd swear, she says, and she grabs my ear, bending it a little toward her. I said, Are you feeling well?

Sure, I say. All this Christmas stuff just depresses me. I really only like the music.

You're not very convincing. You're so angry these days.

I'm not. I'm not angry. I stand up and walk down the stairs to the foyer. See, I say, heading to the main room. See how happy I am?

There's no call for sarcasm. She crosses an arm over her stomach and props up her elbow, her drink resting up near her face.

Hey Nora, come in here. Aphias, come here. My dad comes from around the corner. His face flushed, he takes my mom by the hand. C'mon.

On the television was some footage from the Spirit of Christmas Concert, taken from two years before. The chorus had sung with an adult choir, the Portland Symphony, and a few guest stars from the Biddeford Opera production of *Carmen*. My father had seen my face on the screen and looked for it again. You were right there, he said, indicating the corner of the screen in which my face had appeared. Right there.

3

ENDLESS JANUARY INTO endless February. Sunny days hit the snow and make me hate light, cold that snaps my nose numb and then burns me once I'm inside. I spend the days reading.

I had been doing an English paper on the pantoum, a literary form, originally Sri Lankan, that came to Italy in pages wrapped in silks. The same silks that perhaps had arrived with the infected fleas of the Plague. I think of the elegant horses, stung as they ride, carrying the death of nations.

I take a break from studying and find my grandfather reading through the paper in the gray winter light shading the kitchen. It's the afternoon, just before dinner. He favors our kitchen as a place to hide from my grandmother. She favors her kitchen as a place to hide from him. Anyung haseo, I say, sitting down. I've been practicing some Korean, because it makes my grandparents smile.

He chuckles, almost to tears. Pretty good, round-eyes, he says. He learned a lot of his English from G.I.s, and says things like this, or, I take leak. But he's salty in his own right. He didn't learn English from them by accident. He sets the paper down. How's my smart grandson?

Good, I say. And I pick up the paper to look at the classifieds, because I've decided I want to work a job and have some extra money. And so I see this:

Wanted: student researcher, for book project. Please be energetic, bright, a fast learner, and extremely quiet, with an interest in history, in particular the 14th century in Europe. Please call Edward Speck, at . . .

When I call the number listed, the man I speak to is good-natured and reserved, and tells me to come by to see him. He gives me an address in South Portland, nearby, in a part I don't ever go to, though not for any particular reason I can think of, and the next afternoon I drive over and find myself ringing the doorbell of a large brownstone house that looks out of place, surrounded as it is by new houses. As if this house had been here for a very long time, alone, and suddenly been joined by neighbors just beyond the boxwood shoulders of its lawns.

Edward Speck is a tiny man. His white hair drifts above a cheerful face. He lets me into the house on this afternoon looking like he's decided, seeing me through the door, to hire me. He tells a brief history of himself (study at Oxford, Ph.D. from Columbia) and that he lives here because it was his grandmother's house and he had always wanted it. The furniture was all hers and is original. He asks me no questions. I've added nothing, he says.

I admire in particular, in the mudroom, a bench attached to a mirror and hung down the sides with bronze fixtures resembling moose antlers.

I'm only here, he says, for the cold months. We sit in the parlor, on matching giant leather club chairs. His has an enormous hassock in front of it. A Persian rug, the color of several wines, muffles us.

Why's that, I ask.

Because cold air concentrates oxygen powerfully. It's wonderful for the brain. And also, no one likes to be here in this time of year, so no one visits me, and I am left alone.

I see. And, I do.

We agree on payment (he decides for more than I'd thought) and he outlines some responsibilities: opening and filing all his mail for him to go through, returning books placed to the right of the desk to his library, returning books placed by the door to either the Portland library or the library of the university (check inside flyleaf). Occasionally, he says, I will ask you to look things up for me, and then photocopy what you find, along with related articles, or to take out the book. You won't have to do any writing or household work, although sometimes I may ask to be driven. I will need you for ten to twelve hours a week.

He stands. Now, for the tour.

The ceilings of the dark house accommodate people much taller than him or I. The library I remember and envy. When I first enter it, I realize I would work without pay to be able to come here. For some genius thought to make a room like this: three stories tall, shelves on all sides, brass ledges to them connected by ladders made of iron. And all the books shelved and stored behind glass doors crisscrossed with iron. Windows edge only at the top, so that light glows into the room instead of falling, and then the ceiling with a fresco of a dark city, a mountain in the center of it.

What is that city, I ask.

Edinburgh, he replies.

The mountain? I say.

Arthur's Seat, he says. A hill.

On my way out, he looks at me and asks, What is your parentage?

I am used to the question. I know the look: people searching my features for matches, finding few that correspond. It is confusing to some people to look at me. Watching me takes longer than most.

Half Korean, I say, and half Scottish-English.

You look like a Russian, he says. A young Cossack, really.

I think of Mongolia. Lady Tammamo. A little Mongolian too, I say.

An ancient race. He pauses, lit from within inside his doorway. Excellent, he says. We'll see you soon. And oh, by the way, call me Speck, please. Everyone does. And with that he closes his giant door.

4

THE LIBRARIANS LAUGH as I carry my piles of books out of the library. My mother is incredulous as I bring them in from the car.

I don't pretend I understand, my mother says, surveying the piles of books in my room. But if this is what you want.

It's really interesting, I say. It created a great deal of what we know as culture today.

Uh huh, she says. I can't wait until you and your father go over this one.

This is just something I want to do, Ma, I say. And she pulls the door shut, saying, Come down for dinner in an hour. One hour.

I look over the books before closing the door to go downstairs. A job, I understand now, is a purpose. I feel a sense of mission. My hours with Speck leave me feeling protected. I walk through the quiet house attending to my duties. Under his instructions, I am to speak with him when I arrive, after school at four, and when I leave, at six. At no other time, unless, of course, he comes to find me. But these restrictions leave me feeling free inside the silence, which, inside his house, is as thick as the drapes that protect his dark house from the light that would bleach the color from the chairs and yellow all the books. Even in their pristine cases. The relief of nothing to say. I'd always prized silence for being the absence of other noises. In this house I come to see how one can prize silence for being articulate, as well.

5

PUBLIC HIGH SCHOOL seems to me to be a barbarian ritual of four years that leaves me with no ability to mark its beginning or end except through shame and occasional violence, from which I hide in a series of classes for the precollegiate, and the thirty of us who fall into this category come by senior year to seem a race apart from the hundred others in the class. One girl in the year ahead is ridiculed for having her picture taken with her baby, for the yearbook. The father had died. I look at the picture and they seem to me unbearably beautiful. Her hair carefully folded back by a curling iron, his baby hair tied atop his head with a ribbon. She had always been, I recalled, a fiercely silent girl, pretty and small. Now she seems a giant. I see her in the school, nonchalant. Widowed, a mother, a high school senior. Our lives, I decide, watching her, are tiny beside hers.

I watch my grandparents as well. They fascinate me. Their ears seem tuned to some signal not quite in range of hearing. And their quiet, a readiness. My grandfather rises to do Tai Chi in the mornings on the back lawn, facing the sun as it rises. My grandmother meditates, and then cooks for him. When she smiles, her smile has the force of a joy as old as her and as unbroken.

Zach and I continue. What we continue, we don't know. We don't ever talk about what we do, directly. We say, I'll be over. Or, Are you coming over? As if one or the other of us had decided to visit, and hadn't yet informed the other. I don't love him. He doesn't love me. Now we tear at each other more, for wanting not to want this. And afterward, as I look at his white thighs and brown arms, there's real tenderness in knowing, whatever it is we want from each other, it seems always to be the same. No one asks about how we spend our time. His parents, often not home, would have no way of knowing. That I had been there.

In my bed I keep Peter's letter to me. The one that arrived after he was dead. I keep it with a picture I have of him, in its envelope. My mother doesn't move it when she changes my bedding. Ever.

6

SPECK'S OTHER HOME is in New York City, and he promises to me to take me there sometime. There's nothing like New York, he says. I feel young there. Everything there is much older than me.

On an afternoon when the sun is starting to come and stay longer, and the snow melts enough to show all the dead grass, Speck interrupts both our silences. I am in a pile of his bills, marking the ones to be paid. Subscriptions, utilities. Doctors. Ugh, he says. So, would you like to see this?

I reply with a look.

Come here, he says. Come on. I've been looking it over again, and will probably never allow it out of its case again. Not while I'm alive. He takes me into the library. A letter in two pages, under glass.

They were renovating an old building, and it sort of fell in, in the cellar, he says. They came across the spire of an ancient cathedral, buried shallowly and unfinished. The letter was found in the top of the spire. Here's my translation.

1361. Edinburgh. I do not know the day, since they were abolished. A last letter. To whomever finds it, whenever they have heart enough to dig.

This was to be a cathedral built for Robert II, but now is mine.

I had fallen asleep. A fever had come over me and I had left my house, where I had been a boarder. I was the last one, I think, of those who hadn't left and were not dead. In any case the house was empty and I sought the company of our Lord, even though I was soon to have it.

Our area had been set off, and no one was allowed to enter or to leave. The death rolls for this street of the township had increased so quickly and stayed so high that soon no one was coming in to bury the dead. They were being left, and sometimes a house would burn, to indicate that everyone in that family had passed. Being unable to partake of a regular service at the church, I came here instead. And I had been so unhappy, and so afraid, I tried, here in the unfinished cathedral, to make some peace in myself toward what my fate would be, when this fever ended.

I hadn't expected this.

I do not know how it is they have succeeded, by what art they have buried us. But they have. No light fills the windows. When I look from the door, I see a narrow and dangerous tunnel, the roof timbered. Piles of dirt are there. Refuse. And I am sure the smell is not just from the dead left here, but from those brought over and thrown here. Since we are a street of graves anyway. And so the air is foul and close, and there is now a stink that I suspect to be myself. I am lucky, I think, that the boils on me arrive now, where no one will try to burn them with irons. I am given to remembering now, how a friend had said, of the Black Death, that the leprosariums are now closed. The lepers being dead. Soon, all will be dead.

I am Andrew Hunter. I am a Norman, my family recently given over charge of the forests of Arran. I had come here to study stoneworks. In particular, I had been interested in a Roman bridge, back in Normandy, where my family is from, made of coursed stones, and made so that the water passing could pass through the stones, even as the bridge stood. Many days I spent looking at the bridge, studying the construction. But I am not sore, for surely it is God's work that I be here. Surely it is Heaven's own intent that I be here, alive, to record what has been done. For no one will write of it otherwise, a record of what happened here. I do not doubt, the new death roll is simply the number of the souls buried here, and the name of the road. I do not doubt.

Mostly I fear the rats, gruesome and huge and black. They fear my candlelight, what I can draw from these tapers left here. Meant for future services, now to be burned only for this. There are, as far as I can tell, no survivors beside myself, at least that can move. Sometimes I think I hear a moan, but it is hard to know if it is the new weight of the earth above us, or someone, still long in dying, in their home. I haven't eaten in a time past remembering, but it matters little to me. I have burned three of these tapers. The fourth burns now, recently begun. And I find myself hoping, even here in this hell, and surely, this must be hell; hoping to live long enough to have burned the thirty tapers all. For even here my life is precious to me, precious remembrance alive in this dark. Though now I fear losing the candle to the dark before I lose myself.

3 Tapers more

I have slept. I have woken. My fever is gone. I have survived the Death but am unlikely, it seems, to survive the cure of the city. Exploring the cathedral, I found the tower. It is spoked by timber supports that wind up in the manner of a stair, and I think I can climb it. It occurs to me that there is a chance I could crawl out the top. Though I would, of course, be carrying on me the Death. As I looked up, through the struts above me, my candle jumped, which told me the air moved. A breeze.

I remember the Italian who came to the city to try and instruct us, on how to avoid the Death. He looked like Death. He wore a robe and a hook-nosed mask, and a hood. This is what we wear to avoid the Death, he told us. We laughed at him. He moved among us in the streets, his eyes hidden in the mask, but I felt, in his passing, the laughter that followed. Not of how strange he looked but of how there was nothing we could do. Looking at him, we knew, this wasn't for Scotland. Robes and masks. We'd all be dead instead. And Italy rule the world.

It was Rome brought us this, I heard one man say, after the Italian went by. But I knew it wasn't. Hand him a scythe, somebody, said another, and then there was more laughter. If I were to make my return, I suppose I could dress like that. Protect people from me. Disguise myself from those who know me to be dead.

There's no more to it, Speck says, when he can tell that I'm done reading.

In the kitchen, where his housekeeper has left us a supper, we eat quietly at a Formica table, each looking off into separate corners. And then he looks up from his plate and he says, I'll be leaving soon, in a few weeks more.

New York in the summer, I say.

Yes, he says. Delightful. Everyone bad leaves. All my friends are gone off to colonies and the like, and I can get some work done.

It's the most beautiful thing in the world, I say.

He doesn't pause. Yes, it is, he says. I thought so too.

They buried the whole neighborhood, I say.

Yes, he says. They're giving tours now, sometimes. But it's terribly unsafe. Won't last. Just wait until some visiting mayor is trapped and that will end right quick.

At home, in bed, I imagine the fresco of Edinburgh from Speck's ceiling on my own. Trace a tunnel down through. Before going to bed I had looked through a book of my mother's, a guide to Scottish clans. Hunter, it said, had the motto, "I finish the hunt." It was a dog, sitting on a crown, for the crest.

Disguise myself from those who know me to be dead. I see him crawl the timber supports. See him place the letter. Did he jump down to his death? Or did he indeed leave? Could he? In this way I keep myself awake until the morning. Blue outside my window turns to spreading white, to show me, in greater degrees, the shadow of my grandfather practicing the slow dance of his life. The colors of the morning world.

7

THERE'S A HOLE in me the size of you, from where you came through.

Edinburgh, after the Plague.

I begin building the tunnels. On a hilltop past the greenhouse where I meet Zach regularly now, to drink, I find a cellar, old-fashioned, dirt for a floor, and nothing remaining above except a few burned timbers. The tall grass hides it from the road, frames the squared-off divot here. A check with Town Hall confirms the lot is for sale but has been for thirty years. A farm here burned to the ground, 150 years ago, and nothing's been built since. Until now.

I work on it through the year and a half remaining before college. I build a cross, inside the hill. Crude, but the winds move through. An interrogated hill. I work there with a spade, carting the dirt off to the marsh's edge, my back aching, but the beauty of work is that it builds you while you build. I become stronger. I have my shovel out there now, the wheelbarrow also. Two years of shoveling makes a spade out of my back, narrow at the bottom, wide at the top. You're really filling out, my mother says to me on a day near the tunnel's completion.

Thanks, I say, grabbing an apple with slight exaggeration as I head for the door.

The first tunnel went by in two months of digging. The second had to wander around submerged deposits of bedrock. I pushed the last dirt aside and walked all the way through, end to end to end to end. Four corners here. I had read about the pyramids, burial mounds, but for me nothing matched my Edinburgh, my streets paved over, my city under a city.

In the winter, from the hilltop, you can see through the trees to Spurwink church, a white steeple there on the corner, presiding over the road and the graves in the yard behind it, the marsh farther out. Down below, in the hill, I have set sconces in the walls, for torches, citronella to keep out the mosquitoes. The floor is slate. I go down. The secret of the king of the hill is that he rules it from underneath. In the dark, I smoke. I sing, sometimes, pretending it is the Plague years, and that I have been left here to die in the buried city, to sing songs for the dead. Other times I think of Peter.

One day I come home from Speck's and my grandfather is waiting for me, smiling. You like old things, he says, right? I set my books down and follow him back to his quarters. Under his bed, wrapped in a blanket, is something preposterous. A cannon. Bronze. Unbelievably ugly. Short and thick. Where's it from? I ask.

I get from G.I., he says. But is Portuguese. Very old. Sixteenth century. They give to Korea, to help keep Korea safe. Long, long time ago. G.I. take it, but he need something and so he give me it.

I remember the pictures of my grandfather on his boat. A very long fishing vessel. G.I.s, I was sure, probably had occasion to need a few things. You like it, he asks. Look. Have firing piece. Also, cannonballs.

Yeah, I say. Gramps, we could declare war.

He laughs so hard at this tears come down his face. And later I realize this is probably the only time I have seen him cry.

I want to fire it.

When I tell Speck about it, he laughs. Sure, he says. The spice trade. But really. It's worth a fortune. Keep an eye on it, and don't let him use it in any arguments.

I tell Mom. We, she says, setting out the plates for dinner, have never had a normal family. But promise me, she says. Don't go telling anyone. Because, and she sighs. Because he didn't ask if he could take it. Korean national treasures, she says. They are a tenacious bunch about it. Almost everything they had was taken from them. Here, she says, and lifts the lid on a pot of American chop suey. Taste this.

8

THE SURVIVOR GETS to tell the story. Have you figured out who survives yet? Zach calls me one afternoon. We haven't spoken for most of the summer, the weeks quiet from the sound of us not calling each other. It's over three years since the trial, three months since we last had sex. And then a night shortly after that, he had driven over and asked me, Do you think I'm gay?

He leans his head against the windshield of his car, where we sit to talk in private, in the driveway of my house. Zach's two older brothers had been harassing him about getting a girlfriend. He'd told them to lay off. They'd told him to get laid. I roll down the window.

What we did, I say, wasn't . . .

What?

We were kids, I say. Experiments. You know. No, I don't think you're gay.

You don't.

Nope. You're not like me.

As soon as I had said it, everything about us became the past tense. As soon as I said, did. Did. What we did. You're not like me. When I said that, I saw that he wouldn't be. And so I hear from him next on an afternoon when I am thinking of how we are both to leave for school soon, how I am going to Korea before that happens, to see relatives. Zach calls. Meet me at the green-house, he says. Tonight.

I am apprehensive. He had developed friends who bored me so quickly the protective sounds of my own thoughts swept over me and shut out the sounds of them almost as soon as they said hello. As soon as they started talking to me, I heard my own voice about them, saying things I couldn't say out loud, knowing it would offend them. In the way a pianist won't shake hands, my ears don't listen, if they sense a bone-crushing squeeze lies in wait.

All right, I say. I'll meet you there at around eight. How's everything?

Everything's fine, he says. Outside, the night opens above us like a whale's jaw, a blue, deepening wedge.

In the hours before I meet him Zach takes a walk through his house. He picks a shotgun from its closet, roots through the cupboard for shells, takes the long way out of his house as he shoulders a jacket and finds his keys. He drives there in record time, parks the car far from the road. He knows where to park to avoid the eyes of passing police, and even watches from the car as a patrol car rolls by in the sunset hour. He goes to the greenhouse and sits for some time, I imagine, looking up, through the broken panes. Would he look at the sky or at the glass in front of it? He must have struggled some with the shotgun, as it wasn't long enough for him to use his toe to hook the trigger, but it wasn't short enough to easily pull with one's hands. Though as I write this, I see it wasn't one's hands, was it? They were his, probably aided by a twig, dropped once the shells took off the top of his head from the inside out.

That part is imagined. This is what I see, once I arrive: a crow sits on his chest. The wings shoot up, defensive, as if to say, It's dead, isn't it? The crow blinks its black wings, folds enough air to take to the sky. On my way back to my car, to go and get the police, a fox crosses my path. He darts a look over his shoulder, and when he sees me, turns back to where he's going, and seems to leap out into the air and vanish.

Everything can fly tonight, I tell myself, except you.

I would have to be fast. I gun my engine away, to go right to the police station. So that the animals don't get him.

9

TO THIS DAY I can see the fox take flight. In Korea that summer, where I am sent to visit my family there with my grandparents, my grandfather tells me how the fox is the most important animal in all of Korea. My grandmother clucks her tongue as she sets our ginseng tea on the table. We are at his sister's house in Seoul and she and his sister have been talking since we arrived. My grandfather has been quiet. Most important to you, my grandmother says, headed back to the kitchen. The fox, my grandfather continues, very clever. Eat everything. When it can. Smarter. Not most strong. Smarter.

My grandmother returns. Most important animal in Korea is here, she says, and taps my head with a kiss. This one, and then she laughs, returning to the kitchen to wait while we eat.

I'm there to do a pilgrimage for my grandfather's sisters. Our family shrine is on Moolsan-do, an island off the coast of Korea where my family has been for generations, and so after the visit in Seoul, where my relatives complain of how thin I am, they stick us into a wide train. We take the train until the rails stop and then a cab until the roads stop and then a ferry, out to the middle of a sea so blue and beautiful it looks like God's own tear.

Moolsan-do means water mountain. In my imagination, before my arrival, I think of Moolsan-do as being like a wave, towering in the sea, held in place forever by some arcane force, and as we arrive, the island does look like a wave at first, rising against the horizon as we approach. Up close, the real Moolsan-do looks like a mountain submerged by flood, with only a few beaches, most of the coast rocky and dark. The ferry's in no danger of running aground, the water is deep. There's one taxi, my grandfather tells me, as the ferry gets closer. Two teahouses, he adds, and one hotel, and 200 people, me related to approximately 110 of them. The other ninety being, by his guess, "new arrivals." He laughs as he says this. I step one leg off the boat onto the pier and feel the steep rock of the boat as I do so. The wind pulls on me. I lean into it, and steady my grandparents as they disembark. They smile at each other as they slip past me, getting their bearings. They look like they have a secret, as if they're being welcomed by spirits hidden in the wind pressing at us, haunted for a moment, but by happiness. I step fully off the ferry's plank, and the tanned sailors grin and run on board to remove the cargo of baggage and food. I follow my grandparents, taking in the town at one glance down the short street by the pier. I count off everything my grandfather mentioned.

As they have regularly throughout the trip, my grandparents regard me then with furtive glances that end in a smile for me and a nod. My grandfather knows about hauntings, it occurs to me now. Here was where he knew his sisters, here was what he remembered, every day, in his Imperial school, as the Japanese grammar spread inside him, as he learned the language of the people who took his sisters and destroyed them. All his thoughts come to him in Japanese first, his dreams in Japanese also. As they cross the wooden pier, as he tenderly helps my grandmother into the green taxi, as he laughs with the cab driver, I think of how every single thing he says in Korean comes across a pause where the Japanese is stilled and the Korean brought forward. Each part of speech a rescue.

Sunlight around my grandfather now as he waves to me, where I stand among my thoughts. Come, come, he says. Come meet driver.

I come toward him, shake the driver's hand, and we set out for the temple at the island's other side. He knows, the thought comes to me. He knows I cannot talk. He knows I am trying to learn how to talk. My tongue heavy from death, my words scattering off my ghosts, who can only watch, mute at what I am trying to do as everything I try to say fails.

Driver says you are very handsome, my grandfather says, laughing. Say you look like Zhe.

I meet the driver's eye in the rearview mirror, where it waits for me, and I smile.

At the polished stone temple, we kneel and pray, leave food, enough for a small beautiful lunch, for the dead. We take turns and throw soju for them. I trace the characters with a finger, unable to read them. There's no mounds for the sisters. My grandfather doesn't know the day they died, only the day they were taken. He doesn't have a single grave. Only Moolsan-do. When I take my turn to pray, I ask to be helped. And hope that prayers can arrive translated.

Peter's the one that burned. Zach was the one who pulled the trigger. Still, I feel like the bullet, the fire, like I tore his head open. I set the fire. Sometimes the scattered thoughts of their deaths run like a jagged red seam of fire inside me and I burn from the inside out, like a lightning-struck tree: the outside whole, the inside, that carried the lightning's charge, a coal. At other times, I feel empty, transparent, a child of the wind. Touching nothing, nothing touching me. And alternating between these states, with no warning as to when one will turn into the other.

They're gone, I tell the sea. Nothing comes back to me.

On the ferry ride back, off the island, the sun lights up the hair of two little girls in front of me enough for me to see, sure enough, the red threads there in their hair.

Years later on streets in New York, women bustle by me, in fox coats. I want to ask these women, do you ever, in that coat, think you can fly? Do you ever feel, wearing that coat, the thrum of a leg about to let fly?

On the bus back from the train from Moolsan-do, an old man, dressed in the loose linen suit of a retired man, seated in front of me, raises his lighter to my arm and lights it. At first I start to see a faint flame rise from the loose thread there at my side. He smiles at me. It's like a wick. The thread burns out and off. The fire goes out.

Later, I get off the bus. My grandmother looks at me like an owl looks at a mouse. She kisses me, the owl's wet feather. Skinny, she says. Get you home.

At my great-aunt's house she sets out plate after plate of food. The traditional dinner and then more plates: fried Spam, sliced. Fried eggs. A bag of potato chips. You like, my great-aunt says. Grandmother get for you. My grandfather waits until the food is all out and then approaches the table. The driver paces in the garden, smoking.

My great-aunt says something to him in Korean as she pours his water. He looks at her and raises his eyebrow. He says something to her gingham-covered back as she passes back into the kitchen, to sit at her table there. Your granmi, he says. She say we call someone to come look for you. Your ghost missing, she says. We call tomorrow. Ghost-singer. He shouts to my grandmother, turns back to me, and says, Terrible singer, for ghosts. Bad music.

THE MUDANG ARRIVES in the morning, a laughing woman with a man's stride, a man's way of leaning back from her hips. Who took your ghost, she says to me, her voice deep, almost sounding like it came from inside me. She plucks at the front of her khaki trousers, hitches her linen sleeves up.

I don't know, I say.

We find it, she says. And then she wanders the house. Up to the third floor, full of old furniture, and then down again. She walks the whole house. My grandfather has gone out to his favorite place, the bar at 8th Army, the officer's club. My grandmother paces in the garden.

With no warning, the mudang starts singing. Her voice now is unexpectedly high in tone, almost flutelike, and differs so sharply from her speaking voice that I watch, as if what made the difference were something I could see. She sings, and begins to step forward, in a slow dance, punctuated by her clapping hands. In my grandparent's green courtyard, my grandmother lowers her head, and the mudang sings.

She draws herself up short and says to me, go to your room. Wait there for me. And then she begins her song again.

In my room, I wait. On my bed, made up in thin cotton sheets, a Western bed they've had in this guest room since before it was popular to have them in Korea. The song reaches me through the open windows. I can feel the sweat glaze me, and I lie down for a breeze that passes in through the window with the song. My eyes close.

Two eyes glow at me in that dark, green-gold, irisless. Hello, a voice says. Miss me?

No, I say.

They brought me here for you.

It's something that they want, I say. Yowu.

And then I wake to the singing.

No good, the mudang says, when she comes into the room. How you life? How you life no ghost? And she shakes her head, laughing. Oh, sometime, she says, and I don't ask. Sometime. Is like diamond, walking.

What, I ask.

Diamond. She takes my grandmother's hand, where there flashes an extraordinary diamond. See? Comes from earth. Reflects light, most beautifully. Nothing more beautiful for reflecting light, but, belongs in earth first. Like your ghost, diamond.

Huh, I say. I consider it. The ghost, flashing somewhere under the sun, diamond and cloud together. If my ghost is like a diamond, someone has dug it out of me. I see it flying the skies of the world, mistaken for a daytime UFO. I don't mention the voice I heard when I closed my eyes, I decide nothing good would come of it. We bid the ghost-singer good-bye. My grandmother thanks her and presses money into her hands, which she frowns at as she folds it into her trousers.

Good-bye, she says to me. Sometime, sometime. Is okay. Is hard to die, with no ghost. Almost lucky. And she leaves, humming.

11

THE SCHOOL I'VE decided to go to is Wesleyan. I guess I should be happy, my mother says. She doesn't understand, even when I point out the enormous art campus, where the modern cement buildings like enormous gravestones keep company, garnished by enormous weeping willows. I'll be happy here, I tell her, which of course is why she relents.

Of course the real reason is an enormous series of underground tunnels that connects the campus. I found them on my prefrosh visit and wandered through them. Some were narrow and dark and others widened into rooms. Some were covered with indecipherable graffiti, others were spare gray, pipes everywhere. Home, I thought, at last, on that visit. My lost city. I write a postcard to Speck, explaining. He writes back asking for me to send a picture of me in them, which I do.

On my first day, I drive myself down. I arrive at a small suite in

Clark Hall. I am to share it with another boy, name of Caleb Oswald Evans, of Beaumont, TX. I am reading this on the door, his name and hometown spelled out carefully, and then the door bangs open. Welcome to Clark Hall, this Caleb says. He's sitting on his bed, wearing only a pair of shorts. Smooth muscle everywhere I can see. My eyes focus immediately on the smooth arches of his feet. The windows are all open wide, and I see that it's the wind that pulled the door. No AC, he says.

I see, I say, and my bags drop carefully to the ground where they wait. White rooms, two, side by side. Caleb in a white bed, wearing khaki cutoffs, legs crossed, reading the Tao Te Ching.

So this is the future, I say.

We smile at each other. He looks familiar, and I ignore the feeling. I sit down in his desk chair and we shake hands.

Call me Coe, he says.

I will, I say.

In the first few days I make many friends through smoking cigarettes. During the president's speech to the new students, I look at the shiny ashtrays on the tables, like cheap mirrors. I wait and wait, no one is smoking. And then I light up. Soon, like a smoke signal, I see another faint rope of smoke some tables away, and I look over, to catch the eye of a thin girl with dark hair and eyes who wiggles her fingers toward me. For the duration of the speech, no one else smokes. When we speak later, she says, Well, there were ashtrays there on the table. I mean, they were letting us smoke if we wanted. It means a lot to me, that you smoked.

I decide to let that stand.

Her name is Penny Fields and she's from Niagara Falls. She's the same height as me, and at the party where we find each other she's the only one who walks up to me to talk. I am dressed in a black shirt and black jeans and boots, and she says, Who died?

A couple of people, I say.

Huh. Good one. Fee, she says, testing my name, like it's a shoe she's trying on. Fee. She grabs the hem of my shirt and tugs at it a little. Fee, we need someone to jump on that table over there and dance.

She slips a cigarette into her mouth and stares meaningfully at a long conference table over near the DJ. The party is in a fraternity for the football team, DKE, and besides the table, the large dark room is furnished in chairs that seem to have been upholstered in pile carpeting.

Can't.

C'mon, she says. I saw you earlier. You're a good dancer, you qualify. She lights her cigarette. People who are good dancers are, and here she puffs on the cigarette until the end is gray with ash, you know. Exhibitionists. This last emerges from her mouth covered in pale smoke.

Did you ever notice, I ask, that when a cigarette burns, the smoke is blue, and when we exhale, the smoke is white?

What are you getting at, she says. We walk toward the table. I push myself up onto the table. All the color gets left inside us, I say, and hold my hand out to her. She grabs it, climbs up, holding her skirt down as she does so. The music is so loud it knocks in my ribs.

Good thing I wore underwear, she says. Here, have some color. She hands me the cigarette.

The football team here is not a very good one, but no one really minds. The boys are cute and relatively nice, and the girls appreciate them. We dance, side by side, facing them. No one looks at us while we watch them.

12

I'D ARRIVED ON campus with only black clothes. Boots, jeans, shirts, sweaters, a long black overcoat for fall and winter that buttoned to the neck, made of cashmere, and a black windbreaker for the fall. It soothed me, in Maine, there was no confusion, dressing like this. And so my first August in Connecticut I am a black speck on the campus, emitting puffs of smoke as I walk. Here, out of my mother and father's sight, I can smoke all I want, and so I do. My grandmother sends a red coral necklace from Korea that arrives shortly after I do. I carefully clasp it so that it can't be seen, under my shirts.

That first week, Coe comes with me to Arthur the barber, on Main Street, and watches as I get my crew cut. When I am done, he sits in the chair and says, Same again. Arthur laughs and clicks on his buzzers. Coe's sandy hair is gone quickly. The resemblance is striking. He looks like Peter, I can see now, if Peter had lived and lifted a lot of weights. Oh there you are, I say, inside.

Do you like it, he says, as we leave.

Yes, I say.

With our new haircuts, we walk by Penny's hall over in Foss 8. She and several of her hallmates are sitting in the hall on the floor reading magazines, their hair tucked into plastic bags. Henna, she says, barely looking up, and then she sees Coe. Well, Hello, she says. Didn't know we'd have gentlemen callers today. We decided that we'd all dye our hair red to get talked about.

Foss Red, says one girl, looking at what turns out to be a copy of *Interview*. You made us do it. She does not look up.

You guys have to do it, too, she says.

Coe and I laugh. That's good, he says. Funny.

Penny, I say. I can't. I think of Lady Tammamo. The fox. Bad luck, I say.

What? she says.

For me, I say. Bad luck for me.

Hang on, she says, and goes into her room, emerging with the henna and two bags. Here, she says. Do it. If you don't like it, go get crew cuts again. Coe and I sit down and she rubs our heads with the stuff. You guys will be the Foss Red Men. You'll be like twins. It'll be beautiful.

Great, says Coe.

All right, I say. I'll be beautiful.

Later, in our rooms, we laugh at each other. We go to the showers, and wash. Coe stands in the shower opposite me. The henna runs down him, brownish green. He closes his eyes, leans back, and the foam runs off him to pool at his beautiful smooth feet. He opens his eyes. What, he says. Smiling.

Nothing, I say.

13

I HAVEN'T BEEN angry in years. And yet I've been angry since before I remember happiness.

I can't say it was this or that that was the reason. There is no reason and every reason. Why do you want to die, I ask myself. How else does it stop? If I die, the trouble stops with me. I can see her, Tammamo, her hand closing her husband's eyes, breathing in the air to make the fire-breath, his family, watching her. Enough, she'd be thinking. Fire on her lips. It ends with me now.

Outside my window a spider floats in the air, as if levitating. I look closely to see that spider is actually hanging by a thread connected some ten feet down, probably. It is floating, spinning upward, counting on the wind to catch in its furry legs and lift it, as it unspools the web. Until it can land someplace else, attach the thread's other end, and continue, making the web. I continue in this watching, trying to match this sight with the idea that a spider finishes by eating its entire web at the end.

Coe walks in to my room. Wake up, he says. Time for practice. The clock reads 6 A.M. We've joined the crew team. I pull back my covers and dress quickly in clothes Coe helped me pick: we decided I could wear gray for exercise. We run the distance between Clark and the boathouse down by the river, more or less straight down the long hill of the campus. In the dark morning the sun is the gold center of everything. Death feels far away in that instant, impossible. We arrive at the cold river as summer touches the beginning of its last days, and Coe smiles. The sun. Coe.

From Penny, I learn how attention is like light. How it is light without heat. How to make a shadow puppet out of the self from the way I stand before it.

Caleb Oswald Evans, she says. From Beaumont, Tea-Ex. Nighttime, in her room. She wears a slip, flip-flops, red nail polish on her fingers and toes. She turns the pages of the freshman face book and finds Coe's page. She puts a red nail-polish mark next to his name, letter *A*. He's for you, she says. Mr. Bisexual.

I've just told her that I am bisexual, in answer to her question. What's your deal, she said. And I wanted to say, None. But instead, I tried to imply the opposite. Everyone.

I don't say anything as she does this. She offers me a cigarette and I decline. Good Lord, she says. You're quitting?

Crew, I say.

You're leaving me not for one man but a boatful, then. You won't hold onto the bi in bisexual for long, she chuckles. Uh. You saw *Another Country,* right?

Yes, I say.

You want a romantic attachment to men, but instead, you are attaching romance to things that men do. She lights her cigarette and adds, I guess I'm smoking for two now.

I know what you think I'm doing, I say. But I want to get into shape, too. Besides, nothing would ever get started if we didn't first attach romance. Everyone always ranks on illusion, but illusion is a mighty thing.

You're on your own with that one, she says. She shucks off her flip-flops and folds her feet under her, leaning over the face book. The face book has everyone's last high school picture. Already everyone seems smoothed out, prettier, more adult. The pictures are improbable. Coe's shows him in a jacket and tie, which is more clothing at once than I've yet to see him wear. Tae Kwon Do, it says, she says. Does he really?

I've not yet seen it, I say. But he's not the type to exaggerate. Penny leans back then, into a chair pillow. The arms stick out around her and it's as if she's in the arms of an alien mammal.

Tell me all about it, she says. You know, his father is a very powerful man. He won't like what you're thinking about his son.

Uh huh, I say. I gave him a back rub today after practice. He told me he was half Korean inside, like I'm half Korean outside.

Penny's head falls back. You two should be stopped, she says.

I laugh. For no other reason than I know that there's no stopping. I wish you were a girl, he'd said to me this morning as I rubbed the muscles of his warm back.

Oh, Fee. You have to go now, she says. I think it's hopeless. I changed my mind. I can't hear anymore. Men are hopeless, you know. You'll learn this someday, and she says this as if I weren't one. We both know she isn't talking about me.

In my room in the dark I can feel it sometimes. The red inside. I shave and look at the hairs in the sink, red mixed with the rest. In my beard is every color of hair: brown, blond, black. Red.

14

LOVE IS THE regrowth of the wings of the soul, Plato says, years in the past almost past seeing. Except of course they are as alive as words are. As we are reading words. On the breath of an ink wind, spread on a sail made of a paper page, this, in translation:

> . . . he receives through his eyes the emanation of beauty, by which the soul's plumage is fostered,
> and grows hot, and this heat is accompanied by a softening of the passages from which the feathers grow, passages which have long been closed up, so as to prevent the feathers from shooting. . .

I read everything I have ever wanted to know about the world in this. And then Plato quotes Homer:

> Eros the god that flies is his name in the language of mortals:
> But from the wings he must grow, he is called by the celestials Pteros.

Peter. The morning opens and closes. The library around me rises in acres of books and bricks and glasses in alternation. All the distances between me and everything else seem uncrossable, a permanent exile.

I stand up. It's time for my Classics of Western Thought class. I am a Greek, I tell myself as I go down the marble steps out of the library. A long time ago, there were cities where boys loved each other enough to give speeches about it. They loved books more than money. I pause and go back inside to the card catalog, where I look up Mary Renault, and head up along the aisles where the air is so dusty my throat catches. *The Persian Boy* sits there. Alexander the Great's eunuch lover.

I leave the book on the shelf, unread.

Out in front of the library, students walk, hair messy from bed, in giant sweaters, heads down against the new cold in the wind. Mingle not with those you do not love, Plato warns, or you will be condemned to wander the earth nine thousand years without wisdom.

15

WINTER BREAK COMES like an open grave in winter, a dark cold slot after the fall term's last snowy days.

The first time I try to die I am on a mountain, near my aunt's house, and I've decided to go on an overnight camp just before an ice storm comes through. The Friendship Mountain Range sits on the border of Canada, Vermont, New Hampshire, and Maine near where I am visiting my aunt in Rangeley, Maine, a place she's lived for twenty-five years as a librarian. I haven't planned this too far in advance, but, after Christmas concluded in a pile of nonrecyclable paper and satin ribbons, and as I again pack up the art materials that I regularly get every year for Christmas, the trip, as it was suggested to me then, seemed "a perfect opportunity to lose myself." A pattern of literalism that continues to this day.

I am up here ostensibly to paint and sketch. The storm has been forecast for days but previous to it are days candled by the sun to a painterly brightness, and the only shadows possible, between sun, clear sky, and snow, hide under my feet. My aunt Pat, my mother's younger sister, is concerned and has asked repeatedly that I not go out. She has recently divorced, and is dating again, happy, as if her new divorce has shucked off a parasite that had eaten her entire youth. She now seems resupplied, her face colors itself, her hair soft again. On the morning I make my effort, I reorganize her kitchen shelves as I stock my bag out of her pantry. If you get the idea to buy cooking lard or cinnamon, I say, indicating the things I have found in large supply, Don't. She has the habit of purchasing things she can't find, a permanent shopping list in her brain: frozen bagels and cream cheese, cinnamon, lard, microwave popcorn and canned beans, always there. As if she will always be safe with these, no matter what.

I wish you'd wait a few days to see if the storm will pass, she says, brushing her pants. She has just come in from the woodshed, to add logs to the three woodstoves that heat her reconditioned farmhouse. She is built like my mother, and has about her a similar tightness to her movements that gives no indication of her actual strength. She runs a hand through her hair. I'll feel stupid calling your mother to tell her you died of exposure, she laughs.

If I die I'll call her myself, I promise. And then I heave the pack on my back.

You have enough gas, she calls from the door, as I settle onto a snowmachine I rented that morning.

I do, I reply.

All right then, she says, and then she may have said something else but it disappears in the roar as the machine runs under the choke. She steps back in.

Ice storms appear first as rain, and then sleet, neither of which is an ice storm.

Even as I head down the trails, the machine banging over the hard-pack snow, I don't think of it then. I think of nothing. January-thick white snow is everywhere. The new year is under way, and the snow makes everything seem perfected, cleaned off and put away until the spring. The evergreens are the suggestion or the idea of a tree, a green shadow helmeted in white. And the bare trees, arterial, reach out as if they give up something of the earth to the air above.

I reach what I decide is to be my campsite, situate my tent, and dig a pit to hide my food. I settle in for what turns out to be a long meditation in a quiet so vast my heart and breath make a racket. I bank a firepit and build a fire.

The sky becomes an ink wash, black scattered by water. And then light again. The sun lights down where it can, as if trying to grab hold. Help me, the sun seems to be saying to the little fire at my feet. I am now to be on the side of the cold and as the ice begins to come I am glad. The sun has every other day to hold us. Now is the storm's turn. I let my fire go out, stay where I sit, the cold rising across me.

The storm is a glazier. Then fog passes through, touches the cold trees to add to the ice already there. Here the wind spins glass from the water it has stolen off the sea and the lakes, off the hair on my head and the breath out of my mouth, the storm takes the water from us all everywhere, to make of a mountain range a stained-glass depiction of a saint no one knows. A cathedral for cold January, a place for this gray bitter month, that everyone hates, to come and hide and pray for mercy, to pray to stay, when everyone else wants it to leave.

I walk down to the edge of the lake, picking my way through the dark woods. The ice here is relatively new. I set out on it, praying it will break. It's a coward's way, asking the lake to take me, but I decide that's how it should be. There's an island out about a half mile from the shore and I head for it. Death by exposure seems easy to achieve: to lie down in the snow during the storm was a time-honored Inuit passage to the other side of life. The blue expanse of the winter night would wrap you and you would become simply part of the blue, as easy as that. But it requires a patience for the journey, I can see.

When the ice breaks, I forget what I came to do. My left leg slips through snapping ice. My face slams hard as my leg goes through, cold and then warm again. I curse and roll and as I roll, my legs whipping up through the air, I can feel the ice cut me open.

I tear off a piece of my T-shirt and wrap my shin. And I crawl on all fours for the first thirty yards back, limp the rest. I laugh in the cold dark.

Back at my tent, I see red in my fire coals. I add wood, blow on it. Fire again leaps off the bark. The sky now the blue of the underside of a flame, as if above us heaven burned. Some part of me hopes it is true. That Peter is there, spreading fire as he walks from cloud to cloud.

The next morning the trees split from the cold. The water freezing inside the trees tears the fibers of the wood, and the wind pulls them apart. On the drive back, everywhere I look, sharpened sticks instead of trees. Back at school, Coe asks about the bruise on the side of my face and I show him the cut on my leg as well. You're crazy, he says.

Yes, I say. That's about right.

16

IT WAS PERHAPS my drawing master who made me a ceramics major, but it never matters who makes you, ultimately, only that you are made. In any case he helped me find what would end up being the way I would choose to live, for which I am grateful. He was a visiting professor from Germany and as our final assignment we were to do drawings, ten in a series. A tall man who walked like a limping horse and spoke through a gentle voice a broken patter of English and German, he was often seen walking under the trees and looking up through their branches in just about any part of campus. I could be anywhere from a Ph.D. carrel in the library to a friend's dorm room and there he would be, striding confidently, intent, but of course with the limp that seemed almost a choice, and it would have been suspicious if there weren't any sign anywhere of him spying. He was entirely internally preoccupied and it mattered not at all what was going on around him unless it had something to do with something he was drawing. I once saw him leaving the cafeteria with a paper towel stretched between his hands, seven strips of cooked bacon balanced there. He saw me and said, I'm drawing them, don't worry. You can come later and eat them if you like.

He himself did what he called tender lines. He drew without looking at the paper and with both hands, using pencil, always, that he would rub upward instead of down. He would point at drawings and say of the lines, Do you see, this is another language from this, they are not talking to each other. Or, he would say, You must erase these. There is too much architecture here. He taught the advanced class for majors and he spoke of lines in drawings the way poets speak of lines in poems. This is the best line, he would say, and touch it. The others are only imitating it. You must get rid of them. Start over and keep this only. I hated drawing this way. It made me unsteady, and the figures looked ugly to me. I drew my assignments in one hand.

I had done for my drawing project nude studies of five boys on the crew team. I admit to having had a more than ordinary amount of fun doing this, but it was also for me an attempt to release what turned out to be an extraordinary amount of lines inside me that awaited figures. These figures. I had wanted to draw these guys for years, and so they would come over in the afternoon when the light in my room was best and there on my comforter I would arrange them in a pose. They had the unselfconsciousness of athletes, the body was this thing they used to go fast, they liked the one they had because as yet it had met almost all their demands of it. They accepted the idea as I put it forward to them and enjoyed the afternoons we spent this way, two drawings per athlete. I remember Mike as being particularly beautiful nude, without an ounce of spare flesh to him anywhere, almost a physician's muscle chart, and Rich had hair all over his body, like a pelt. Ian, my former coxswain, looked particularly the part of a St. Sebastian, and then Coe, who was so breathtaking that I could almost not draw him. It was all I could do not to rush over to the bed. Aaron studiously enjoyed himself. We both knew that there were two reasons I was drawing him this way, and he knew that the second reason would never express itself past the drawing, and was fine about it. His enjoyment would be in offering for my eye what he would refuse the rest of me.

I don't know what these are, the drawing master said, when I presented. The class would have laughed had they not known something of what was next. The drawings were beautiful, I had thought. They were tender, I thought. How could they fail? He reached a finger up and he said, they are like perno.

I knew he meant porno.

They are not drawings, he said, sad. These lines are all not even lines. And those that are, they are in different languages from each other. He looked incredibly sad then. I cannot believe it, he said. He hung his head down under my beautiful men.

That night I watched the ceramics students out in the yard of the art complex, where the ceramics studio did raku firing. I sat with my drawings rolled up at my feet, smoking one cigarette after another, as if they could take out the stitch this day had left in my head. He had been right to have been sad. I hadn't wanted to be a pornographer. I had wanted to take something inside myself, like I had once drawn a breath, and then to send it out, as I had sung. To say that you make something out of thin air: you can, if you sing. You can make an enormous number of things this way.

I watched as the raku students pulled their pieces out with tongs and sunk them into shredded paper. The hot ceramic set fire to the paper instantly. Use this too, I said, pulling my drawings apart in long shreds. I tossed them into the can, and the potters cooled their pieces on them, the paper turning to wet-looking black shreds that floated on the air around the kiln.

When you draw, you destroy as you go. Even as you make. I saw now that as long as there was a form that I wanted to make love to, I wouldn't be free. I would not be able to make lines for it, and as long as I was me, these lines would always be in separate languages. Clay, wet, spinning on a wheel that you kicked as you went, that rose and thinned or flattened and spread with the faint touch of a thumb, that seemed fine. You set it in a hot oven. Almost a thousand degrees. You underglazed or deglazed or glazed, you baked or bisqued, you waited, to see, would it crack. Would the glaze fall off in a pile. It would be fine, this way. And I wouldn't also have to destroy anything, except for the clay that cracked while drying, tossed back into the reclaim pile, to be used again. There wasn't anything you could do but set the piece in the fire and wait to see how it would come back to you. As I watched, I thought, and I saw how there was something that could return to you from fire.

I signed up for the ceramics major the next morning.

17

THE NEXT YEAR I kept the Polaroid picture of Peter and I from his last night alive in a diary that I wrote in only when I wanted to die. I wrote in that diary, that year, almost every day. Some days I made myself laugh by writing, instead of the date, Hello, Death. I would drive along Route 84, looking at the ditches, thinking about what it would be like if I just didn't turn, if I continued, into the cement embankments, my car wrinkling shut like an eye closing, my body, chewed as if by a giant lazy jaw. I wanted to wake up and not feel. My life would have been acceptable, I felt, if someone had come in and in the night severed all my nerves where they attached at the skin. If I was numb, then great. More life for me, another helping, please.

There were undergraduate crushes. Always, blond boys: the expression *dew-lapped* comes to mind. As in, the dew's tongue passes over and leaves a drop behind. Romantic, to the point of putrefaction, I wrote long terrible poems about whoever it was I was infatuated with. Penny laughed at it all, and came to ask always, which one is this now? She knew there was a way in which these boys were all the same. These boys were all stand-ins for Peter, and none was greater than Coe.

My friends cultivated an active disgust. You're in love with white power, they'd say. You seek white acceptance. For this reason alone I maintained a careful distance from the political life of the campus, which was considerable, until the last year I was there.

My friendship with Coe turned inward on itself. We lived now in an apartment building owned by the university, a heinous building known only as High-rise that sat across the way from a home for the mentally ill. I walked to the parking lot in the morning wondering which lunatic fantasy I now lived in, as the patients across the way loved nothing better than binoculars, and watched us from behind their barred windows and porches. Coe lived down the hall from me, and I regularly went there to type my papers, as all through school I didn't have a computer. Neither of us was on crew anymore, and his roommate, Rich, also a former crew-team member, was now on hockey. We walked around constantly in a state of dazed half-dressed stress, trying to make grades. I felt myself to be inside an airtight and airless bubble, invisible to everyone. The gray buildings faced my room, the wrong way for light of any kind at any time. The year a long shadow I walked through.

Below me lived two boys who were in more or less the same state as me and Coe, a boy named Richard, and his roommate, Rafe. Rafe was an elegantly tall, handsome, and dark-haired boy; Richard was an angry redhead who had a reputation for being a nasty drunk. The two of them spent almost all their time together, as Coe and I now did, and the parallel seemed unbearable, not the least for me living directly above Richard and Rafe. Rafe and Coe had girlfriends. Richard and I, increasingly, hung out with each other, reluctantly. He wanted to hate me, I could see, on those nights we stared over each other in the direction of our beloveds. I wanted to give him a reason and have it be done with. It happened like this.

A party in a house we called Eclectic, once a fraternity, now a tumbled-down beer hall of a southern-style mansion with Neoclassical columns, paint peeling off them, holding up a roof full of people high on speed and coke or smoking pot because they hate cigarettes. Richard is there on the porch, a few others sitting nearby. Richard shakes his long red hair, a faint part to the side, dressed in a T-shirt and black jeans faded to gray by washing. He hates the idea of style in himself, even as he worships it in others. Oh hi, he says. He's drunk already when I find him. Don't you look terrific. I raise an eyebrow in response. Go get a beer and drink so you're not so obnoxious, he orders me, pointing in the direction of the keg with his cigarette and I laugh as I head along.

Rafe is across the way. I say hi to him as I pass. He has the face of a boy still on the long body of a man, and he smirks at something the girl beside him is telling him. He's really too preppy to care about this place, but he's here because of Richard, ostensibly, and there's nothing he won't do without Richard. Except have sex. He nods as I pass, and seems deliberately engrossed. Richard floats at the perimeter of their gaze.

Coe is here also, inside. He is smoking. What the hell is that, I say, pointing at the cigarette.

Trying to be like you, he says, grinning. His girlfriend, Laura, is next to him. A short, pert blonde, glasses shining in the dark, she smiles at me. I amuse her just by walking by.

Tell him to put it out, I tell her.

He listens to you, she says.

The rest of the night piles up around us like this, people like cars looking for parking spots walking back and forth and soon the smoke is so thick that I tell Penny, who has just arrived, that I'm not smoking anymore. I'm just going to breathe, I tell her.

Shut up, she says. You know you like it. I hate it when people who smoke complain about the smoke. She says this as she heads off for a beer. Richard wobbles over, always a bad sign.

Do you think he loves her, he says, suddenly very, very grave.

I don't ask who he means. I don't, I say.

Sluts, he says. Both of them. I mean it's a school of whores, but what sluts. He steps on the cigarette he just lit. I don't want to smoke anymore. He pushes a thick piece of hair off his face. Come over, he says. Have a drink. I've got whiskey.

I look around the party. Coe is gone. There's no reason for me to be here. I mean, there's no reason because I want to be dead, actually, but there really is no reason. So I say, sure. Let's go have whiskey. And then Richard walks as straight as anyone and we leave the party.

In his apartment the dark seesaws around a desk lamp he flicks on and then faces into the wall. No other light other than the awful street lamps, always too bright, shining in. If sleeping in the light of a moon makes you mad, I think, what does a street-light do to you?

I turn around. Richard is opening whiskey. He has taken his shirt off. A boy's body with a man's face, Richard has the opposite arrangement to Rafe's. His hairless chest a bone in the dark. He hoists the bottle to his mouth and drinks hard, like cowboys in movies do. He flicks at his nipple as he does this and then sits at his desk. Holds out the bottle. There's nowhere in his small room to sit but the bed, so that's where I sit. I reach for the bottle and then lean back. If he wants the bottle he'll have to come and get it, I decide.

I'm not prepared for this, which thrills me. Almost more than he does, or the same way. I tip the bottle up to my mouth, holding it by the neck, and slide some whiskey down. I breathe through my nose, swallowing. As I take the bottle away, Richard is reaching and pulling off my shoes, my socks. I balance the bottle on his bedside table, which is covered in Thomas Mann books, and I lift my hips as he slides my pants off. He then kneels on the bed and walks over to me, where he leans down to kiss me, but then stops, just above my lips.

If you tell anyone, he says. His breath on mine, wet.

Won't, I say. I know he doesn't care, and that I'm lying, and that he knows I'm lying and that I know this. He just wants me to be able to say he said it when I tell about it, later. He wants to be able to believe it for now, also. That boys do things together and it's a secret. That we are boys and not men dressed like children, surprised by the passage of even a year. And as he kisses me I try to decide, if he likes secrets better than kisses. After, I decide it's kisses. For the night, he is wild. A storm. His grief at losing Rafe, I see, is a daily one, as for a Sisyphean task. Each day Rafe is at the bottom of the hill, each day, Richard tries to roll him up. No end, barely no solace.

I reach up under his balls, in his jeans, and slip a finger into his anus, where it goes easily. I think about how there is skin here only a few cells thick. Sex is asking someone to touch you where your skin is thinnest. His eyes roll back.

I leave to go upstairs before Rafe gets back. Richard is asleep before I close the door. I have dreams of him, flying through the night sky, his blue-white skin cuts the black.

Some days later. In the café, at the top of the student center, we sit and have coffee together while Richard reads *The Magic Mountain* and I flip through the course catalog. We say nothing. I can see, in the sunlight, the profile of his penis through his pants, which I watch. I am thinking of how in the light off the street I saw the glint of the red hair around his penis. Eventually we leave. We go to his apartment, and undress. He starts to cut us some lines of coke before I think of whether I want any or not. He cuts the lines on a mirror on his lap, then holds it out to me. He smiles. Please, he says.

I do my line and hand the mirror back to him. I love this drug, he says.

Why, I say, as he slides his coke back and forth on the mirror.

Because I can't ever cry when I do it, he says. Like there was nothing I couldn't watch on this drug.

I wish I could be in love with him, I tell Penny, when I tell her about it later.

Don't be annoying, she says. That's out of the question. It's bad enough he's so ugly. She is reeling anyway. Richard isn't known for this sort of thing, but he is about to be, when she gets off the phone with me.

He's not ugly, I say. But I don't say any more to her. The best of him doesn't share well, I see now. I regret having said anything, immediately.

18

MY DRAWING TEACHER had asked me to sit for him, and so on an afternoon after the end of reading period but before my exams began I sat naked in his studio. The May Connecticut weather was awful, humid, and despite myself I sweated. My German teacher seemed unaffected. He drew, pulled the paper, drew again. I had had allergies for some time and they were a problem and now I was sure another attack was coming on because I could only sit there and cry. I sat there naked and cried in front of him. He never asked me why I was crying. After an hour I felt that even if I wanted to I couldn't speak. In the enormous silence he made no conversation, nor did I, only crying there in the studio. I made no effort to wipe my tears for fear of losing the poses and I was after all being paid well and wanted to be able to pose again at another time. And I was sure he was drawing the tears.

Some time later in my room, as I looked out into the longest gray shadow I had ever occasioned to notice, I could breathe again. Some days later I thought back to the incident of the crying and thought to call my doctor, who told me that if my eyes had been itchy then yes the crying was an allergic reaction, but that otherwise it had been an emotional one. The teacher had marked each pose with a careful Polaroid, and the tears that day were my only tiny reminders that the photographs Big Eric had taken of us had never been found. Of everything that had been turned in for evidence, the pictures were not among them. I wondered then if somewhere, pictures of me with him filled a book. Being shown to someone else.

There were more reminders, certainly, to come, and I would not know them, not even when they were happening, and would likely not be able to do anything about them. From somewhere inside me the photos altered me all the time, like a virus that hides in the organs, emerging, from time to time, to kill and reproduce again.

A few days later I went downstairs and did some more coke with Richard, which is when he told me someone had told them we'd slept together, and did I know who I might have told?

I took the envelope and shook some more of the white powder onto the tray. He was right. You couldn't cry on coke, not in the first fifteen minutes; and those fifteen minutes *were* lit up, as if the coke burned the seconds in torn strips, each second cut from the other and set on fire. I cut a line, and then another, and divided them both into two short lines, and then finally met his eyes. He had lit a cigarette, and a smile sought out his mouth. A Doris Day song found me there, and I started to sing it. I've counted, a thousand sheep . . .

Fee, he said.

But it wouldn't be make-believe, if you believed in me. Cause without, your love, it's a honky-tonk parade. Without, your love, it's a . . .

Fee. Don't do that.

Everyone saw us leave together, I said. Rumors start. Et cetera. I took the rolled dollar from him, did the lines, and passed the mirror.

He didn't believe me, but it didn't matter, either, he saw that, in the tray I handed to him. He saw it in the way I stayed there, waiting for him to finish, and the way, when he was done, I had the sense to leave, as he put it, without his asking. I wanted to leave, too. When you draw, you learn first that sunlight is the true judge, of color, of texture. Neither of us wanted to see each other that way, in the first light of waking.

19

THE SECOND TIME I try to die. Sunset in my apartment. I fall asleep in a gold chimney of light, perhaps the first to ever find its way into my apartment. I'd been up for two days on coke to finish some drawings I supposedly had been doing all semester and then I passed out, and I wake up to Richard standing next to the bed. His fly is open, his dick hanging out. When my eyes open he smiles.

You have a choice, he says, which you want first. He shakes it near me. I watch the pink head move up and down, the unmistakable bounce of a penis. It has its usual appeal, and yet.

Coffee, I say.

Sluts don't get coffee. Come on. Choose.

Coffee, I say, again. And then I roll over. I hear him in my kitchen. It occurs to me I have no idea how he got in. How did you get in, I ask.

I can pick a lock, he says. Boarding school. I'll show you sometime. He lights a cigarette. I'm sad my stupid porno-flick manners didn't work.

Uh huh, I say. Me too.

You know what I hate, he says. I hate it when people make like they are going to knock themselves off and they leave a note and everything and then arrange to be found. What is that? I mean, I'm sort of glad Sylvia Plath died. The bitch was playing at it.

The lamp on my desk lights only the lower half of him. His shadow head says all of this. The cigarette is a pale orange, like a firefly on its last burn. I'd been wondering why I had him in my life, and then suddenly I know why. And I am so happy. What's the other choice, I say. Knowing.

Coke, he says. But this time we freebase. He stands up and comes back with coffee, which he sets down on my bedside table. We both look at the spoon handle in the mug, like it's a compass needle.

Sluts get coke, I say, and he smiles again.

Coke cooking as you smoke it smells like burning carpet. A house on fire. What time is it, I say.

Who cares.

I thought I'd care more about it, but this adds nothing but an opportunity. Needles, knives, thugs in the dark, thugs in the light. There's the whole world waiting to do you in if you get the chance. For instance, almost everything in my kitchen can be used to kill me. The hour that comes next arrives sheathed in a white fire that burns cold along all my nerves. While Richard fucks me I feel like a god. Like I can set things on fire with a touch, leap into the sky and not come back. Like I can cook my own dose, an extra one, while Richard goes down to get cigarettes at five in the morning.

I send myself shooting out into that gathering 5 A.M. light. And not crying the whole time. Everything is already moving so very fast, but you need a great deal more speed than this to escape the earth's gravitational pull. Seven miles per second. More fuel, please.

The white fire meets the black hammer. Come apart. I fall down but by the time I fall down, I am already not there. Immeasurable dark, I float into it, I feel my body tumble far from me. No note. Richard will understand.

20

RICHARD CALLED AN ambulance. When he came back to the room, the curtains were on fire, but he put those out quickly. It turns out he's good in emergencies. He didn't know until now. No one knows how the fire started. It's assumed I was smoking a cigarette but I do not remember having the cigarette. We were out. It was the reason he went downstairs.

Before I open my eyes I know I am back. I fully expect to be burned but of course in the mirror opposite my hospital bed I just look bad, like someone beat me up. I'll find out later that Richard did indeed slap me quite a bit when first finding me. Someone did beat me up. But he did CPR. High as a kite on freebase. The bruises will stay for months.

Coe is beside me. In the chair next to my bed, he sits reading and looks up. The sunlight behind him scrapes my eyes.

You're trying to kill me, he says.

That's absolutely what I was up to, I say. My voice sounds oddly alive. And I see now that I've been strapped to the bed with restraints. Huh, I say.

Well, I mean. I mean clearly you were trying to kill yourself, he says. And he takes my hand in his. I told them I thought you were trying to kill yourself.

I nod, this being an ancient form of agreement, and we sit there with this for some time.

Richard, of course, never forgives me, but it hardly matters. Coe graduates with me. I leave to go home for the summer, to San Francisco afterward. He heads off for Bangkok, a job working for Citibank.

Richard deserves his own place in my heart, a shrine where a fire burns and blossoms are tossed into it for fragrance. Apple wood would burn there. But he is too late, for now. A famine has left the people weak and they pray to a god who will not answer them. They lay boys at the altar, a sacrifice.

I wanted to tell him, you see, I am lost in someone else. You are too. We kept company in each other's reminiscences for the nights we spent together. There's nothing more for this.

I MEET THE David brothers when I go as my mother's date to a fund-raiser for the Gulf-of-Maine Aquarium. The party is on a yacht tied to a slip on Central Wharf, in Portland, the parking lot shining, full of Mercedes and Saabs and new Volvos. I see the brothers right away when I come in, the two of them so beautiful side by side, shining like the cars outside, in this crowd. If you waved a wand and turned them into dogs they'd be golden Labradors. They are more beautiful together and safer, I decide, because then you can take turns looking at them. My mom knows their mom, and soon we are shaking hands, Hello, My son Fee, this is Kathy, her sons Matthew and Lebow. Around us cocktails float by on trays and people offer hot tiny foods, spiked by colored picks, and I am looking at these two, with their dark straight hair and dark eyes. We raise our eyebrows as our eyes sweep together toward the same corner and we shrug upstairs, without a word, all agreement, where we get Heinekens and pull out cigarettes. Matt lights mine, bowing his head, courtly.

We're having a party on the Fourth, says Matt. You've got to come.

You do, says Lebow. There's a half pound of shrooms at home, and we don't know anyone. Our folks just moved to the Cape and there's only so many trips we can take on this bag.

Matt is the younger, my age, Lebow three years older, just graduated, from Grinnell, where Matt still schools. Lebow is starting to look like a real man, thicker, where Matt is still thin like a boy, his lips dark like rose hips. A sharp scar, pale pink, a puckered line, runs just under the cheekbone, an inch long. We talk most of the night, the three of us, and when Matt announces the impending arrival of the mothers, we toss, all at once, our cigarettes into the sand bucket, ready to leave as they emerge from the stairs. I am somewhat thrown by the ease with which we all silently move in agreement about how to greet our moms. I am unused to this sort of brotherliness, but I like it.

I'm so glad you boys got a chance to meet, Matt's mom says.

When I get to their house a few days later, in the sunny part of the afternoon, we pick up where we left off, sitting around drinking beers on their deck while Lebow makes the shroom punch, grinding the fungi in a blender with ginger ale and sherbet. Slowly, girls arrive, it would seem, almost exclusively, a four-to-one ratio, and Lebow and Matt grin, waving, the girls coming in with the familiarity of visiting family, picking up beers from an ice-filled garbage can, shaking them gently to lose the wet, jumping back at the foam spray. The David house is a big stone house on the ocean, on a spit of land far from the road, protected by birch-pine forest, with a separate pool house, where an indoor pool, glass-enclosed, occupies a stand of trees. Within a few hours it is completely occupied by ponytailed girls glossy from lavender lip shine, buff manicures, bathing-suit tans, and shaved legs. The boys seem invisible, the opposite of the way it is with birds, the male of the species here more inclined to vanish into the background while the girls flick hair back from their shoulders and smoke skinny white cigarettes that they stub out before moving on in a kind of rotation.

There isn't anyone who doesn't take some of the punch, and Matt and I throw down a fast two Dixie cups' worth, the strange chalky hallucinogenic fungus going down smooth. Grinnell College recipe, Lebow says, as we three toast in the kitchen. Who are these people, Lebow asks, and we laugh.

In a half hour, it won't matter, Matt says.

A half hour later finds Matt and me on the lawn, watching girls play Frisbee as the sun starts to go down. A stereo system has been set outside and music plays as the shiny girls toss shiny discs. God, they're beautiful, it's so beautiful here, Matt says, and the girls do seem like goddesses, like everything there is here is only to gild them a little more. Matt wrestles off his shirt and lies down on it, to reveal that he is shiny also, shiny brown with nipples as big as eyes and a smooth belly puckered by an outie belly button. I restrain myself from bending over to put my mouth on it, but it looks like the place you would begin inflating him by, if he were a gas-filled balloon.

Instead I take my shirt off also, and Matt says, God, you're built, and he says, Feel this, and he curls his biceps, hiking himself up so I can reach, because for some reason I can't move, and I touch the muscle, like a fist under his skin, and as my hand drops away I can feel how his nipple gives off heat like a lamp. The shiny girls watch, toss their Frisbee some more, and one of them yells, Arm wrestle, and it does seem like a command from the goddesses, so we face off, lying down, hands curled together, and as we struggle, I start to feel like we're both vanishing, and the girls sit around us, watching, and we're vanishing because the ground is swallowing us. We're evenly matched, but also, I don't particularly want to win, I never have, and so when Lebow walks over and grabs our hands and presses mine down over Matt's, Matt rolls with him, bringing him down on top of us so that we make a pile, and I am wedged against Matt's shoulder as Lebow grabs his brother's head and forces a big wet kiss on his lips that smacks like gum snapping. He jumps up laughing as Matt tosses me off him to wipe his mouth and spit. All of us pause, me and the shiny girls, as Matt barks to his brother, Shithead, and Lebow just keeps laughing, shrill and repetitive. Gratified, the goddesses return inside, looking after another beer, leaving their cigarette-filled empties on the counters of the kitchen.

By now I can tell this is the identifiable trip, the thing, and I stand in amazement, looking at it all: the whirling world of blue sky and sunshine and pretty white girls with expensive cars, the whirling from the heat I can feel where the parts of me that were pressed to Matt feel irradiated, like they should glow bright enough for me to read by, the way I can hear each tree breathe. Trees breathe, I say to Matt, an amount of time later that I am unable to quantify, except by knowing it is still not yet sundown, and he says, It all breathes. Feel the world take a breath all at once. And we go quiet together.

We head down to the pool house where the beer-drinking Frisbee goddesses have not yet arrived, and Matt flicks on underwater dome lights that spread a green-gold glow from below, and he strips out of his shorts, naked quickly. C'mon, he says, and I do, in awe, of him transformed into a baby Neptune. He fumbles open a jar and dips his hand in, and spreads a thick paint stripe across the forearm that glows blue as it starts to dry, and he hands me another paint jar. I open it and test it on my stomach, to see orange come up. I look up and see Matt has painted bars on his face, and he smiles as he runs his fingers flat down my face, painting it. His hand pauses under my chin, and he pulls me in by it, for a phosphorescent, dry-lipped, teeth-knocking kiss.

He laughs and dives in. The glow from underneath scatters light and dark across him, the blue glows darker, his white smile like an elbow of lightning. In the water he looks like a storm I once saw from above, inside a plane, and that's about how far up I feel when he soaks me with a splash. Stop looking and start swimming, he says.

I dive in, and when I surface, I see the beer goddesses by the side of the pool, removing, slowly, their clothes, their white breasts flash like whale bellies, and behind them the sky finally goes dark. They find the paints and start decorating each other. Music starts and I realize it isn't in my head but that there are speakers, in the walls of the pool house, and then there's Lebow, who drops his shorts, and starts laughing as the goddesses paint him, one taking his chest, the other his face. I hear the water on the deck behind them for a moment just before Matt knocks them all in the water, and kicks their clothes in behind them. Soon the pool is littered with bikini tops and cutoffs, and the laughing beer goddesses jump into the glowing pool, screaming and laughing, grabbing for their clothes, and Lebow swears at his brother, but the two goddesses with him restrain him, they aren't interested in what he wants from his brother. I pluck my shorts and Matt's from the water's surface, and head off in search of a towel.

I find Matt on the lawn, naked, glowing blue in streaks as if lit from some secret blue sun, holding a cup for me and for him. Cheers, he says, and we drink. The sky looks full of comets and the crescent moon is a little pink on the tip, like it cut someone before rising. We watch as the goddesses play in the glowing pool with his brother, and Matt asks me, Are you getting cold, I have some clothes in the house, and so we walk the lawn, the earth rolling under our feet as we go, and in his room he says, Here, hands me cold cream, and he says, It's the only way to get this shit off, and he takes a shirt and starts removing the orange paint from me, and I lie back as he does this, until he is kneeling in front of me, humming my dick into his mouth, and I am not glowing anymore, just greasy, in the dark.

And now the fireworks go off, banging the dark open, fire tossed everywhere, and somewhere probably one of the invisible boys the beer goddesses brought finds the stereo, and whoever it is puts on New Order, and the singer sings How Does It Feel, To Treat Me Like You Do, and Matt glows blue as he swallows me from the foot of the bed, and when I look out the window, Peter is there, hanging inside a star, singing along to the New Order song, his thumb on fire again but now a roman candle, and he tells me, Love is the regrowth of the wings of the soul. And the song lyrics are now spelling themselves out in the sky in blue letters, and on Matt in the dark swallowing me, the heat from him melting me into the sheets, and I ask Peter though I know I'm not speaking, to take pity on me, to take me with him, and he says, You can't come, you're not ready yet, and I say what, and then he recites Plato to me, he says, "He receives through his eyes the emanation of beauty, by which the soul's plumage is fostered, and grows hot, and this heat is accompanied by a softening of the passages from which the feathers grow, passages which have long been parched and closed up . . ."

And then Matt is spread out on me, and the blue is running off him onto me, he shows me into a kiss like a treasure vault hidden from all of heaven's searches, and I hear a dog crying somewhere and turn to see out the sky Peter, now waving, he's saying, You're free now, you are, and he grows wings of corkscrew stars, he has a fire around him, he rises. He lights the sky. And Matt appears before me now, he says, Fucking God, and he says, don't cry, and then we disappear, all three, into the deepening blue.

AND NIGHT'S BLACK

SLEEP UPON THE EYES

Warden

I

A VOICE LIKE a summer's day, my grandfather says to me.

I am twelve, singing out in the yard. York Beach, Maine. My grandfather and grandmother have taken custody of me and are preparing to send me off to a boarding school upstate. Someplace experimental, my grandmother says, knowing of my fondness for science. Small. You'll like it.

My mother and father are in prison, serving terms. That's all I get to know about it. I've never known them to miss them, that I know of; they were arrested and tried and sentenced well before I was old enough to remember anything. I occasionally find myself missing something, but hard-pressed, I can't say for sure that it is mother, father, family. My foster mother, who had me for four years, was good to me, but also quite plain about my status. My borrowed sugar, she would say to me. Found you in a cup.

I know they can't see me, forbidden, by court order. I receive letters, occasional pictures. Occasional. The pictures are occasions. Until recently all I had was a picture of my father as a teenager, thick brown hair, leaning against a granite boulder while hiking. Long brown hair wrapped in a handkerchief. My mother, also a teenager, dressed as a nurse for a Halloween costume. They met in college, my grandmother tells me when I ask. And she shows me the pictures of their wedding. When I get the new photograph, my father is bald. I ask, What happened to all that hair?

It goes, grandfather says. He rubs his thick hair, a gray spume.

Why am I so light, I ask. I know enough to know that parents and children are supposed to resemble each other. My hair is fair, eyes are light, green-blue, like the leaf of the lavender plants that border this house, where my grandmother grows roses and sweet herbs. My grandmother says nothing, but later emerges from the attic before dinner. I put these away, she says, but there's no point to not having them. A picture of a little blond boy, hair cut in a towhead Prince Valiant cut. A gleaming helmet for a tiny warrior. Who's that, I ask.

Your father, my grandmother tells me. My son.

2

THIRTEEN. MY MOTHER gets out of prison. Divorces my father. Returns to Sweden. She's from there, my grandmother tells me, explains. She's got people there.

3

FOURTEEN. HOME FROM school for Christmas, in York Beach. A resort town, empty in winter except for the few year-round residents. A present under the tree looks different from the rest. Store wrapping, unlike the home-done tinsel of my grandparents. I fumble the large package and hear muffled banging from inside. I fumble because my grandparents are staring. Finally it opens to spill out a butterfly net. A killing jar. A book of lepidoptery. Framed specimens, on tiny pins, to be hung on the walls. Beautiful, my grandfather says, and my grandmother looks at him as if she is choking.

Lovely, she says, her voice coming off the back of the room as she stands up and goes into the other room.

Will you use it, son, my grandfather asks.

Sure, I say. I am thinking of my father in the picture, our hair the same golden color. I am thinking, I don't want the change. I don't want my hair to change.

4

I AM A junior at Thomas Bethune Day and Night Academy, a private school for two hundred boys and seventy girls in East Knot, Maine, between Orono and Blue Hill. This school has been my home for years: a modern residence hall separated into two wings, New East and New West, by a dining hall; the Arts and Humanities building, called, strangely, Blue, and the Science and Math building, Farren, both the old original buildings. Blue was the manor house, a stone house with, originally, thirteen bedrooms, a ballroom, a dining room, a kitchen, servants' quarters, library, study, and sunroom. Farren was the barns and greenhouse; botany and animal husbandry are specialties there. The gymnasium is brand new, courtesy of a recent alumnus who made a fortune in leveraged junk bonds, and comes with a pool and indoor track. I spend my time there. Swimming helps keep my darkening hair blond. My name is Edward Arden Gorendt; my friends call me Warden.

5

THE NEW ASSISTANT swim coach arrived as the solution to a scandal: Ms. Fields, our swim coach these many years, had become pregnant out of wedlock and was determined to have the child and not marry and not give up her job; the school, in a rare conciliation, agreed. The board was mostly pro-life, something Ms. Fields wisely tailored her appeal toward. He was to begin early, in order to learn her training styles and workouts, and then the board hoped that seeing a man beside this increasingly pregnant teacher would give the illusion of codified heterosexuality the board supported. Mr. Zhe would also take the opening in the art department, being that rarity, an athletic fine artist.

He works in ceramics, Ms. Fields tells us, when we ask her. In her one-piece Speedo, her belly has started to dome. I imagine the baby's head there, as if it were trying to sit up in a made bed, trying to press through. I wonder if she will jump in and help us out with troubled strokes as before. And then he arrives.

Not so tall, actually; a bit shorter than me. Dark and yet pale, he looks young, like he is still in college. Not quite thirty, he has broad shoulders, a swimmer's bowed chest, strong, wide legs. He is dressed in running pants, flip-flops, a white tank, and a coral necklace at his neck. His hair is cut short, military-style, a widow's peak on his forehead points to his goatee that points to his feet. He has the look of a Russian, a Eurasian. I think of a picture of Cossacks I once saw. He smiles at me, and it is a knock on my chest, as if he had reached out and rapped it. My chest opens, my heart admits him. Hi, I say.

Hello, he says. He goes around shaking the hands of the team members. When he gets to me he asks my name and I say, Warden. His left eyebrow goes up. Nice to meet you, he says. A nice jail you got here.

6

HE TAKES A house near the school but not too near, on a tiny two-block street at the edge of town called Willow Street, and he lives there with a "roommate" by the name of Albright Forrester, a name I learned by taking his junk mail out of the garbage one day before practice after I saw him discard it. Albright Forrester, it read, you have been selected for a special subscription rate for the new *House and Garden.* I said the name that day as I practiced, Albright Forrester, Albright Forrester, mumbled into the chlorine-blue water.

The house is a saltbox Cape, with a widow's walk like a hat on top even though there is no sea there, and while it's run-down, they refurbish the house and grounds with incredible speed, as the roommate seems to have no occupation other than keeping the house. A cutting garden sits next to a vegetable plot in the backyard, and the small yard is home to two mixed-breed dogs that seem to be siblings, probably Labrador–pit bull mixes. Albright is younger than Mr. Zhe and prettier, slightly taller, his hair worn shoulder-length and always falling forward to obscure eyes the color of the swimming-pool water. He walks the campus on occasional visits with a casual air, as if there were nothing at all strange anywhere in the world, nothing that could take his interest from whatever middle distance he seems always focused on. To say he attracts a good deal of attention on these visits is an understatement. The smile he gives Mr. Zhe on greeting is more intimate than a kiss hello.

I go to their house some weeks later, drive down the street. I pause over the clutch and let my old black Volvo wagon drift. Albright comes out of the house, cutting shears in hand, headed for a lilac bush by the front of the driveway. His eyes flick toward the car. I shift and pull away. He returns to his cutting, the blooms coming away into his hand. I declutch and drift, watching in my rearview mirror. I can't stop looking at him, imagining Mr. Zhe coming home to him; do they kiss in the door? Do they act like brothers? I shift, the car engine grinds slightly, slower now, I don't want the brake lights to flash, attracting attention. I take the turn, U-turn, drive back by to see Albright in the door, plucking leaves off the lilac stems, unmindful of me. I drive away. That night, as I lie in bed, I think of a Mason jar of lilacs in the middle of their table, their dinner spread around it. A dark shape in my window ledge catches my eye: my binoculars, for butterfly catching.

The next day I take the afternoon and park after school in a meadow not far away. I tell myself, as I unpack net and killing jar, grease my face with sunblock, that as I walk the fields bordered in heather and wild rose I will only be after the luna moth. I won't try for anything else. I march the meadow with more than a little enthusiasm, and for the first hour or so find nothing, and then I see what looks like a buttercup take off into the air, fighting a breeze. My net swings out and it is so easy, as I tug in. The pale yellow greenling floats in and settles into the jar, almost resignedly. Personality in a wing flutter. I walk, binoculars up, to a rise of lichen-encrusted bedrock, the bone of the hill emerging, focused on the far edge of the trees, where the house of my coach hides, and so barely hear when a voice nearly below says, Watch out.

I jump back. On a green army blanket, eating his lunch, wearing just a pair of shorts on the beautiful body and sunglasses to cover the beautiful eyes, is Albright.

Hello, Collector, he says.

Hello, I say.

If you were to fall over out here on something less congenial, you could hurt yourself. Come to think of it, even if it were congenial, you could have hurt yourself.

I'm sorry, I say. Bad habit. Can't see for the looking.

Indeed. He laughs. I'm Bridey, he says, and reaches a hand toward me.

I'm . . . Ed, I say, not a lie. But suddenly I don't want Fee to know I've been here. That we've met.

Are you a student at Bethune? he asks.

Yes, I say.

Well, he says. It's early for butterflies, don't you think? I'm not a lepidopterist though.

Not so bad, I say, indicating my killing jar, where inside, the wobbly captive opens and closes its wings like a fast-motion flower. Today we caught a moth, I say. I'm about to jump up. I'll see you, then, I say. I've got to be going. Very sorry to have nearly clobbered your picnic there.

He shines in front of me. All of him reflects light: dark hair, bright eyes, smooth skin. The dead blond grass around him, as if we were picnicking on a giant's crown.

Sure, he says. No harm done.

7

I HAVE A girlfriend now, Alyssa is her name, also a swimmer. If anamnesis is a memory of paradise returning, this is what she seems like to me. Sometimes. She knows something is wrong but I don't know how to tell her about how it is I've fallen in love with our assistant coach. We see each other every day, after practice, and today, as we leave the building, she smirks at me through the wet dark hair she shakes behind her, in order to wrap it in a ponytail. She's the master of the skinny smile, which she offers me now as we walk the linoleum hall out to the yard.

You're quiet, she says.

I'm just listening to you, I say, and we laugh. It's a line from Truffaut's *Two English Girls,* something a man says to one of the sisters. He's a lover to both of them. This makes me familiar to her again, I know, and so we walk through the spring night wet, us wet, the grass wet. Her there, me pretending. Is this how it is now, I ask myself.

She turns, smooth skin covered in shadow, to ask me, Did you ever know your father, before he went off to prison?

Yes, I lie to her.

What do you remember.

Music, I say. But not any specific kind. People singing. That's how I remember my father. That part is true, I think. I think.

That's beautiful, she says, and pulls open the door to New West, the light coming out, restoring all her colors. She's beautiful to me again here. She kisses me. Good night, she says. Call me later if you want.

Okay, I say.

My father is a paper father. Letters, with a prison address. A crime I'd never been told about. My flesh-and-blood mother, the one who left all those years ago, after the divorce and her release, about her, my paper father says, She loved you. And she left because of it.

8

IN ORDER TO make the best use of the teams during the spring-break training, the school announces that under the direction of Mr. Zhe, the new art teacher, a sculptor-ceramist, we will begin the building of a nonsectarian chapel made of loose-stone construction. A Vermont stoneworker is coming to oversee at points. Bethune had lacked a chapel until now, as the radically liberal board that had put the school together had all had various chapel experiences at their respective boarding schools that hadn't pre-disposed them toward either religion or spirituality. A blind spot, one was quoted, in the school paper, the *Bethune Tribune*. At the grand old age of ten, the school decided it ought to have a place for "restful meditation." Mr. Zhe had providentially mentioned his interest in doing some loose-stone construction, and so now the search for a site begins, in earnest. Spring break, two weeks away, will mark a groundbreaking. When done, it will be the largest modern building of its type.

They're going to smudge the site, says Tom Ludchenko, wrestling the paper shut. We are in our room, waiting by the electrical outlet for the hot pot to boil for tea.

What's that? I ask.

They blow sage smoke to the four corners. I'd not be able to conduct any restful meditation anywhere that wasn't properly mortared. He yanks the plug from the wall and a spark chases out from the wall, after the plug fork.

Gravity holds it together, I say. I watch my tea brew. We get either an art credit for doing it or a science one.

Now the alumni can have weddings here, Tom says. Though it'll only be big enough for ten people to sit.

Four people's a wedding, I say.

Tom Ludchenko and I have been roommates for four years. I've seen him grow four inches in a year, the year between twelve and thirteen. One summer he was a blond stick with nothing for his shirt to hang on, and the next year he was a girl-eyed soccer player, playing goalie so as to avoid getting scrimmaged, knocking balls off with shoulders you could climb on. One Saturday a month we go down to Baxter School for the Handicapped, where we are student buddies to deaf peers; we help them with speaking, they help us with lipreading, this last an innovation of Tom's, and an excellent espionage tool. Tom and I use it to spy on every girl we go out with, on the faculty meetings on our yearly performance, and of course parental stuff. Sometimes, he'll stand across a room, and I'll talk to Alyssa while he watches my mouth, and as I repeat occasional things that she says for what seems like emphasis, she of course getting impatient (What, she asks every time, is there an echo?), while Tom prepares to meet me for strategy afterward.

We ride down today in the Range Rover of the headmistress, Mrs. Walter Thoreau, pronounced *threw;* the program was her idea, and she "administers it." Her brother is deaf and works at Baxter now, and she enjoys shopping at Freeport outlets while we spend our three hours in conversation; her brother is now actually part of a radical group of the deaf who don't want hearing aids or the new surgical corrections, and this is how she waits out yet another of their political contretemps. She also likes to grill us for gossip.

How's the new swim coach, she says, as soon as she guns the engine and gets us out of the tollbooth area; every time, the conversations begin here, as if the school's borders extend to the tollbooth. We're very excited about him, she adds, indicating the direction she'd like the conversation to go toward.

He's good, I say. An image of him hovering at the water's surface, coming out of his suit, splits the view I have of the road ahead of me. I am sitting in the front seat, having beat Tom to saying shotgun. He has tattoos, I add.

Trendy, she says, smirking at the middle distance. No piercings, I take it.

None I can see, Tom says from the back. She laughs. And he asks, Do you know who Ms. Fields's baby's father is?

Tom, she says, you are headed for a world of trouble if we talk that part up. But I'll tell you, she doesn't have one.

Immaculate conception, I say, imagining her briefly, holding a jar and a baster.

Top secret, she says. Alumni support for the new chapel is very strong. We might even get a new dormitory out of it. She's rallied much of the support, which is brilliant politics on her part: she deflects attention from whatever scrutiny her pregnancy might go under.

But anyway; are either of you going to do the building? I know you're both here for spring training.

Neither Tom nor I responds immediately. Around us, the cars on the road today are full of ordinary families. I wonder if passersby assume we're Mrs. Walter Thoreau's children. I might look it; she's a sharp-featured forty-something woman, well groomed, a little lipstick and mascara, with a good healthy complexion and short dark hair. *Gamine,* I think, is the word for it. As in, like a young boy.

I want you to promise me you will, she says. The more we have, the better the project will be.

Okay, I say.

Only if you will, Tom says to Mrs. Thoreau, and she laughs again.

9

DOWN AT THE school for the deaf the afternoon passes loudly. In a long-windowed classroom overlooking the sea Tom and I tutor students in speech patterning. Welcome to my home. How are you. Microbiology is one of my college degree goals. We teach them how to shape their mouth, watch as the sound comes out in pitches a degree high or low, to shake like a branch in that wind between flat and sharp. We practice our sign language, and as our hands flicker and our mouths stretch and close, the silence fills in with movement, which is what all sound is anyway. Being deaf, reading lips, everyone is at least like a word to the rest of the world. Everyone you meet is a sentence.

When you read, I ask one of my students, Fiona, what do you hear?

She laughs.

What is it like for you reading, I ask. When I read, I hear a voice in my head. Do you?

She puzzles over this. I don't know how to tell you what's in my head, she signs. Her hands bounce near her chest, like butterflies.

You've never heard a sound, I ask.

I feel them, she says.

And when you read, lips, or a page, I say. What's there? What orders it? Is it like someone making noise, and you feel it all over you?

I have to get back to you on that, she signs, smiling. She's a pretty girl, Irish skin and the blue eyes like the sky reflected in a sword. The quiet around her seems to make the focus of her prettiness sharper, the air's stillness focuses her in the eye. As if talking might make it harder to see someone.

Okay, I say. E-mail me.

10

WHEN I GET back, there's an e-mail from my grandparents. Dear Edward: re: Christmas . . .

It is starting to look as if your father will be released, as he has suggested, by the holiday and so it is a matter of some importance that you reach a decision about how you would like us to include him, or if. We have rarely spoken of how we feel about these things but not because we feel we are protecting you, exactly; we simply wanted you to form independent feelings from ours, for as it was, we were sure you would pick up on these feelings subconsciously.

The e-mail is long, basically a treatise on their theory of raising me, the borrowed child. They were always tentative around me, as if I were going to explode one day, into a hundred angry Edwards. In retrospect there was a certain danger of me developing MPD or something, from the sheer cognitive dissonance of having a father while not having a father, et cetera. But I know we both feel we'd been careful, and as I read, I began to understand more of why. And then they finally give me the exact reason.

. . . in 1982, your father was convicted on twelve counts of child molestation, and then related charges of sexual assault, and the corruption of minors. Your mother was convicted as his accomplice and served a shorter sentence. There is some question also as to the death of a foster child in their care, although the judge, after some investigation, ruled out foul play. We loved him as a child, we are trying to reach a forgiveness of him in our hearts, but with this problem, there is a high rate of recidivism, and so we are concerned. We aren't concerned particularly for your safety, but we do feel you need to make informed choices. We feel, as you approach the age of majority, that you are an exceptionally mature young man, and so we approach this topic confidently. This is only the beginning of the discussion; please call us after you read this, and we'll discuss this further. We took the trouble of making an appointment for you with a counselor, should you so wish.

We aren't concerned particularly for your safety, I think. They mean I'm too old for him now. Not that he's cured. When Tom comes back to the room I'm calm again, showered, cleaning the toilet in the common bathroom where I threw up. Wow, he says, from the doorway. Clean freak. You know, we have someone who comes through to do that.

They never do a good enough job, I say.

II

I HAVE BEEN having, I know, problems with my flip turns. When I somersault at the wall, I pause before striking the wall with my feet, to look and measure the distance. I look around. My head turning is bad for the water rushing behind me. And so Ms. Fields watches as Mr. Zhe, who has told us today to call him Fee, jumps in the water beside me. Watch me, he says.

He heads in toward the wall as if he will hit it with his head and then bangs through the turn, not even seeming to upend so much as to wriggle his way through. He comes up for air, to say, Don't breathe before. You can breathe after. Keeping your head down, watch the cross at the bottom. Try to measure yourself according to that. If you look up, you start to become less stream-lined. So now watch again. I measure my distance from the wall by knowing that when my head is over the crosshead, it's time to start the turnover.

And if you butterfly-kick on your way in you'll be disqualified, Ms. Fields's yells from the bench. Her stomach now has a tiny perch to it.

Watch from below, he says. I take a breath and start under, watching from below as he heads toward the wall again. He lands on the wall without looking, parts the current following behind him with his arms spread ahead of him like a knife turned to the side, and pushes off, foam at his feet as he kicks. He swims over me, two feet above, and the waves of his passing bump me against the floor, gently.

Did you get that, he asks, when we are both above water again. He didn't even glance at me as he went over me, and even now, it seems to me he doesn't see me somehow. As if I'm transparent, made of glass. To make sure, he says, before you continue, I want to see twenty somersaults right here, in front of the wall.

Around me the rest of the team pounds the cold blue water. I stand in the shallow end, turning myself over and over as he watches, to make sure I've got it right. I squeeze the memory of him above me out, not so much even the sight of him as the feeling I had, of an aurora of heat and skin above me. I know there is no way for me to feel the heat of him through the chill water. And yet I do. It comes to me later, as I lie under a thin sheet in my dark overheated dorm. I wasn't feeling it with my skin. The part inside. *Entelechy,* a word from my SAT vocabulary worksheet, springs into my head. The original energy inside of something. The source of movement.

I hear Tom turn over. Tom, I say.

What.

I'm working on that chapel, I tell him. You too, okay?

Okay. Sleepy-sleepy, he says. He says it every night, has for four years. And like a magic charm tonight, I go to sleep, almost immediately, on hearing it.

12

THE PIT IS dug in advance by a bulldozer, and the stones, having been quarried nearby, arrive in several trucks, where they are dumped into a pile, the entire thing causing less sound than I had thought. So that's what it sounds like when all those rocks fall, I tell myself, as I stand, watching, from my window. I bet you didn't know that rocks could rustle, did you? These do. They fall off the truck as if they were dragon scales, to shine wetly across the distance from my dorm here, the far hill for the chapel, there. And so it is we gather, on a somehow-clear day in March, to put this together. Thirty of us, in sweaters and fleece vests. We look like an ad, Tom says to me, as we look at all the pretty people around us, so well cared for, clear-eyed.

But for what, I say. Clean living?

Tommy Hilfiger, he says.

Alyssa slaps her face with sunscreen. Rosy as always. She wears little makeup, probably more than I suspected. She says a sharp hello, passing me by. I follow.

Yes, I say.

You make plans to go to Florida with Tom and I find out from Tom. What is that?

A mistake, I say. I've been really busy, I forgot. I actually thought I'd already told you, I say, as the other twenty-eight students follow Mr. Zhe, who eyes us briefly before starting. Can we talk about this later, I ask.

You have all the time in the world, she says. For Tom. Interesting. Her eyes narrow, nostrils widen, as if something were leaving through the one, taken in by the other. I see I never think of her anymore, in this moment. She had departed my thoughts completely, to the extent it took seeing her to remind me of her.

When I find out who the bitch is, she says, looking over my shoulder to the sea behind me, I'll punish. Fully punish.

Alyssa, I say. There's no one else.

It's all over this, she says. Someone else is all over this. And she turns, to sit down, in a cross-legged drop. I drop beside her.

Mr. Zhe wears a gray zip-up turtleneck sweater that makes him look like he's a sailor preparing us for departure. He shrugs back and forth in front of us, laughing occasionally, nervous as he outlines what the job is. It's like putting a puzzle together, he says, and introduces a handsome blond guy, his skin brown like he'd been left out in the sun since birth. The expert. We watch as he and Mr. Zhe put together a few of the rocks.

Listen to the rock, the expert says, as you hold it. I think of the rustle they made as they fell. The rock has a shape, search for where it meets the rock below, how it will ask for the rock to go above it. The idea is to set them in such a way that gravity holds them in place.

The first day, the foundation is set and banked. At night, from the dorm, it looks like a giant's footprint. Someplace a god stood on the earth. In the morning that follows, we set the stones quietly, all jokes gone. We work in pairs, one holds the stone as the other orients it, and it is built in strips. We cut one way, then the next, and when we break for lunch, the walls to the chapel rise to our shins. The shape they imply is in the air above them, like they're singing a song of the next thing to come.

When Alyssa slaps the back of my head, passing by, I don't do a thing. Tom Ludchenko mouths to me, What happened? And I mouth back, I don't know.

We return to building.

13

THE CHAPEL IS completed in a week. At night Tom rubs my shoulders and talks to me about the girls of Florida. I say nothing I remember in response. Alyssa has told everyone in our class that I am cheating on her, and that when she finds out who the girl is, there'll be real trouble. This last is emphasized with her right fist slapping her left palm. Smack.

Who is it? Tom asks me after our last day of building. You can tell your Tom, sure.

She's high, I say. Even Tom believes her now. I am taking her pictures down from the wall, sick of her smiling reproach. I still love her, I say. She's the only girl.

What are you doing with those, he says. Presuming you aren't lying even to your best friend.

I pull them all down, sunny picnic smiles, the class trip to Katahdin, the road trip we took out to Montana with her family. I put them in a file folder and slide them into my filing cabinet. Best friend, I say. I am teaching her a lesson in silence.

You mean, she's right, he says. He walks up to the wall and puts his hand on it. What are you going to put here instead?

Don't know, I say. She's not right, I say. She's just going to embarrass herself, when the truth comes out.

Uh huh, Tom says.

You are such a fuck, she says, when she sees the wall the next morning. Really.

Tom runs out of the room for the bathroom. Listen, I say. All you have to do is admit you are wrong, and I'll put the pictures back up.

I don't give a fuck about the pictures, she says. Are you some kind of moron? I don't mark territory. Where are they, and here she plucks at the desk. Where? My homework spills across the floor.

I leave the room while she isn't watching. I walk to the bathroom, where Tom brushes his teeth. Through a mouth of foam he says, You are a brute, man. Unbelievable. I walk back to the room, where Alyssa sits in the floor's middle on her knees. Paper around her as if she's shed it. I hate you, she says.

I love you, I say.

14

ON THE NIGHT before I go to Florida, I slip out to visit the silent stone bump we've made. Since finishing it, I've wanted to be alone with it, and after Alyssa's meltdown I want to go somewhere on this campus that doesn't remind me of her.

Open to the four directions, domed, slate benches in rows facing toward a central granite altar, it seems, already, as if it has always been here, since before the school. On the slope of the rise toward the sea, it looks down to the houses of the school, like a large trail marker. There is no electricity for it, no heat, no light, and so in the dark night as I come up to the entrance I do not see that someone is inside. From just outside the door, I feel it, instead, whatever warm air this visitor makes by just standing there reaches me through the stone chill.

I wait. I hear the pitch of the night tide at the beach over the hill, the creaking wood planks of the boat spit. I slide myself to the ground, hide my warmth from the one inside, lean my back into the chapel's serrated wall. I'm pretty sure it's him. The one whose idea it was to build this place. Fee. I like to think I can tell him from the heat he gives off.

And then I hear it. A faint sound reaches me, above the ocean: singing. Or rather, humming, the music, but no words.

It makes me want to laugh a little at him. Except even the stones shouldn't be hearing this. The song pricks me like wood sparks off a fire. I wait, quiet, cold, the stone's cold reaching me slowly. And then he leaves, quickly. A sprint, he runs from the same cold that's holding me still.

I watch him go. It's Fee, all right. His car in the far lot spits light across the lot and takes the road in a whirl of white and red. I stand, shake my blood back into my legs, and walk through the chapel with my lighter out, lit. He loves someone, I think, as I enter the chapel, warm from him.

I find a taper, which I light. So this was the warmth. He'd obviously just blown the candle out. I can smell the candle smoke that hangs around me now in the new light. And in the light, the floor shows me where someone has disturbed it, near the base of the altar.

The altar's granite was quarried nearby, in Peterboro, and it is a large dark polished gray. Five-sided, it reflects me as I squat down. There's a picture here, curled up and set in a spot where the stone sides of the floor don't fit perfectly, a rock envelope. It's not obvious at all, as I look at it, but to me it is, as obvious as the weather or the dark outside. Because, as I take it in my hands, I decide, it is for me. I slip it into my pocket. I didn't know why I'd wanted to come out here tonight and now I know, I came for this.

Back in my room, Fiona, my deaf student, has e-mailed me. Re: What's in my head when I read:

I didn't want to say. I mean, is that what hearing's like? I guess it is. I guess I hear. In that, if anyone speaks to me, it's like a transmission, on the optic fiber of my eye, played in my head as if it's a speaker. Speaking frustrates me. Because I know, it's nothing like it should be. I wish only to communicate with other people as gracefully as they communicate with me.

> Have fun down in Florida with Tom,
> Fiona

15

NOWHERE TO LOOK at, it seems, when crossing Florida.

The sky looks strained, as if it'll just let go, and the vacuum of space come down, ripping everything off the ground. But the weak sky continues, somehow, a tea-stain white with a peek of blue down near the tops of the trees, as occasionally a crane flies out across the sugarcane fields that stretch endlessly to either side. Chokingly thick smoke, from the burning cane, obscures our view here and there.

Interterm practices ended and we are allowed a five-day break while we taper, in which our bodies store the enormous energy we have been raising daily for practices, and let it out all in a rush, when we compete upon our return. Tom Ludchenko and I have come here for our yearly pilgrimage to his grandparents' place. We knew, they said to us this morning, over breakfast, if we got a place in Disney World, we'd see our family. Tom rolled his blue eyes in his pink face as they laughed at him with their matching blues. Blue, blue, blue, I counted, blowing on my coffee.

In actuality we have come to hate Disney but there is a swim camp near here where Tom knows some girls from another team, the Mount Desert team, who've all come down here to do strokework. Alyssa will kill me if she finds out but Tom is the only one who'll tell, and he speaks to her less than I do all the time. And there is a lot she'll kill me for besides all of this.

We pass a sign. SPIRITUAL READINGS, PAST LIFE REGRESSION, TAROT, HANDWRITING ANALYSIS. ONCALA, WHERE THE SPIRIT MOVES US ALL. WELCOME TO VOLUSIA COUNTY.

What's that about, I say to Tom.

There's a town nearby called Cassadaga, where there's been mediums for years, he says. But recently it got too large, internal squabbling, et cetera. So some moved here to found a new town on the same theme. He shrugs his huge shoulders. Want to stop?

I do, and say so.

At a rose-covered visitor center a kindly white-haired man asks me a few questions as Tom waits in the car and soon he hands me a brochure. Clairvoyant. Tanya Roux is a Certified Clairvoyant of Oncala's Council of Clairvoyance and Clairaudience . . .

We head over, according to the map, a few blocks away, where Tom waits again in the car while I am seated in a velveted parlor, midnight blue from floor to ceiling, a dazzling crystal ball in the center of a small white table. I set my brand-new credit card down on the table and when Tanya comes in, a strikingly young, dark-haired girl so thin it shocks me, I find myself desperate to get this over with.

I explain myself quickly, and hand over the photograph. The picture is of a boy, dated August 1983, and the boy, so blond his hair is the color of the noontime summer sky. He is yelling something to the photographer, his eyes crossed in a manner both charming and sad. The medium takes the picture and lets go of it immediately.

So hot, she says. She holds her hand a few inches above. This is as close as I can get to it. It's burning.

I leave with her advice in my ears. The boy is gone but the fire is not. Get rid of the picture or the fire will come for you. Tom smiles at me as I climb into the car. Done wasting your money, he asks.

Sure, I say, and put the picture in the copy of *The Wapshot Chronicle* that I had brought with me to read. We drive out, the sunset beginning to make a red mark on the sky's bottom.

The next day at Disney World I find myself watching the children.

Small. Skin like a petal. Hair that won't do what it is supposed to. Eyes like lake water at night. A need to eat but not to stay clean. Holding legs as parents try to walk. I try to imagine what it is my father saw that he would have done what he did. There is nothing about them, that I can tell. I try to see the Eros here, he is often, after all, shown as a baby boy. The child of love and war. But no effect. No Affect. Just Popsicles melting. Smeary faces. Yelling. Punches. In the line for Space Mountain, Tom notices me watching and he says, Biological clock ticking? This is something Mrs. Thoreau says all the time.

Space Mountain. Rushing through the dark at high speed. Someone else is driving. You could die, if they aren't paying attention. This is what childhood is, and we line up for it. In the line, a little boy of eleven stands in front of me. I can see he's already sturdy, he has the hero's triangle of a body, the broadening shoulders, the tiny waist and hips, the sturdy legs. The man in him waits, barely. But isn't anything you could touch. It's not love, I see. It's not like when I want Fee to touch me, when I would take hold of Alyssa by her neck and pull her in for a kiss.

Tom's grandparents take us out for dinner. Lobster, four and five pounds each. To get this large, they have to be thirty years old. We sit foursquare around the table, over huge broken red bodies, pull the meat out and soak it in yellow butter. Around us, children yell for their parents' attention.

16

BY THE TIME we return from vacation it feels like a month has gone by but it isn't a month, just shy a week. Tom feels the same way. We float in and out of classes, the teachers' voices a syncopation, and we drift down to the quad, where we sit on wet grass and watch the clouds hurtle by like islands cut loose from below. Blue Hill is one of the most beautiful places in the whole world, anyone knows it, Tom tells me. We shouldn't be glum. But we are. Tom misses one of the girls he met on our adventure over at the stroke camp down in Florida, and I have the picture I found in the chapel. Somewhere in Fee is a picture of this. I can't help but wonder who the boy is but I don't know him and so he fades,

becomes transparent. And as he does I do, the boy I knew myself
to be dissolving.

Did you ever see a bee lying drunk on a rose? Lost in the petal,
so close you can't see its tiny burrowing. In this way, I hang as I
can. As close as I can.

After practice we go as a team for a carb-loading premeet meal
to an Italian restaurant that has an all-you-can-eat buffet, where
we pay our six dollars apiece to the elderly cashier and head off to
stuff ourselves in the glass-candle twilight of the room. We sit in
three booths at the back of the restaurant, eating, talking loud,
and Ms. Fields takes an uneasy seat next to me. Hey there, she
says.

Hey, I say. Precious Cargo, I say, pointing to her stomach.

You doing okay? she says. She twirls at her spaghetti and drops
a ball of it into her mouth.

I, uh, yeah? Yeah. Why?

Go ahead and convince me, she says, chewing. I was just talking but I guess there is something there.

Is it weird, having someone inside you like that, I ask.

She emits a laugh, choking a little as she swallows. Wow. Nice
question. Um, well, it is bizarre, but it's beautiful, she says.

Beautiful, I say. Ms. Fields still hasn't told anyone who might
tell who the father is. And then Mr. Zhe sits down next to me.

Get enough to eat there, he says. His large head here in the
dark restaurant like a lamp inside the dark cave of me.

He starts talking about the chapel's finishing ceremony, the
inauguration of it. Easter there'll be a service, he says. The head-
master likes the idea of having an Easter service, brief, of course,
because of weather (It might snow, adds Ms. Fields), as Jesus
rolled the stone away and this chapel is rolled stones.

Not hungry, Ms. Fields asks me.

I see that I've stopped eating, and so I pick up a fork. Resting,
I say, and stab a shiny ziti among the rest in the sauce lake on my
plate.

Mr. Zhe puts his hand on my forehead. You're not warm, he

says. Maybe a bit clammy. His hands are warm, dry, they have a faint smell of sweet cinnamon. Around us, the other swimmers din the air with their conversations, and suddenly all the sounds flatten. No one sound any louder than any other. A leveling takes place. I hit the floor on my side.

And so it is that the faint, caused by my thinking of the theft of the picture, is the first reason he takes me in his arms. I'll remember it later. At the time, he lifts me to carry me outside, his arms hard like wood. As the air comes back to me, the light, as we go through the doors to the outside, breaks on us like rain. He lays me out on the grass, stays above me, searching my eyes, lifting one lid, then the other. Ms. Fields appears above me, the pillars of her legs looming suddenly, the blue sky above her, heaven's sieve. Is he all right, she asks.

I think so, Mr. Zhe says. Are you all right, he asks.

I close my eyes. Yes, I say. I will be.

In my dorm's phone booth, the door pulled shut, I talk through some fast options with a hot-line operator for "gay, bisexual and questioning youth" I find on a number from a newspaper ad. He's down in Portland, he tells me his name's Kevin, that he's thirty-five, that he wants me to know that the conversation is confidential.

Do you know how he feels about you?

I don't, I say. I mean, I have no reason to think he feels anything. I'm just his student.

You mentioned you know he's gay; is he out at the school?

No, I say. I, uh, I went over to his house. Saw him with his boyfriend.

A little Harriet the Spy, are we, he says, chuckling. Sorry. I mean Encyclopedia Brown.

No, I say. It's fine.

Do you fantasize about other men, he asks.

No, I say. I don't. I don't fantasize.

Hmm. Well, how about this. What do you imagine, happening, when you think of him.

And here, for some reason, I think of my father. Your pause, he says, is a little damning.

I, uh, was distracted for a moment. I don't know. That's why I called. I don't know what this is, I say. I twirl the phone cord, and the phone numbers, written in ballpoint and pencil on the wall, start to look like a map to some country, topographic: here, the mountains. There, a river. A notice, above the phone, reads PLEASE LIMIT CALLS TO 20 MIN. I look at my watch. I've got thirteen minutes.

How about this, the operator says, all business. How about, if you imagine him getting fired and you getting suspended or expelled. Because you are not yet eighteen and he is your teacher and no one, no one, thinks of this as the happy ending for the story you're telling me. Not even you, right?

No, I say. I mean, right.

So, what's worth that.

I love him, I say, surprising myself. When he's around, it feels like he's in charge of everything in me. I don't know what to do with that. Do you kiss it? I don't know.

Oh, boy. The operator's quiet a moment, and then he says, I don't know anyone who wouldn't fall in love with that.

I laugh.

I remain worried, he says. The school thing is large. I really think, with a year to go, that you should consider doing nothing until you have graduated. Your graduation is the most important thing right now, and the year will give you time to really know what you want to do about this.

He'll be gone by then, I say.

See how smart I am? the operator says. Look, I know what this feels like but at your age, you're going to feel like this every three days.

Feel like I'm going to die, I ask. Every few days?

You're not dying, he says. I guarantee it. But if you do anything about this you could get into trouble so deep you might wish you were dead. And that's, well, that's not what this should be about. Love should be about making you want to live.

In the hall I see Alyssa's brown-skinned back as she passes by, headed for my room. I don't have a lot of time. I say, There are Mexican Indians who believe that gold is the earth's blood.

Huh, he says. Beautiful. What's that go to do with anything?

We cut the world to marry, I say.

Marriage, he says, is not a big topic for this hot line, despite what people might think.

I'd cut the world for him, I say.

Don't even cut a class for him, the operator says. Do yourself a favor. Stay young. For another year, and try to find a nice boy your own age. Okay? And one other thing, he says.

Yes, I say.

Call me here at this number if you decide to try anything. Talk to me before you do. All right?

Alyssa, in the window of the booth, mouths, Who are you talking to? I raise a hand to her, signaling a moment, and I say, All right. We hang up. I imagine him logging the call. 6:15 P.M., April 30, 1997. A 17-year-old male, questioning. Talk time, 18 minutes. In love with teacher. Alyssa pulls the door open.

Hi, she says. Who's your new girlfriend?

What, I say.

This phone booth has someone else written all over it. She pulls back.

There's no other girl but you, I say.

She turns, her hair falls over her face, and then she pulls it back, and looks at me. Let's go look at the comet, she says.

Outside the comet Hale-Bopp sits in the sky. Alyssa and I sit and watch it from the lawn. Comets are burning ice, gas frozen and made solid and then burned by the friction, so cold it's fuel. So hot you can see it from planet Earth. I know exactly how you feel, I tell the comet.

It's amazing, isn't it, she says. A comet, and for a few weeks, we get to look at it every night as though it were the most ordinary star.

At the low edge of the sky, a bright smear. The slow burning, light pealing like struck bells at the speed of its passing. A bright tear in the night's dark belly.

Did you ever notice, I tell Alyssa, shortly before we leave the comet's company. How *tear,* as in to cry, and *tear,* as in to rip or pull, how they're spelled the same? You could write them and someone reading would not know if you were crying or separating.

You'd know, she tells me. You would know.

17

EVEN A SLOW angel moves faster than we know how to.

For my senior English thesis, the topic of which I had to choose this year, I decide to choose my subject at random. Inspired by a game the swim team played on the bus, Lucky Bug, I pick the letters and numbers off license plates I see on Volkswagens that our bus passes on our way to swim meets, until I arrive at a Dewey decimal system number. I take the number into the library and enter it into the computer to search for the title, and the title comes up, quickly. *Sappho, The Poems of.*

I want to write a paper about Sappho, I tell my English adviser, Mrs. Autry, at a meeting shortly after. A brisk, red-haired woman with large eyes in a thin face, she reminds me of an elf. She approves it with a smirk. Good luck, she says.

What, I say.

You'll be trying to write that paper your whole life, she says. Sappho's an enduring question.

Later, I am reading her and Mrs. Autry is right.

Sappho, fragment 168:

And Night's black sleep upon the eyes.

He writes a letter.

Dear Edward:

I can't tell you how much I'm looking forward to seeing you after all this time, at Christmas. It's the answer to a prayer, at least. Your grandparents are some of the best people the world has to offer, and I'm sure they've done a terrific job at raising you, and that they've given you lots of love. They wrote to me regularly here to let me know how things were going with you, and while it hurt me to not be able to be in touch with you directly, I always hoped that when I was done here, that we might meet, and at least be friends. I don't want you to think that I'll magically emerge from here and be, overnight, this father you never had. I think I can say that. But I remember you as my baby boy, and it's been so long since I've held you. I know it'll be a shock, to see you as a young man. I've gotten pictures at Christmas, so I've seen it, but it's another thing altogether to meet you.

I wasn't ever happy with the arrangements the court made, please know that. And also, know that your mother loves you. She and I aren't in touch anymore, but shortly after her term ended, she wrote to me to say that her way of loving you would be to leave you to my parents. I know that sounds odd, but she really felt that it was a duty of love, to remove herself. And that's your mom.

There's more. It's just a letter, I tell myself, as I get out of bed that morning, pull on a shirt and shorts, and head out to the pool. It's not an omen.

Years later I would come to regard it as one of those moments where you learn to trust your first instinct. For instance, you always tell yourself something isn't what you think it is because you are trying to scare yourself off what you know is true. For now, though, I am headed across the summer lawns of the school, bright green for the visiting students and the summer kids. I applied for and got a summer term special program of independent study, for reading Sappho, and Fee had the idea that I should work at the pool as a lifeguard. And so that, and the letter from my father, is my summer. Sappho, swimming, Mr. Aphias Zhe, and a criminal pedophile's correspondence. My father.

Phile, for love. Fil, for son. Pedophilial, pedofilial. Fil de pede. A rhyming voice crowds me as I go across the campus. I get to the pool, unlock the doors, and enter the fluorescent rooms and halls stinging from the chlorine. Trophies here by the entrance, pictures of young boys and girls huddled, pink and a little pinched, before the camera. It's cold, the AC pump the only sound besides my flip-flops going pit, pit, pit. A whistle for the kids. Unlatch the locker room doors, turn on the radio, to top 40, flick the hair back with a bandanna. I slump into my chair.

Phil de pede. The love of children. What is it called, when a child loves a man? Notice how the word goes one way. I won't be a child much longer. Paper father, paper son. What I want doesn't have a word. But made of paper, I can be written on. I can find, make, write this word.

The first of today's swim guests are a faculty family, Mr. and Mrs. White, the algebra and algorithm husband--wife team with two tiny blond seven-year-old boys, twins, who bob in the pool, squeaking. Mrs. White is really nice and seems just now to be catching up on sleep lost raising the twins, while Mr. White seems unchanged, still almost a teenager. The twins take after him with his blond hair and his peaked nose. Mrs. White is a striking woman with pale skin and dark blue eyes, which the children have also, the one place her colors touched them. Mr. White, as he smiles at me while the boys giggle at apparently nothing, shows eyes so pale I am reminded of the sea salt my grandmother cooks with. She uses it to crust mackerel.

How's Sappho treating you, Mrs. White asks. She rises out of the pool on strong arms, pulling herself out in one yank, twisting to sit near my feet. She wrings her hair and the water falls out of it in a slap.

Sappho's great, I say. There's nothing like an old Greek Lesbian.

Mrs. White furrows her brow at this. I mean, I say, resident of the isle of Lesbos.

Her sexuality is the subject of some controversy, Mrs. White says with a faraway look.

Is it? I ask.

Thoreau says so, Mrs. White says, meaning the Mrs. They are old friends, refer to each other from their days back at Chapin, in New York, by last name. White, Thoreau. As if taunting each other for taking the name of the husband.

Seems pretty clear, reading her, I say.

Whose translations are you reading? She turns to look at her husband, rising from the water, a twin under each arm, as if he found them there.

Guy Davenport, I say.

None better, White says. A friend of mine studied with him down in Kentucky. He would hand out his translations of Herodotus as he finished them. "There isn't one sufficient," he'd said, at the beginning of the class, "and so I'll be giving these to you as they're done." Isn't that amazing? A genius that knows itself.

We look at each other and I say, Imagine. The luck.

If you're wrong, it's sad. More than sad. Tragedy. Her dark hair now almost like wet wood, a dark branch on her pale neck. Give me those babies, she commands her approaching husband, and as they come out of the water toward her, she seems like a nymph, in command, these pale babies fathered on her by the pool.

Sappho isn't really meant to be read. It's meant to be sung and there were dances for the songs, also. Sappho was a performance artist, and now she exists as a textual project. She was saved by her critics, and by people who wrote of her in letters to each other. As the morning sun lathers the pool through the long windows and stripes the opposite walls in gold, I look at the fragment translations. She's paper, too. A paper poet for a paper boy. People claim to be translating her but they don't, really, they use her to write poems from as they fill in the gaps in the fragments. A duet. She may have meant for these to be solos but they're duets now, though the second singer blends with the first. The first singer in this case is offstage, like in the old days of stars who couldn't sing, a real singer hidden behind a curtain, which is the velvet drape of history.

I'm not really paying attention then when the door slides open and someone I barely recognize comes in the door. At first I want to say hello, and then I realize, it's Bridey, and he doesn't know who I am. Doesn't recognize me from the day we met on the hill. I think of the day we met, me pretending to be a butterfly catcher. The ancient Greeks thought of the butterfly as an image for the soul. I looked at my collection differently after reading that. Tiny souls pinned tight to velvet. Drying ever so slowly.

His attention flickers on me and then off. He signs the sheet and goes into the locker room. I expect him to recognize me but of course he doesn't. He walks with the gait of a dancer, a walk that looks simple but is a coordination of a hundred muscles that know and like each other pretty well. He's a beautiful man, and it feels odd to think it, but this is who I am now.

I get up and set my book in my chair. Mrs. White, I say. I'm just in the bathroom, if someone comes in. She nods her dark head, the hair heavy.

Sure, she says.

Each beat of my heart seems to echo off the tiles. At first I think I imagined his entry because the locker room seems empty, it's so quiet. What I tell myself is that I'm going to reintroduce myself to him. And then as I turn the corner for the bathroom, Bridey appears in front of me, his long hair in his face, tipped forward, like a flower after the sun has set. His eyes search through his bangs and he smiles. Hi, he says. He's naked. There's a flicker across my vision, as if someone has shut the light on and off quickly, correcting an accident.

Hi, I say. He's just being friendly; he doesn't remember me. And then I remember, with the bandanna on my head, I look pretty different. He heads back toward the locker rows, and I head in to the urinal, where I stand for a moment. Nothing comes out of me. I hike my bathing suit back up and flush, trying to act casual. Back at my seat, Mrs. White smiles as I sit down.

Everything okay, she says.

Yep, I say.

Bridey is a strong and sure swimmer, he swims quietly, with force, breathes symmetrically, his freestyle like an Australian crawl, a lot of it on the surface. Fee swims like a bull, head down so far it seems to disappear, so that there's a flat space between the sprays of his arms as he goes.

He's a good swimmer, Mrs. White says. Her head like a pointer, she watches him travel back and forth across the pool. A charming man, she says. Too pretty, really. It's wasted.

What is, I say.

Beauty like that. In a man. Women always resent a beautiful man. Her eyes take me in, even as she bounces one of the twins on her leg. Don't tell me you don't know that.

How would I know that, I say. I don't know anything.

What a lie, she says. Terrible of you. Boys are different, they don't . . . and here she turns back to Bridey. I suppose, she adds, I shouldn't talk to you this way.

You can, I say.

Everyone expects a boy to be beautiful. It's allowed. A man has so much else to do. You don't trust a beautiful man. It's like he's still a boy, somehow, in the important way.

You don't trust boys then, I say.

Not for what women need from a man, she says, and she frowns here. I don't.

Bridey swims across the middle distance, lane 4, still churning. He doesn't care what we have to say about him, he doesn't seem to care that we are here. It's fine, it's how it should be. Except preposterously I find myself cheered by Mrs. White's assessment. I have a chance.

Do you know who that is, she asks me.

I don't, I say.

He's the partner of the new swim coach. I'm surprised you haven't seen more of him.

Mr. Zhe's not very social, I say, feeling a bird in my throat. As if it could peek out, as I open my mouth, to talk to Mrs. White. Its shiny eyes behind my teeth. The rumor, I add, and here the bird goes away, is that he's the father of the art teacher's baby.

Her pretty eyes get a little small, and she laughs in a pip. Oh my, she says. Children. He's not, she says, and here she looks over to Mr. White, who is swimming lazily through the water in lane 2. He can't father a child, I shouldn't think. You understand, she says.

I think of my new friend, the hot-line operator. Yes, I say. I do.

And the subject shuts like a book. Bridey slides out of the water, sleek, walks around the edge of the pool. Mrs. White, he says. How charming you are there, with your children. She smiles at him, youthful. Women don't hate beautiful men, I see as I watch her. They may envy them, but that isn't hate. Hate is love on fire, set out to burn like a flare on the side of the road. It says, stop here. Something terrible has happened. Envy is like, the skin you're in burns. And the salve is someone else's skin.

Aphias. Bridey says, I know Fee is planning something for Labor Day, but I don't know what. Probably a garden party with a tent. He pushes his hair back behind his ears. Hi, he says. I'm Albright Forrester. He holds his hand out. I shake it.

Hate. Envy. Hello, I say. No bird in the throat now. I am the bird, now. A raven? A sparrow. I say, I'm Edward. Edward Gorendt. He lets my hand drop and hitches at his suit.

Nice to meet you, he says. You're on the swim team, I suppose.

I am, I say. Mrs. White's gaze on me feels like a sunbeam, warm and from far away.

And all the day afterward fills with hours where the air evanesces like it will open and Mr. Zhe emerge from the sparkly hard center, a flightless angel slipping from God's portal. Fee, Bridey had said. Fee.

Of course, years later, I will know, the bird in my throat was a crow.

I go through the days left before school like they are rooms along a corridor where I stop in, look around, to see if he is there, and leave after waiting. I walk the days with his name lying on my tongue, like a swallow of water that I can't take down my throat. Bridey continues to come to the pool, on occasion. I do not go into the locker room while he is in there. Sometimes Mrs. White is there also, smiling, her twins on each of her knees.

18

THE ROSES ALONG the wall of the library disappear pretty regularly and soon it is discovered the problem is a Japanese beetle infestation, the roses being eaten the same day they open. In the morning, a flower. In the evening, not a petal.

So one evening on my way back from the pool I find Mr. Zhe standing in front of the rosebush, with what looks like a yellow Santa hat in his hand.

What's that, I say.

Japanese beetle trap, he says. It's got a synthetic hormone in it that attracts them, and then they go in here, get poisoned, and die.

They think they're finding a mate, and instead, they die, I say. I pluck at the yellow fabric. Huh.

He smiles at me. Doesn't seem fair, does it.

Summer lasts forever, I say.

It won't, he says. It only seems that way in August. He rubs a stem in his fingers. Pretty healthy, he says. You miss your friends, though, huh?

Yep, I say, though I hadn't thought of it that way. I didn't really know most of the students in this summer term. Didn't want to. Mr. Zhe looks at me for a long minute. All I know is that all summer I've wanted to run into him, and now that I have, my stomach feels like it is kneeling on my guts, like I could burst into tears right here. I want to say, touch me. Please. And it seems for a moment that he's going to put his hand on my shoulder.

You'll be fine, he says. It's really just two more weeks. I hear you have some stuff you're dealing with, though, and if you need to talk about it, you can talk to me about it.

Rose-breath around us, faint. The dusk like a mist of the night, as if night evaporated at dawn, to collect and then rain down again, to make night again.

Were he to put his hand on me, I would be revealed as nothing more than a newspaper, erect. A screen on which is projected the image of a boy. How could he love me? There's nothing to me except a place where the light resists moving forward. Okay, I say, instead. I will.

Do you have a number for me at home, he says.

I don't, I say.

Here, he says, and writes it out on a slip from his pocket. Later, at my dorm, I lie on my bed looking at the number. It was a receipt he wrote on. $10.00, Japanese beetle, trap and bait. Augusta Hardware.

19

AROUND THIS TIME is when I start to throw up for what at first seems like surprising or unlikely reasons. At first, on the day in question, a day I spend in a sea kayak with Tom, I think that it is seasickness, even though I've never had travel sickness of any kind.

We are in Bar Harbor, today, sea kayaking. Tom has developed, since the stone-house episode, into something of a junior geologist. The sea kayak was a birthday present for him, and we've been practicing in it a few times a week. September is on us now up here, and we feel, as our paddles pluck at the waves, the chill wind off the sea, the cold front coming up just after the warm morning. We are out in the water off Burnt Porcupine Island, a tiny drop of stone spiny with spruce pines, and Tom navigates us to the edge of the shore through the bright-colored sea kayaks of the tours passing by, with their friendly instructors announcing loudly to speed up or slow down. We let them pass. We idle in the water in front of an enormous egg-shaped granite boulder, sitting, without a friend, among shattered sandstone and siltstone at the top of a short stone beach.

Glacial erratics is when a boulder or rock of a very different era or climate is carried for great distances by a glacier and set down far away, where it remains, Tom says. And so it looks out of place. He indicates the near shore. I look.

The glacial erratic.

It looks very out of place, I say.

I try to imagine the area, covered in an ice blanket thirty stories tall and as long as the coast, shaving down the mountains, pushing the rocks into each other, like when the guys at the ice cream shop pound the toppings into the ice cream. Glaciers, carrying these boulders along on their underside like the pebbles that stick to my feet when I walk the beach. Thus preoccupied, we don't notice, behind us, the Cat.

The Cat is a jet-propelled catamaran-style ferry built in Transylvania that can make the Bar Harbor–Nova Scotia passage in two and a half hours, half the time of the boat it replaced. The

Cat blows out of the harbor and the waves come out of its wake like water sprites cut loose to make mayhem. We almost don't notice in time.

Fuck, Tom says, and he whips his oar into the water to shove us around. Get the stern facing the wave!

And too late I turn as he turns, too late as the kayak follows the wave up on its side. It doesn't turn us all the way over, exactly, but the weight of the boat follows and then we are under. Here in the blue light of the water, I see Tom's golden hair like kelp. I pull at my splash skirt, tug it free, and break the water, spitting. I wait to see Tom join me and he does, he spits, he says, Fucking assholes.

We aren't far from the shore, and so we right the kayak and pull it in to shore. The water, even in summer, is the temperature of an ice cube melting in your shirt. The stones of the beach warm us as we walk up and lie down on them to dry off. Their dark color catches the heat better than white sand.

And then I feel the air catch that peculiar hardness, as if Mr. Zhe floated on a beam out of sight, waiting to take shape in front of me. And my stomach rises and tightens. I throw up.

Oh, man, Tom says. Are you all right?

Yes, I say, and I spit the rest out. Seawater.

I ask Mr. Zhe about glacial erratics on the first day of school. I've waited to ask him. We stand outside the pool, waiting to go in for practice. It's forty minutes beforehand, and I know he gets there that early. I pretend I have the time wrong. I pretend he believes me. I've lately begun to feel he knows what I am thinking.

Oh sure, he says. Cool stuff. And he leaps the fence running the edge of campus. The grass there is from when this was old cow fields, and enormous rosebushes grow here and there in the middle, unruly giants. Mr. Zhe has taken cuttings from them, he tells me, for his garden at home, and is excited that he may have found some old roses. Among the fields in the roses are a few of these giant rocks.

This one is gray and ribbed with marble, it looks like, or

quartz. This, he says, is a glacial erratic from Ellsworth. It's old. But see here, how smooth it is? It was rubbed down. But here, and he points to places where the rock looks punched open, these are called shatter marks.

Chatter marks? I ask.

Shatter, he says. Where another rock pressed against the larger one with such force that they both broke as the glacier moved. The smaller one would have powdered, and here is where it shattered. The larger one looks like it's been shot.

I like chatter marks better. Where the small stone was trying to talk to the big one, but because they were so close to each other, in the rub of the glacier, the small one exploded, trying to talk.

I'm having a reception on Labor Day, he says. An open house. I'll tell the rest of the team. But Bridey and I will need some help and it would be great if you could, you know. Come by early. How's that sound?

Fine, I say.

We'll be expecting everyone at around three, so if you can be there at one, that'll be great, he says, rubbing his hand along the shatter marks. And here the sun catches on him, coming through the trees. Gilt. Guilt. Gild. In my medieval lit books, it says that *gilt* first meant, blooded. And here in the sunset, he looks red, almost bloody. Not blood spilled, but the essence of blood, the red heat, the transaction of all life. A gas passing from one color to the next, blue to red, even the act of breathing a certain alchemy, sure of itself and its result.

I'll be there at one, I say. I could bring my tarot cards, read fortunes in the tent.

He blinks and says, You know how to do that?

Sure, I say.

That'd be terrific, he says. And he pats the rock like a dog.

It's not so much like a crush: I don't do anagrams of his name. I don't write our names together, on trees, in bathrooms, a heart drawn around it like a fence: Fee and Warden, forever love. I make sure there is no trace of what I am thinking. No paper (except me) for someone to find, no drawings of his face or poems, only the worn photograph from the night at the stone chapel, of someone he had once cherished and tried to give up. Fire, the fortune-teller had said. Fire clings to what it burns. No weight to it, just color, light, heat. Indeed.

The fire was inside me, though, the paper boy lit up like a paper lantern.

The practice is over too soon. I swim clumsily, I know. Mr. Zhe says little about it. I catch him watching me, a feeling not unlike sunlight falling on me, a warmth as particular as it is gentle, and for its gentleness, not unnoticeable, not unable to create, in me, a feeling like I am going to throw up. And after the practice, I do.

I stand in the stall and my stomach, mostly empty, throws whatever it finds into the bowl, which I flush repeatedly to cover the sound.

I lose weight. Everyone notices. At meals, the team jokes that I am vanishing. I am turning flat. I throw up a couple of times a week after practice. The paper boy. And in this state my grandparents demand and receive another visit.

You look thin, dear, my grandmother says, as she hugs me. And I can feel your shoulder blades. That's bad. It means you're near turning into an angel. She searches first my left and then my right eye, as if that's where it will show.

In their home, the air is stuffy, fans everywhere try to cool the turgid air. I watch one in particular, where the blades, in their turning, create a shine not unlike sun crossing water.

Honey. My grandmother says this, an assertion. This is not working for me. Not one bit. Eric, she says. My grandfather walks up to stand beside her. In front of me, like a pair. The pair they are. Pare. A pair pares. Any thirds away.

I mean, do they think this is what a normal boy looks like? she asks my grandfather, as she raises a hand to my brow.

Talk to me, I say, and I begin to cry. To me. Not to each other.

Edward, she says, and I sit down on her couch.

I am what a normal boy looks like, I say. And then I run to the bathroom.

I hear her outside, in between retches. We've got to get him . . . doctors who might have . . . often, sure, but Eric . . .

At a doctor's office in the afternoon, they extract blood, poke, look inside me with lights. As I lie there on the bed, I wonder. If they can see the bird, in my throat. If when they look in there with the light it bounces back the dark eyes. The small terrible beak. No matter how much I throw up, the bird never comes. Never feathers. Just more of what might have been me, tossed into the bowl and flushed away. The bird excavates me this way, to make room inside me to grow.

My grandparents again. Floating into view, beautiful white hair, so clean. I wonder what it's like, when it grows in. How you feel, to see this light from the door of the beyond reflected there in your hair. And my hand reaches up to touch them both on the head, a gesture I know they are mistaking for tenderness for them, but it doesn't matter, for after, when the bird controls me, I know, this memory will console them when I no longer can.

The doctor says, over his clipboard, that everything checks out. But what about the vomiting? my grandmother asks. Nerves, he says. I recommend counseling. But his bloodwork shows no problems, except maybe dehydration.

Well all right then, she says. And a few days later, in a counselor's office, she says it again, as I am prescribed Xanax.

Lots of people take it, Tom says to me. The phone-line counselor says it too, though he says, I think you wouldn't need it if you would just come out.

As what, I ask.

As gay, he says.

I'm not gay, I say. I'm just in love with a man.

Uh huh, he says. And what is gay, then.

Gay is wanting men. Sexually. As a rule. I have managed to turn off the booth light, so I can sit here in the dark.

So let me get this straight. You throw up so much that you are fainting, and now you have been prescribed drugs, because you want this man so much, but, you aren't gay.

No, I say. I'm not.

Okay, he says.

You told me not to do anything about it, I say.

You can still tell people, he says. In fact, your life may depend on it.

And the words I want to say fly in my throat like swallows lost in a church. The bird is many now, small now, hops inside me. Each one carries a possibility in its sharp tiny beak.

20

THE DAY OF the party is so beautiful, I wish that morning it didn't have to be the day that it is.

Bridey and Fee have set up a large white tent that glows from the yard as I approach, like sails full of light. Bridey comes out of the house as I park my car, slapping flour from his hands as he lets the screen door bang shut behind him. Piecrusts, he says. First I'm blind from cutting paper roses, and now I'll be crippled from rolling the crusts. He kisses me on the cheek. Fee's inside, he says.

In the tent, Fee bends over a long folding table, draping the clothes. Put your finger here, he says to me by way of greeting.

I put my finger down on the cloth. He pulls it into a neat triangle edge and drops the rest over the side, a clean fold. He pushes a tack in to keep it in place. Bridey's paper roses, white and pink, cluster in chains strung around the inside of the tent. It's beautiful, I say.

Thanks, he says. The missus has been working all week.

Just another faculty wife, Bridey says, entering the tent.

And so we spend the hours before the party. I shell piles of shrimp for shrimp cocktail, sip a lemonade, and joke with Bridey. Fee walks in and out of the kitchen on his way to the various tasks of the house and party, saying nothing, while Bridey asks me questions, about Alyssa (She's still so angry with you, he says) or the Thoreaus (Aren't they strange, he says, so like characters from a novel about another country). I don't remember my answers, only a wind full of the meadow, and the light, bright enough to strip paint.

Read my cards beforehand, Bridey says to me, and brushes shrimp shells off his hands, rinsing them under the faucet. I sit down at the table. He bends his beautiful head over the cards. Shuffle them, I say, and put them in several stacks. He whicks the cards like a professional. Sets them out. Okay, I say. Now pick the one stack that seems to call to you.

Of the three stacks he takes the one on the left. Hand it to me, I say. He does. I deal the cards out, ten, in quick succession, in a Celtic cross configuration.

That's a beautiful card, he says, and sets his finger down in the center. I take the cards in, slowly. Ace of cups in the center. Crossing it, the page of wands. Crowning it, the five of cups, below it, Temperance. In the past, the Lovers.

Well, he says.

This is about love, I say. But the Lovers is actually about art, and decisions. The final outcome card is the Tower. Everything you've known until now is about to change, based on a recent decision. It's not bad, I say. Only if you don't accept that change is on its way. True love here, I say, and I can barely say it. But I can't lie to him about his reading.

This is about change, he says, pointing to the Tower.

Yes, I say. It's Poseidon tearing down the world. This, I say, and point to the ace of cups, that's Aphrodite coming out of the water. His daughter.

Fee comes over, dressed in a tank top and sweatpants. He smells faintly of dill. Potato salad's done. How's the future look?

Poseidon, I think. Good, I say. The bird says.

And then the guests arrive.

The party charms us all. The warm afternoon lets the chill of the night ahead enter early, and so everyone draws a little closer. The paper rose banners flap up, as if to say, this land is claimed for paper roses. The Thoreaus, the Whites, the Ms. Fields, extremely pregnant. I could let go at any minute, she says, and Fee widens his eyes with alarm. It turns out they have known each other for a very long time. Since college. Don't worry, she says to the group. No stories. He and I could destroy each other. The teachers and their spouses fill their plates, they chill glasses with punch they drink slowly, at first. And then Mrs. White whips a cigarette from her purse, and soon, Fee is sent to climb his kitchen counter for the bourbon he's stashed up above the cabinets.

Why's it up there, Mrs. White says, smoking from below.

So you wouldn't see it, he says, and Mr. White laughs.

You're real funny, she says, and points her cigarette at her husband.

Mrs. White and Mrs. Thoreau take up a spot in the tent, with bourbon and cigarettes, and wave the smoke away from Ms. Fields, who fans herself gently with a paper plate. When I approach, their talk stops. Hello, Mrs. Thoreau says to me. You look wonderful.

Thanks, I say. My grandparents are worried I'm too thin.

You're a teenager, she says. It's practically what being a teenager is, being thin.

21

I CLIMB THE mountain in the dark, but the moon is full and helps me, as much as it can. The party ended hours ago. Near the moon, when I can see it, there is a planet posing as a star. I know it's a planet because only a pretender wouldn't be faded by the moon. Only an impostor would remain when all the other stars recede.

I had set the note down, in its envelope, in Fee's stack of mail. The two stacks were neatly sorted. The party outside whickered in the breeze, polyphonic conversations. Their bedroom. The bed was neatly made, the pillows stacked to make a crude, soft geometry.

The eagle's nest is here on a ledge, like Tom said. I pause before getting in. Large as a bathtub. I can almost lie full length in it. The nest's soft walls stretch when I settle in. No eggs here. Lulled, I close my eyes, and I must fall asleep, though it feels like no time at all when I open my eyes to the eagle looking at me.

A gold coin in the snow. The enormous eye. Feathers that look like armor. I'd never seen feathers look like they could protect anything until now, but here, I can see how they hold the air, strain it like a whale's baleen strains the water. The wings draw open. In the dark, wings spread, he could be an angel sent here to bring me home. To tell me, go home, Fee loves you, and nothing's wrong. But he isn't and Fee doesn't. Unless eagles have been angels all along. I can see why someone, on seeing one, would think that God had sent for them in this way.

He pulls his wings close again in front of him and a huff of oil scent comes off him, a musk. A faint powdery itch in my nose, like down.

I slowly climb out of the nest, the eagle surprisingly quiet. It's okay, I say to the eagle. I'm leaving now. And as I head down the mountain in the morning, it seems like this bird I am now should be able to fly.

22

AT THE DORM my grandparents wait. Grandfather in a tan suit, a blue silk tie creasing the white shirt. His hair shining against his head like the inside of a shell. Grandmother in a dress of navy silk, hemmed at her ankles, which she crosses as she sits in the chair there in lounge. They look up as I enter the room. You're late, my grandmother says.

I can't imagine why, my grandfather says, and she elbows him.

I'll just be a second, I say, and head to the showers.

The stink comes off. I dry, thinking of waterproof feathers. The guillemot, cousin to the parrot, dives in the water in pursuit of fish, where it swims on its wings, flapping them under water. I push hair gel through blond hair, wondering whose it is.

Hi, I say, reappearing. They inspect my father-meeting attire: gray sweater, red polo, jeans.

Lost more weight, my grandmother says. Are you sick?

No, I say.

I ask him to show me the collar on his ankle. Electronic, he can't remove it. He's tagged, like the animals in *Mutual of Omaha*

Wild Kingdom. Here in his new home, a tiny cottage, in Belfast, Maine, he smiles. Pours me coffee. God, he says, looking at me. Milk?

Sure, I say.

My grandparents are driving the roads in search of antiques. So they say. I know this is a lie. My grandmother hates them. If they're not inherited, she says, they're just junk. We have breakfast together, this man and I. My father.

He sits, pushes his cup forward. Edward, he says. I want to answer any questions you have.

That was when I asked to see the bracelet. He pulls up the leg of his pant, where it shines, like a plastic baby snake. Huh, I say.

You're so tall, he says.

Six feet and two inches, I say.

There aren't any pictures on the walls yet. A mix of wildflowers in a glass Mason jar is the only color in the room. He's a tall man, this father. His hair, going silver, gone in the middle. The forehead shines. His hands, large, white, soft. Some men go to prison and become huge, caricatures of muscle. He is thin, ruddy, his glasses occasionally gleam in such a way that his eyes are hidden. The lenses go white. Windows into a world made of some other light the sun's not fathered.

What's the most important thing I need to know about my son, he asks me, and I realize, I've just been watching him.

You, I say.

He tells me about how much my mother wanted to stay in the States, as he calls them, but how much she hated the idea of wearing a collar. Of neighbor notification. I'll not walk beside my son in that, she said to him in a letter. They didn't see each other much after the conviction. Epistles.

You are so handsome, he says finally. We walk the road. A skinny asphalt lane, no line in the center, even the trees look dry.

Thanks, I say.

23

BIRDS NEVER KNOW their fathers. After birth, under the mother, after learning to fly, they usually never know how they share the sky with their father. Their father, careening after the same school of fish seaming the water below. Is there a memory, as the father cuts through the same cloud?

They all said it would be like this. Alyssa says it, back straight, carrying a duffel bag into my room. She empties it by my closet door.

Like what, I say. I am reading on my bed. I set the book down.

That you'd just stop. One day, you'd just vanish, and it would be over.

I'm here, I say.

So you say, she says. So you say.

All right then, I say. It's over. Are you happy now? I stand up and walk over to the bag. Is everything really here? Let me check. I look over the books, the CDs. A bead necklace with my name strung on it. All right, I say. I stand up and she's crying now, but it's not enough. She needs to be far away. Before something worse happens. I haven't disappeared, but she has.

Can you leave now, I say. It'd be better.

I take the things she's brought back down to the laundry room, with a sign that says, PLEASE TAKE. They all look like something I've never seen or owned, stuff someone else left behind, dingy with strangeness. Except the necklace.

I know him in the dark.

In the chapel he sits waiting for me. No candle.

What is it you want, he says. He doesn't turn to look my way.

You really can't tell, I say.

He doesn't move. He sits still, like the hill we are on, as if he were a part of it. A rock in a coat.

I'm in love with you, I say. In the dark, my wings ride inside the shadow. Here in the shadow the earth casts, my wings, large as my love, extend to the upper reach of the sky. The boy I am is small, made to fly on wings the size of the sky.

I step beside him, slide onto the cold stone bench. Fee, I say.

I have to go, he says. And is gone. I sit for a while, as the heat of him disperses into the air, the stone, me. He thinks he can leave me by leaving me.

The next note I leave for him I leave in his campus mail. I've seen Bridey leave him notes. Campus mail is fairly unprotected: the honor code means, no locked doors. Nothing is ever stolen. That's not the danger in Mr. Zhe's mail today. The Whites are out of town, and asked me to house-sit for them. I know that nothing can happen in the dorms, but in the Whites' house, a few things seem possible. I just need one more chance. And so I make it. I walk to the wooden honeycomb of mailboxes and slip the note inside, folded just like I've seen Bridey fold his. So that it perches there, almost origami: crisp and geometrical. I write only the address and a time, typed on a typewriter I find in the typing room of the town library.

The time between then and when he arrives presses on me. So much so that I wait outside, in the dark, across the street. I can't wait in that house without him. I smoke and wait in the dark. I don't have to wait long, though it feels, when he arrives, that I am another age, a new age that I've never been. Suddenly older. I walk across the street, crushing the cigarette as I go.

He turns.

His panic makes me sad. He tries very hard, I can see. To act as if I am just his student, he just my teacher. My coach. Hey, I say. It feels a fraud as soon as I say it. I pull the keys out. And the cold sweeps us into the warm house. I try not to cry and am successful. And this makes the difference, I think. Through the warm house, the dry house, the house usually full of children's sharp noises, we slip, quiet, and in the Whites' bedroom I let myself fall onto the bed.

I'm not as pretty as Bridey, I know this. But it doesn't matter. Not anymore. He kisses me like he's tasting something strange, and for a moment, I remember, the bird, and my heart tatters. I worry that he will taste the bird, hit it with his tongue. But the bird lies quiet tonight. Tonight I get everything I have wanted. For the first time.

24

MY FATHER IS a Mainer. He doesn't lock his doors. I have questions, too many to ask. And so he wakes up in the night at some point and comes down to find me in his living room. What the fuck is this, I say.

I hold the pictures out in my hand, fanned like poker cards. I've been looking at them all, looking for some reason to understand what made me. The two of you, I ask.

He's frozen in the doorway, like victims in those goofy movies where criminals gain control over the mechanism of time. Did you hear me, I ask. I toss the pictures down, and they scatter, as if trying to get away from each other. From him. From me. Answer me, I say, and stand up, and reach for the first weapon I can find. The lamp's shade falls like a hat, the bare bulb shines.

Answer me! I walk to the wall and plunge the lamp bulb-first into the wall. Answer! Me! The glass pops, the drywall singes, the lamp sits there, hung in the wall. I pull it out and throw it at the window, and it carries the broken glass with it into the yard. I grab the box of pictures and toss them out after it, and they spread on the lawn.

I look back at him and he's still frozen. The dark room shows him better than the light did and I register now, the beetled brow, the eyes. Why did eighteen boys keep quiet as he ran his hands over them? These eyes, each a knife. Silence shrinks me. I want their names, I want to know, want to find each one of them. Give each one of them a piece of him.

In the dark quiet room my wings return to me. Yeah, I say. Come on. I unbutton my shirt. C'mon. I open the shirt totally, the cold air a blade laid on my skin. You're a fuck-face! You and her both! Do you know what I want from you?

Leave, he says.

I want you dead, I say.

Leave now.

Children, I say. It would've been like eating them.

You don't know what it was like, he says. And you need to leave.

B L U E

F e e

I

SOMETIMES I IMAGINE my grand-aunts. Escaped from their tormentors, unable to go home. They would be like my grandfather,
of course, thin and tall and silver. Their hair would be wrapped
into modest buns, let down only at night, when some daughter
might help them brush it. The red hair would be gone, turned
silver now. The white fox, very rare, is the good fox, the most
holy one. Helper to the rice god.

If they were still alive, though, they would have come home.
Could they be alive out there, somehow unable to have found
their way home? Sometimes I see them: old women, vigorous as
teenagers, stepping across the night in a rush of wind, their hair
turning to fire. When the fox flies her hair is a fiery tail behind
her. Watch them come. They dodge church spires and office tow-
ers in their pell-mell, sow sparks, set mysterious fires at the
homes of their now-elderly tormentors, who emerge to put them
out, a little afraid. They laugh as they go.

We love him, they would say of their brother, their words scattering across the roof of sky. We miss him. But we can't come
home.

2

WHEN A FOX marries another fox, fox trouble ends for one whole
day. Kitsune no yomeiri, the Japanese say. Rain and sun together
at the same time. Good luck.

I met Bridey when I was leaving San Francisco, a place where
I'd spent far too much time, for New York, where I was intend-
ing to spend another as-yet-indeterminate period of time, that
would turn out to be three years. I'd abandoned all pretense of a
fine arts career some time ago, had drifted into making raku pot-
tery for some of the home goods stores in the area and developed a
line I called stormware, for all of it looked as if the sea had gotten
to it first. It was popular. Magazines used it in pictures, and
sometimes I made some money. I couldn't make enough, though,
on my own, but didn't want to expand the business, and began
looking for a way to leave. But of course, the only way to leave is
to just leave.

I no longer spent all my time wanting to die, but I was fairly
apprehensive about being alive. It wasn't that my life lacked
meaning, but rather that I disliked the meaning it offered to me
every morning as I sat at my studio wheel, spinning. My father's
scientific mind had given me a knack for the chemistry of glazes,
my mother's orderly ways and laid-back approach made for a
loose style. The housewares were popular and profitable and vanished more or less as they were made. I kept none of them, eating
off odds and ends I found in church sales. With the exception of
the occasional political demonstration, I lived quietly, and was
relatively solitary, avoiding the Castro as well as the Mission, and
the bars of SOMA. I was not making great art, but I didn't want
to, either. I wanted to make lots of things that added little beau-
ties everywhere, on a daily basis. This seemed to me better. I'd
had enough of great art, I had decided, through music. One afternoon, though, my resolve was stronger than on the others and I
made my plans. I gave my notice at my apartment and called
friends from school in New York, who said, Well, it's about time.
Penny in particular was impatient.

I had heard in gossip from these school friends that there was a boy from the crew team who was doing erotic dancing at a strip club in Chicago, at a place called Slick. It was a place that had male dancers a few times a week who all showered in front of the clientele before walking around to collect their tips. I loaded my car with my suitcase, dropped my boxes at Greyhound, and headed off. Checking my mail on the day I left, I discovered a letter from my mother. I decided I would open it later.

I thought of Bridey fairly often. Who would he be? My friends had tried to describe him to me. He wasn't out when you were there, they said. He was closeted. He's beautiful, they said, but sort of arrogant and very crazy. As I wound my way through Reno, and then Omaha, and then Iowa City, I thought of the stories again and again, how he had married and divorced a beautiful and wealthy Boston girl from an old family, how he had been forced to divorce her because he was caught with a boy I did remember, a breathtaking boy he had seduced apparently for the first time at their wedding reception. I had decided well in advance to stop and so I parked under the SLICK sign, locked my car, and went in. I realized, pushing the door open, I had no idea if he would be the one I thought he was. I'd no way of recognizing him.

I had my mother's letter in my back pocket, and set it on the table in front of the stage, where I ordered a Scotch and water and watched as boys made their way in and out. Most of the clientele were older men, some of whom openly stared at me. The bouncers raised their eyebrows but did nothing. And then he came out.

I remembered him as soon as I saw him. He was beautiful, he was arrogant. I remembered paying him almost no attention. I don't remember there was time enough to do so, as I was graduating, and occupied by thoughts of my worthless life. He remembered me as well, for what he did was step off the stage to perch on my table and squat down. He wore only a towel that night.

You're a bastard for coming here, he said. He looked me right in the eye. No one else has, he said.

I shrugged. I was trying not to laugh.

Aren't you going to open that, he said. He pointed to the letter.

I might, I said. He had squatted so that my drink lay under his towel, which is to say, under him. To get it, I had to reach there, so I did. I left my hand there. He didn't seem to notice.

Who's it from, he asked.

My mother, I said. Listen. What exactly are the rules here about touching you?

He laughed. There aren't any in the house. I have personal ones though. In order to keep the local peace. He brushed his hair out of his face. A drop of water fell from somewhere underneath the towel and hit the bar, and then another dropped on my wrist. I noticed the thing around his neck was a wet G-string.

I stood. My arms reached out, as if I were waiting for a baby.

What is this, he asked.

I want to pick you up. I mean, carry you. Just for a bit. I reached for my wallet.

How are you going to do this if you don't hold out your hands? he asked, and began to swing himself toward me. I reached and he sat himself down in my arms. People stared as I wandered around the room, him laughing. There'll be trouble, he said.

Yes, I said. I bet.

He was warm, he smelled clean, of course, having just showered. He reached out and plucked the letter from the table, and when I set him down again, he handed it back to me.

Thanks, he said. I'd like to see you again.

Nothing seemed likely, except that I would have to open the letter, and so I said, You could see more of me now. It's unfortunately the only way. You could take me home.

He laughed. You're like a boy someone lost in a toy store.

I live well over three hours away, I said.

All right then. But I have to finish this shift. And saying that, he climbed back up on the bar.

He told me that his name was Albright Forrester, but that everyone called him Bridey. I sat at the bar and waited through several more drinks as he showered again, and the other men in the bar pushed dollars into the G-string he had put back on and then eyed me, suspicious. He remained cheerful, as if this were the most fun he could have. The money, the fingers, didn't seem to touch him, as if his skin wasn't really skin but a field of energy with color and texture. If you had to do a job like this, his skin was the right skin.

Later, in his apartment, I told him. I'm not from around here.

I know, he said. I saw the address on the letter. Which way are you going?

To New York, I said.

Oh the fear, he said. You'll have to leave now. He punched a pillow, puffing it flat, and rolled over into it.

I sat a moment.

Well, he said. I mean, a boy's got a heart to protect. Go on.

I, I said. I could. Visit.

Mmm. That'll be fun. What, like you are a sailor at sea or something.

Something, I said. Something.

It turned out he had always wanted to go to New York. I can't let you drive on your own, he said later, as he packed his suitcase. You could have an accident. My sister's words about love came to me then: When it's right, she said, you don't have to have a com-mittee meeting about it. Later, when we'd been in New York for a few weeks, Bridey said, I had no idea there was so much to see in New York. I'd better stay on a while yet. It turned out that New York required several years of seeing. And when I told him about Maine the first time, he said, You're always dragging me around. But I see the best of the world with you.

With me? I said.

In you, he said, and stuck his finger in my ear.

3

FROM THE LETTER my mother sent me, opened, finally, after my arrival in New York, read to me by Bridey:

Darling:
I ran into Freddy Moran's mother recently, and she was, well, she wasn't herself and looked as if she hadn't been in some time. You

see, Freddy's been HIV-positive for a few years now, and recently his health took a turn for the worse. And now she's been frantic, caring for him. She doesn't feel up to the job, now that she's buried her husband, to now bury her son. It doesn't look real good.

Your father's been good enough to help get him into a drug trial at Maine Medical's research wing, and we're all praying for his good health. I know you two haven't spoken much, but I wanted to let you know.

I don't answer this letter. When my mother and I speak next, I don't ask after him. And the new drugs work for a while. Freddy lasts the three years that will pass until I see him next.

4

SPECK DIES ON an early-summer day when he is, uncharacteristically, in his garden, in Maine. He hated his garden, I remembered. He had a gardener who cared for it and he had told him, when he hired him, Just do enough stuff so that these neighbors of mine don't complain.

The news of his death reaches me in Provincetown, in a summer share I'd taken with Penny and Bridey. A stroke took him, very quickly, and he felt nothing, the letter I receive from his current assistant tells me. There will be a ceremony in a few days' time. My mail being forwarded to me, the ceremony, I can see, is tomorrow. I had just written to him, telling him of how I was spending the summer. You shouldn't be leaving New York then, he had written back, just a few weeks earlier. People like you, the city belongs to you.

He'd helped me get work after I arrived in New York as an artist's assistant to a wealthy sculptor and landscape designer. We'd seen each other a few times. His book, the one I'd helped him on, had been published years before: *A Letter to the Digger: A History of Edinburgh During the Plague,* by Edward Speck. I had it on my shelf, and sometimes people would pick it up, and ask, Why do you have this? I like history, I'd tell them, and then we'd move on from there.

The day I get the letter, Bridey and Penny are at the beach together, having left to go early and run. Thick as thieves, is the expression. My oldest friend and my best one, together. Who knew what they might come back with? Some days they returned with a new friend, usually for Penny. Bridey and I had been faithful, another expression. I like to think of it as attentive. We were and are attentive. We occupy all of each other's attention. And sometimes, to make me laugh, he allows some man to flirt his way home with him. I need to keep in practice, he says, after they go home. In case I get dumped. In the second-floor apartment we'd taken, I wait for these two to return and then I tell them, how it is I have to go to Maine tonight. I call my parents and tell them to expect me, and I drive out the next day in our rented car.

Speck's final assistant is a graduate student, a much more professional young man than I was when I worked for him, and he greets me at the funeral home with real pleasure. He's dressed like a true Speck student: gray herringbone tweed coat, with patches on the elbows. A black turtleneck, black jeans, brown oxford shoes. I go in, uncertain of what to expect until I see, at the front, on a pedestal, an urn. I go back out for a moment. Already? I ask.

He left instructions he was to be burned immediately. The student shrugs his tweed shoulders. He abhorred the idea of his body lying around without him in it.

And . . . speakers, I ask.

No, he says. I go back inside.

In the attendees I see that we are all former assistants, most likely. The moderately sized room is full of men and young men of descending orders of age. A familiar reserve, the articulate quiet I learned from Speck, makes the room familiar, and then of course we resemble each other: dark haired, pale, clean-cut but rumpled from reading and bad lighting. Some balding, many with hair that seems to be rising to Speck's example. Bachelors all. Looking at his urn we look at our future. We smile at each other some and trickle out after paying our respects to this last quiet with Speck. No one asks if there are any heirs, as we all know there aren't.

At home, I have a quiet dinner with my mother and father. At the end of it my mother tells me, Freddy's not doing well.

Why not him too, I tell myself.

Do you want to go see him? I'm sure he'd appreciate it. She picks up all our plates and goes to the kitchen. I recognize a pattern for the first time, of how my mother asks me a question and my father waits for the answer.

Yes, I say. My father smiles reassurance. And I call down to tell Bridey and Penny that I'll be a little later than I thought. Tomorrow, I say.

We're using up all the sun, he says. You'd better hurry back.

Penny says something in the background I can't hear and I ask about it. She said, Bridey says, You're never leaving Maine. But she has a plan you'll hear when you get back.

Thick as thieves, I tell myself as I hang up the phone. They're stealing me.

Do you remember what it was like, to be young? You do. Was there any innocence there? No. Things were exactly what they looked like. If anyone tries for innocence, it's the adult, moving forward, forgetting. If innocence is ignorance of the capacity for evil, then it's what adults have, when they forget what it's like to be a child. When they look at a child and think of innocence they are thinking of how they can't remember what that feels like.

I have to know how Freddy's doing. I could call, but instead I go over to Mrs. Moran's new house. After her husband's death, my mother tells me, she moved. A quick trip through Portland's rain-stained houses, all of them a wrong color for happiness up in this part of town, the part between the stores and the sea. The Eastern Promenade, Munjoy Hill. There's a cemetery here where kids come in and kick the stones down regularly. Because they probably hate the dead for being free from the sights around them.

Her house is near the sea. In a sense all of Portland is near the sea. Red-brick buildings, mostly, in a crest over the land on the rise of hill here, a gentle brick murmur to the slope of the whole town no matter where you are, the slope from where the glacier came through. Don't think this means Portland isn't beautiful; it's why it's beautiful. In any case. She stands taking in her mail as I arrive. I barely recognize her. And she doesn't recognize me.

Fee, she says, when I reintroduce myself. Shocking, how you've changed. She takes me inside her dark clean house.

Freddy's my only one, she says, as I sit down. And she flips open a scrapbook. Pictures from the choir, the robes, the rope belts. All that smooth hair gleaming on head after head. Freddy Moran, the book says on the front. And she shows me the clippings of Peter's and Zach's obits.

I'd last seen Freddy in a restaurant in the Old Port. I was home from California, visiting, out to lunch with my mother, who sat, radiantly blond and happy to see her son again, across from me. It was a two-story seafood place, red carpets sanguine in the stained afternoon sunlight that tugged the gauzy sheers in the windows. Captains' mirrors on the walls distorted us all into faraway and tiny shapes. I watched them for a while, thinking, those are the real mirrors.

He moved through my center of vision like a shadow, like a floater bouncing through the fluid of my eye. The room went black like a wick blown by the wind, returning quickly. It was him, I thought. He had turned into an elegantly attractive, clean-cut young man. His gait gave him away, his walk a little faster than the rest of him, as if his legs were always dragging him forward.

To my mother, I said only, as I rose, I have to go say hi to someone. She gave me a crooked smile and consented.

I found him in the downstairs, seated at the bar, a dark, wooden affair. He took me in as I entered, in a way I recognized. He was checking me out. Hi, Freddy, I said, and his eyes opened large, as if they needed more room.

Aphias, he said. Jesus.

As I stood in front of him, I realized I didn't know what it was

I would say to him. I was so happy to see him, I had followed the feeling, and not arranged for anything to say. For it remained that we really had nothing to say to each other. Up until that instant, when language there was gathered, like condensation forming on a window, inside us both.

It's been so long, I said. I don't know where to start.

You look great, he said. I heard you were in California.

I'm visiting, I said. It's been great out there. For me.

We were a study in contrasts. I'd adopted a shabby mode of old-man-style clothing in high school and never really gotten far from it. That morning I wore a black T-shirt, a pair of old suit trousers made from charcoal wool, and cordovan leather shoes, on the worn side. I knew I looked sallow from smoking too much. Freddy glowed, rosy-cheeked, smooth-faced, he smelled clean from where I stood, and was dressed in a red polo shirt and khaki pants, brand-new running shoes on his feet. He looked protected, from germs, depressions, extremes of poverty and misfortune. None of this was true, though. Just a marvelous show. Marvelous even as mine was drab.

It was good to see you, he said to me. Uncertain as he said it.

I went back to my table, the world altered. The lunch, flavorless, my mother soundless: I couldn't hear her. I'd look up periodically and see her mouth moving, and I knew she was saying things, but I couldn't hear any of it. All I could think of was what a terrible person I was. How I needed something terrible to happen to me. And years later, looking at the pictures of this in my head, moving in time, resolving one into the next, I can see how it never occurred to me that the reason Big Eric had gone to prison was because he was found, by the law, to be guilty of the crimes. Not me. I was not the one in jail. I wasn't guilty. Was it enough, that the law said it?

Not then.

He'd been wandering the streets in his coats, no pants. In his apartment, his clothes were found, all of them soiled. He was wearing only the coat because it was his only clean thing to wear—he hadn't lost all of his mind. His mother came and burned the clothes, packed up his things and tried to clean the apartment. He'd scraped all the plaster off the walls and painted it blue, she tells me before I leave her house. It looked as though someone had exploded in there. She shuts the book and goes into the other room.

When he gets out of the hospital, she says, returning with a mug of coffee for me, he'll be coming back here.

In his bed at the hospital, he's a tiny map to himself. A reduction. The dementia is now the least of it. I recalled a friend telling me how either his meds or his virus caused his face to hollow as it went for the fat under his skin. Freddy's face has hollowed, and the bed rises a little in a way that is meant to be his body. I stand in the doorway, unsure of how to go into the room. This is the content of our first visit.

5

PENNY PRESENTS HER idea to me a few days after I return on a warm summer afternoon some ten years after we first met. She's aged well, and here on the patio of the Provincetown seafood restaurant where she's asked me to meet her to talk about this, age seems to have brought to her mostly poise. She'd quit smoking some years ago, reviving what turned out to be a rosy-cheeked complexion, and she'd stopped dying her hair that henna red, finally, and allowed it to be dark brown, a color more like that of a stone than a coin. She plucks at her hair as I approach her through the dozen Perrier umbrellas on the deck and she rises to kiss my cheek, so that I catch the faintest scent of sandalwood. I never think to wear scents, but I like hers and make a note of it. Hello, she says, against my ear.

You look fantastic, I say. Teaching hasn't done a thing to you that's bad.

She's an art teacher now at a private school on the northern coast of Maine. Your fault, she says of it, when she first tells me. You always made it sound so beautiful up there. Where she is now, though, East Knot, is more beautiful than where I grew up. She'd helped me get settled in New York and had then left me there, and I resented it. I tell her so.

It is so beautiful, she says, and her eyes take in the view. I can't imagine being anywhere else. She lifts a glass of iced tea and plucks at it. The men are far away though, she says, and surveys the men around us. Which, this being Provincetown, is mostly what's here. Single men, she adds. Of a particular kind.

She tells me that she's become the swim-team coach. I can't believe it, I tell her. You hate and abhor athletics.

No. I hated and abhorred me, she says. And the tone is so sad, the phrasing so alien, I realize it is both true and something someone else has told her about herself. Like a check mark on a calendar, the ten years since our first meeting is duly noted. Penny, who had red hair and smoked and hated athletes now has brown hair, coaches swimming, smiles, and, she now begins telling me, wants to have a baby. Wants me to be the father.

The lunch arrives: fried fish sandwiches and fries, sparkling water. I am trying to place all of this. You want me to donate the sperm, I say.

Fee. I want to have a child, and when I think about what man I want the child to resemble, considering the amount of time I'll be with him or her, I thought of my oldest friends. I've not known anyone as long as I've known you, besides my family. She smiles and scratches behind her ear. I'll be with the child so long, and it only gets harder as I get older. I don't want to wait to meet some guy I've not yet met. I've got a good job, secure, with housing, at a nontraditional school. I'll be able to have the baby with me. How's a baby at swim practice? Fine. There's every reason to think it's a good time for me. I've been healthy now for years, my gene plasm repaired, I hope, from the hard years.

I'll think about it, I say. The hard years of course means the years when we first knew each other. And in the bright light of the patio, where everything seems to have a sharper harder edge and color, I can see that she will have her way in this, as she had her way in other things, that of what has changed about her, her ability to get me to do what she wants is not included in that.

You'll be my replacement, she says. At the school. I've already told them I think I'm pregnant and that I know of someone.

What? I say. You did what?

It's not like it's not going to happen, she says.

And so it is decided, and soon Penny is telling me all the details. Bridey, too. In the attic room of the apartment we have taken for the summer, Bridey tells me he has decided, if I will have him, to accompany me on the move, as I'd asked. I'll be the faculty wife, he says. I've always wanted to grow roses. When I tell him northern Maine isn't much for roses, he tells me he will show me how it can be done. Sure of each other, we go to tell some friends from New York, here for the week, who are frankly confused by my decision, and further by Bridey's.

Well, says one, when we announce the news before getting dressed for a party on the other side of the village, That will mean you guys are off in the middle of nowhere with nothing but each other.

Delightful, Bridey says. Imagine all the lack of interference. The absence of sweet young things looking to poach a husband. This last is a pointed comment to another, silent friend, who walks the house naked until it is time to leave for the beach, where he takes all his clothes off again. Bridey takes my eyefuls in stride, punishing me later by moving all my bookmarks. I'm trying, he says later upstairs, to make sure your attention is properly occupied.

You made me read the same forty pages of *Ulysses* over again, I say, and clap him with it lightly on the head.

You're the one who didn't notice, he says.

I'm practicing, I say, in case I get dumped.

Wedgies tonight, Bridey says.

Bridey. What is he made from? A secret, apparently. He meanders the party that night, looking through everyone there like dresses on a sale rack. I don't know why he comes. I'm the one who likes parties. This one is loud, lots of New Yorkers, the same people we see all year but here they are sunburned, thinner, in bathing suits and T-shirts and Adidas sport mules. Ropey, gleaming bronze flesh alternates with the occasional pale, hairy limb of a newcomer or midweek visitor. I watch Bridey's neck, where his white coral necklace hangs like a wide smile on a string.

I don't remember, Bridey confides, that people used to get this sunburned. Ozone layer really is going. Look at her! She looks like a radiation victim.

When I go to put my arms on his sides he draws them away with his hands. Holds them. Kisses me once on the lips. You really want this shirt, he says. I'll leave it on the bed for you later to look at. While I go buy some more.

And then at the party, someone talks of something, another of another, and then this.

. . . It's amazing, isn't it. How people just tell you about it.

Aren't you tired of it? I am so tired of it. "Oh, my father raped me." So? Why tell these things?

I see two women talking to each other at the food table, dipping chips into a guacamole bowl and scooping it out. Empty beer bottles fill the table and so I start picking them up, as a politeness to our host, gone missing now for about an hour.

These people are just crawling out of the walls these days. It seems like this shit was just invented for the end of this century.

Well, if you read John Boswell's book about foundling children in medieval times, he talks about how early prohibitions against prostitution were in place in order to avoid having sex with children you'd abandoned, sold to brothels. And here she breaks her chips with her tiny teeth. You realize, she continues, that children have always had a lot of sex. I smile at them across the now-clear table, and head out the back door to the porch, where I sit down, a bottle on every finger. I set them down next to the recycling bin, and notice that several are partially full. Unable to move, I begin finishing them. Like tongue kissing strangers.

Crawling out of the walls. I think of the catacombs on Judgment Day. I think of Andrew Hunter and my tunnels, still waiting for me. Why am I still alive? I light a cigarette. Look across my hand to the pinkie nail I still keep silver. Bridey asked me about it a long time ago. When I told him the story of it he kissed the tiny nail. He said, It's beautiful. I think of Freddy.

Did you drink all these? I hear from behind me. Bridey sinks down then and his knees cover my ears. What are you doing out here by the trash, anyway?

I had help, I say. When do we move to Maine, I ask.

Come on, he says. Inside. Right away.

6

UP IN EAST Knot on one of the first nights in our new house Bridey calls me into the yard. Look, he says, and there's the Northern Lights, Aurora Borealis, pieces of the sun striking the outer surface of the atmosphere and exploding. We stand there and watch. They're magnetic pulses. When Penny has her baby, I decide, I will tell him or her that the Aurora Borealis is her great-grand-aunts, dancing with each other, for us. The colors their fiery fox tails.

My grandparents died within several months of each other. Theirs had been a long marriage, arranged for them at their births. That they died near each other in time was no surprise. Both deaths happened while I was in California, near the end of my time there, and both times, I was awake late at night and found by something near to a hallucination. Or a vision. It reminded me of the mudang trying to call my ghost to me, and what I saw that time. My grandmother went first. On that night, my room filled with a huge shadow cat, eyes as big as lamps. She regarded me for some time and then left. When my grandfather followed her, the ceiling light fixture in my room became the center of an enormous face, ancient beyond belief and exhausted. He seemed to be trying to speak, and then he didn't, and was gone soon after.

My grandmother had been a Christian, my grandfather an animist. Chongdokyo, Korea's oldest religion. He remembered his sisters by placing a bowl of water by the window, and a lit stick of incense. When we went to the family temple in Moolsan-do he had done the more traditional observances, but every day, the bowl and the incense. Chongdokyo is an attempt to mirror the ways of heaven, which flat water does effortlessly, reflecting the sky. The incense is meant to symbolize that aspiration. I'd made a bowl for this purpose recently, and so after we come inside I look for it among the boxes we are still unpacking. I find the bowl, a simple thing made to look like my grandfather's bowl: eggshell on the outside, sea blue on the inside. I light incense, and set them out, by the back kitchen window.

You're a good son, Bridey says, when he sees it, and kisses me on the cheek. He's thrilled by the new house, by his freedom from New York. I feel like everything dirty is so far away, he says.

I kiss him back. We kiss all the time now, some three years into this. Penny's pregnancy is healthy and seems to come along quickly. The school had been apprehensive about meeting me but then the faculty were quickly assured that I should take Penny's place during her leave. The affordable house had, after the vagaries of Manhattan's real estate market, come to us with startling suddenness. Our friends had thrown us a party at a restaurant before we left, where the waiters came out singing the *Green Acres* theme song and clapping tambourines, and everyone made vague promises to come visit. Bucoholism, Bridey called it now. Addicted to the Bucolic.

I think of my grandparents, the listening quality they always seemed to have whenever I saw them. What were they listening for? When they had decided to leave Korea, they did so and then left quickly. It was difficult but not impossible, and they never seemed to express remorse. Their whole difficult lives seemed not to weigh on them at all. Taken as mornings and meals, suppers and evenings, all of the world could be carried, both the sad and the delicious, their lives seemed to say.

I turn and go upstairs, to prepare to meet the students the next day. Bridey undresses for bed, reminding me of no one but himself. I sit down and take off my shoes.

Sometimes, I think I know what my grandparents were listening for. Sound waves don't ever go away. Not one sound goes away. The wave simply expands, infinitely. The sound remains. Imagine a cosine arc the size of Jupiter, and that might be the size of the wave of the last thing Peter said. I'd need an ear the size of another solar system to hear him again.

Tomorrow I would meet my students.

Good night, Bridey says, when I pull the sheets up over us, and it rolls off into eternity to join every other sound ever made.

That night we both dream. I have my recurring dream, Bridey has his. This is how we find out about them. My recurring dream: I am in a barracks, walking back from having gone to the bathroom, and I know it in the way you know something in your life: where you had coffee that morning, where you ate your breakfast. And the corridor is dark. I begin to feel it then, the dread, a chill like someone has opened a door to the outside, except that the chill is in my mind, the door, in my mind. The chill is coming from somewhere else through an opening somewhere inside me, and I start to slow down, to try and turn and face the demon. And then instead, I try to run faster, to the main room, where everyone lies asleep. But I never get there. I always wake before that happens, with the knowledge that I am dead. I didn't make it.

I have the dream again. I wake up, to see Bridey looking at me, one eyebrow raised. Coffee, he says, and leaps out of bed. I wait as I hear the smooth feet echo across our wood floors. I drowse off, and awake again to him naked, holding two cups of coffee. Hiya, he says. Had a nightmare. A recurring one of mine.

Yeah, I did, I say.

No, he says. I meant, I did. You did too?

What was your dream, I ask.

I dreamed I was in a massacre. That all around me, people were dying. And I couldn't move. There was some monstrous invisible force, ripping through people. Blood everywhere. We were in some kind of barracks. And everyone was dying. All soldiers, all of us. And then I couldn't see it but I felt the monster come for me. And I woke up. He slurps his coffee then, and settles himself into the bed beside my knees.

I love you, I say.

What was your nightmare, he says.

I don't want to talk about it, I say. Not now.

I think of it later, though, when he's left the house, to go swimming. What if you meet someone from your future life? You are in your past life now, as far as the future is concerned. That morning it seems to me that Bridey and I are somewhere in the future, both a part of a massacre. We are different parts to the same dream. That we were given this present to make us strong for the future to come. I'll think differently of it later. But for the purpose of the events to follow, this is my opinion, now.

7

I SEE HIS blond hair first in the morning light warming the natatorium. Towhead. The color of a beating.

Penny is funny in her suit, her whistle. The boys and girls yawn, push at their hair and faces. She leads them in stretching and visualizations. I pretend the boy on the other side of the room doesn't look like Peter. I stretch as they stretch, close my eyes when they visualize and see myself walking out of the room. Selling the house. Leaving. The silliness of it cures the moment and when I open my eyes I am still smiling from it. I am in love with Bridey now, anyway.

As I stand behind Penny, I imagine telling Bridey about it, and him telling me, it's easy. You have blondphobia. You have the irrational fear of blonds who have caused you pain and their look-alikes.

Kids, Penny says, meet your new assistant coach, Aphias Zhe.

What's your name? I say, not hearing the first time this new apparition speaks. We are stuck in the handshake then, hands clasped.

Warden, he says, and he takes his hand back.

Nice jail you got here, I say. Penny rolls her eyes.

He's not the new comedian, she says. That's for sure.

They follow me, I tell myself, as I drive home. When Bridey opens the door I say nothing about this, in the manner of anyone avoiding calling the name of a ghost.

I go to Portland every two weeks on a Saturday and sit with Freddy. Bridey comes with me sometimes. Is this the reason I moved back to Maine, I ask myself, as I drive the long black road south to Portland or north to Bangor. As I head out to East Knot. As I watch Bridey move through the kitchen. I think of some of the stories I know to fill the silences of being with Freddy: a man who found out he was positive and shot himself in the head, his house rigged to burn to the ground. Another who found out his status when he collapsed from walking pneumonia, and died a few days later. I wanted to be a teacher; my namesake was a teacher, and ever since knowing that, a tiny part of me has known, I was meant to stand in front of a group of children. I love my job, my fast students, my bright swimmers. Love watching someone figure something out and then use it, watch the idea go from me to them and see how it belongs to them afterward. Not mine at all. And afterward, you can only wonder at how it happens. It doesn't happen all the time. But when it does, it feels like this is what magic wants to be, when it grows up.

I bring flowers to Freddy, cut them down and set them in a water glass by his bed. I straighten the edge of his sheet, check his vital signs. He never makes a noise while I'm there. I understand he sometimes sings. I don't know what I'd do, if he started singing.

Afterward, I go out to Two Lights. A small state park out in Cape Elizabeth, on the water, it boasts a lighthouse and an abandoned six-story gun tower, left over from World War II. The park was never really closed when we were younger, which is to say, it was easy to break into, and we used to go out there to drink sometimes or smoke pot. The police were ordinarily an amiable bunch about it, having grown up in the area and come here to do the same things when they were our age. It was called Two Lights because Cape Elizabeth had two lighthouses, one on each side of the cape.

Here the lighthouse sits, new luxury homes around on its hillside, and down by the water, on a bedrock point, the Lobster

Shack, where you can get fried seafood and steamed lobsters. At night, you can sit out on the rocks, and the lighthouse here as it sends its beam out into the night becomes a pinwheel of light, the beams reaching out across the dark water and fading as they head for the horizon. Where, as soon as the light seems to thin and vanish, it appears again, thickens and turns, into a distant pinwheel.

As I sit on the rocks and the light swings out over my head, it seems to me there is another, far, lighthouse, its arms of light reaching back to this one, though I know there isn't, the two of them reaching for each other and never quite touching as they match each other in these huge sweeps of the sky's night arch. It's a trick in the sky. The light bends, somewhere out over the bay. I come here after my visits with Freddy. Here in the dark, what I see: the light, the distance, the night. And what it shows me: that even light bends. That even light is made to carry weight. And if there is a God, and he does attend to all things, if he is with even this beam of light as it heads out across the Atlantic into the night to warn distant sailors of danger, then the place he touches it is where it bends, where it disappears for a while, because that is where it needs help.

Do you want to see something, I say to Bridey, one day when he has made the trip with me, after we leave Freddy. In the blank white of the hospital corridors, anything seems possible.

What, he says.

It'll be a surprise, I say.

I drive back out to Cape Elizabeth. I haven't been in years. Over a decade. I don't know what to expect. There at the top of the hill is the door, still strangely new. I swing it open. Benign neglect, we call it in Maine. No money to change anything, so everything stays the way you left it.

As we are getting out of the car, Bridey turns to me and says, about Freddy's apartment, Why blue?

Because it's the color everyone turns in the dark, I say. I push through the broken greenhouse and he follows, slowly.

A nice view, he says. He takes in the marsh. He thinks he knows what this is.

Oh no.

Down in the center of the tunnels, I don't understand them anymore. Or, rather, I do. But all of it feels small. There's the clay cold of it, there's the unbelievable earth smell. He turns to face me after taking it all in. You built this, he says.

I nod.

I decide I should fill it in. I tell him that. It's not right, I say. What I felt, about wanting to die, that's not right. Look at Freddy. He wants to live.

You're guessing about that one, Bridey says. But you are right, you shouldn't want it, shouldn't want to die. But you can't fill this in.

Upstairs, in the car, Bridey lights one of his occasional cigarettes. And that's when he says, Build something else.

What do you mean?

He slumps across the seat, his head falling into my lap. I see his beautiful eyes. Want to be in them, jealous of my reflection, for being there. Build something else, he says. At the school, maybe. Make it a project.

Along the edge of the field here is a wall from the Revolutionary War. Unmortared stones. I see it as he's talking. It stays in my head, the image of it, for months, before I get curious about it. My thoughts return to it like a tongue to teeth. Build something else.

And so one day, Bridey comes to meet me for lunch at the campus. You know, he says. I went to prep.

I know, I say.

It's weird, he says. There's no chapel here.

Blue. Blue because it's the color people turn in the dark. Because it's the color of the sky, of the center of the flame, of a diamond hit by an X ray. Blue is the knife edge of lightning. Blue is the color, a rose grower tells you, that a rose never quite reaches.

Because when you feel threatened by a demon you are supposed to imagine around you a circle of blue light. You do this because the demon cannot cross the blue light.

Freddy dies on an afternoon after my regular visit. A few weeks before, I had gone with his mother to his old apartment. Together Bridey and I had moved all the furniture to the middles of the rooms and replastered the whole apartment white. When I hear from her that he is dead, I remember sitting in the middle of the apartment and feeling something huge and invisible swing through the colorless room. White is a death color, I thought then. It is the absence of all color.

Fee, she says. Thank you for being there for him at the end. I know he knew. I just know it.

How, I think afterward, sitting on my roof. How can I set this world on fire. How can I get the whole thing to burn.

Back in San Francisco, I remember how a friend of mine once went out and broke every window he could find when his boyfriend died. He walked street to street through the empty shopping district and left behind blocks of broken glass. He wasn't caught. And the next day the papers couldn't explain it. And it never happened again.

Bridey gets home and sees me up there as he pulls the car in. He stands in the driveway. Hey.

Hey.

I'll start dinner, he says.

Okay.

8

THE PLANNING OF the chapel takes a few months. The building of the chapel takes a week. My students are enthusiastic, as is the faculty. I seem to be moving to some sort of permanent position here. I wonder about Penny, how she'll feel about it, if they don't want her back. I have no sense of her carrying our child. I think of it as hers. Entirely. Every now and then she cracks a smile, pats her tummy and says, Hey, Daddy. But I don't know what to make of it.

I know how to make the chapel, though: I base the constuction on designs I see of Roman bridges and also of things made in South America, by the Incas. I find a man from Vermont who specializes in this particular method of construction through an article about him in a garden magazine, and now, the chapel sits in the corner of the school grounds, overlooking the water and the beach.

During the construction I would be doing whatever I was doing, and then Warden's hair would fire in the spring sun. I was reminded of how hunters aim for the white tail of a deer. His girl-friend, Alyssa, worked beside him. They're good kids, I told myself. You are their good teacher.

I sit in the chapel now in the middle of a cold night. With me I have the picture of Peter, and his letter. I don't want them any-more.

I light a candle, like I used to do in the cave. The chapel is warm somehow inside. We built it better than we thought, I tell myself. I read the letter a last time. There's the stuff about how much he tried to die before. And then there's this, which I had forgotten about.

You ought to know, you were my best friend. You were. I know you loved me. I loved you.

No one should have gone through what we went through, but we did. And it kills me to think of it.

But I didn't love you like you loved me. I don't hate you for that. It just makes me sorry, that there isn't someone else who could love you better.

I know when you think about how I went, you'll get it. I was always uneasy about being alive. The idea of being dead makes me feel clear. When I think of it. It makes me think peace, peace, peace. It makes me happy. I am looking forward to it, to the absence of everything. And so I want you to be happy for me, that this is better for me. That I found what I needed. I know you won't be. But it's the last thing I want. You happy.

I burn the letter in the candle and stick the photo in between some stones. I rub the ashes to spread them. Good-bye to all that,

I tell myself as I walk to my car. When I get home, Bridey says, Fee. What the hell is on your face?

In the mirror my face is gray from the ash, like I'd been doing a raku fire. And where the tears ran through there are branches. I go to the bathroom and the ash turns the water blue like smoke.

Bridey comes in to check on me. I grab him and pick him up in my arms, taking him to the bed. Our bed. Holy shit, he says. Call me princess.

Take me apart. Put me back together again. I take him all night, as much as we can stand and then a little more. And it does feel like taking. As if I am sending something of myself through him again each time that enters him and comes out through his throat, where I catch it back into myself, in a kiss. To send it through him again. I land on him afterward when finally we lie still.

I love you, Bridey says.

Blue light of the night around us. Blue light has half the wavelength of red, it rushes to get there. Blue us, violet, blue where the light comes off us, violet where it doesn't reach. I take his blue hair in my blue hand, open him with my blue tongue, blue again.

9

CHRONOTOPE: AN INTERSECTION of time and place. Here is time, here are the places of your life, a connect-the-dots; here are the people, made from time into radiant, concatenated glowworms, all the forms they've been from first glance to good-byes run together in a sine–cosine curve of color-lights, as if they had walked through a camera frame with the shutter stuck open, one age at the beginning, another at the end. You decide, I want to remember this or that, and so the part of you that faces the future is now like a dragon flying over the sea, moves in on a flash of color here or there that looks familiar, bites down and spits the bite to its glance, which catches fire. Here is the flaming pearl, famous from every Chinese calendar. Imaginary appendages attaching it to past and future-past fly to the pearl's side. Imaginary eyes to see past conditional, the "if this then that," blink open. An angel, it seems, but, really, what you make is a golem out of your own life, and then you ask it a question, you say, Speak to me. Tell me what I did. How did I get here?

Like lightning, there is light suddenly everywhere, the light of your life speaking to you. What it tells you is almost the same as what happened. Never mind that almost isn't good enough; it's all you have.

Warden had come to your house, butterfly net in hand, dressed in shorts and a rain slicker. He looks young this day (some days he looks old). He smiles as he comes down the long hill of the back field. You live here, he asks. You say yes.

Invite him in for coffee. Watch through the window behind him where he sits in your kitchen as the sun runs down the sky in spills from holes in the rain clouds, watch the fields go dark then light, watch grass and wild lupine rise in cones of blue to twirl there in the April air. Listen to him run the water in the sink to wash his hands. You ask him if he will sit for a sketch. You haven't sketched in years. You bring out your book, grab the easel from where it has sat since you moved in. Like this, he asks.

Yes, you say. In that coat. It's your intention somewhere in what you call a head that you are sketching the outdoors by sketching him this way, as if he were a piece with the field and sky and storm outside. You remember something a drawing teacher told you about drawing with two hands and you take a pencil in each hand and you draw.

Why are you using both hands, he asks.

Because otherwise you draw only the same line, you say. Drawing this way destroys the line. You are free. He smiles at this and you draw the smile, as close to it as you can, which it turns out is pretty close.

Lovely, he says, when you show him later.

What were you thinking of, you ask.

He says, I was thinking of you telling me I was free.

This is when Bridey opens the door. Oh hello, Edward, he says. To you he says, I see you met the butterfly catcher.

You look at Warden. He is looking strange, smiling again. I'm sorry, he says. I'll go now.

Warden, you say. Edward?

Arden is my middle name, he says. My grandparents gave it to me. I didn't like Edwards, so I didn't really want to be one. But it is my given name, and when I meet a stranger, that's the name I give.

He leaves shortly thereafter. He heads out the way he came, up the hill, a cloud tuft barely visible there, sunlit, like a white shout from the top. He heads for it, the net a pennant. Bridey leans against you. What the hell is that about, he says. Stalker?

There is a part of you, you see now, that is reckless. A part of you that still always wants to die but never wants to really go after it. So it makes mistakes instead. Or it says, when trouble comes in and has lemonade, I wonder what this will look like. If I sit still. If I do nothing. So you say, Oh, I don't think so. I think there's nothing more to it than that he's a very strange boy. Father's in prison, apparently. The school has basically raised him.

Bridey is now looking over the drawing you did of Warden. I love it, he says. I'll have it framed. Sign it. And you do. As you do you realize how clever Bridey is, how much of you he can take. You forget, you realize, all the trouble he was up to before he met you, before he decided you were all the trouble he wanted. He knows how to handle himself, you think. Which is why you are sure of him. You, apparently, are the one you have to worry about. That day, as your pencil inscribes your tiny name at the drawing's foot, you know what is ahead, he knows, Warden knows. The drawing was like an invitation you wrote.

The next time Warden is at the house it is the party.

That summer, Bridey had taken you down to see friends in Ogunquit, and one of them has admitted to being a gay Episcopalian priest. As the five of you sit on the patio having cocktails, you say, Does that mean, you could marry us?

Jesus, Bridey says. Have another cocktail. And he gets up and goes inside.

That's romantic, Bridey, your friend John Mark yells to his back.

Getting another cocktail is very, very romantic, Bridey yells back.

Yes, the priest says. Well, I could . . . I can't give you an Episcopalian wedding. But I have done commitment ceremonies.

Bridey returns. And deliver us from Evil. Oh, hi. And he sits down, stirring a new cosmopolitan.

You jump down on your knees. Bridey, you say.

Don't make me waste this drink on your head, he says.

Bridey, you say. Please. Marry me.

John Mark coughs, behind you.

Get the hell up, Bridey says. I've been married before. You want to be my official husband? Where's my ring?

John Mark pulls, from his hand, one of the several rings he has there. This one is a knuckle guard crossed by a pirate skull and crossbones. Use this for now, he says, and hands it to you.

He stands above you. You can't read his expression. His eyes meet yours. For that moment you imagine you can enter and walk down them like halls.

For the ceremony you all stand on the beach at midnight, each of you with a black-eyed Susan in your hair, each holding sea roses you found on your way to the beach. The flowers were Bridey's idea. The gay priest is nervous, a little drunk, but seems possessed by the occasion now, as if you couldn't stop him from marrying you even if you wanted to. And the sea's night is a cold kelp embrace of the invisible, this wedding a way to keep death at bay, surely now, death will leave you alone for the long moment this takes. The cold feels like bravery tonight. Here on the beach, you and Bridey, John Mark by your side, his friend Justin by Bridey, and the gay priest, Darren, in the center. There are no accidents, he begins. We find each other because we need each other. We find each other because Love is the Lord's command. The one thing God asks of us in our lives, besides loving Him. Bridey and Fee are here because they have followed the

Lord's command to love each other and in doing so to find the Lord, and we are here to witness their love.

You hadn't expected him to talk about God, but what did you expect? He is a priest. He takes your hand, takes Bridey's hand, puts them together. Let what the Lord join, no man put asunder. Do you, Bridey, take Fee, as your husband, before God?

I do, he says.

And do you, Fee, take Bridey, as your husband, before God?

I do, you say. And then you kiss him. Done.

And so the party. Bridey had strung the tent with his paper rose streamers, which had taken him weeks to make, and you were reminded that day of how for the weddings of Korean royalty, flower garlands were made and hung on the palace. The white tent caught all of the light that day and glowed, the paper roses flashed as they shot up and down in the wind, and you had forgotten, that morning, how you had asked Warden to come by early. Forgotten until he was there, with you in the tent, waiting for you to notice him.

Hi, he says, when you look up. He'd had his hair cut so it shot up at odd angles across his head, mussed and held there by gel. His shirt reads BETHUNE SWIMMING. Brand-new jeans across his tiny hips, covering his long legs. Speedo slides on his long feet. He is tan, and beautiful with a tan in the way you can only be if you are blond and seventeen and it is summer in Maine. A way you remember, from growing up.

Let no man put asunder. No mention of a boy. Put your hand here, you tell him, and nod at the corner of the tablecloth you are trying to box-fold around the folding table. I don't feel this, you tell yourself. This isn't me feeling this.

10

DESTROYING THE LINE.

In the legend of Narcissus, it wasn't that he was in love with his reflection, entirely. His reflection, as his love object, had the ability to move him. Who of us can move ourselves? His love is a legend for it.

Peter is there just past the red of my closed eyelid. Peter at the center of the light that spreads the red, hidden in the center of the flame. Burning hides what it burns there. The letter like a torch. Peter was never mine, I see now, because I was his. I belonged to him as certainly as the dog that always sought out the palm of his hand.

Big Eric searched us like a pannier looking the creek bed over, searched every flash of gold for the sight of a lost love. Burning hides what it burns there. Somewhere deep in him was a memory of light that pierced him from end to end like a spit. He couldn't see that he was large and we were not. His body to him felt out-sized, a bear costume borrowed for a party, and then it vanished. In the moment he touched us, he was a boy again. And in the moment he touched us we were run through also. The pain reached out, passed, like fire does, from the burned to the burning. Burning hides what burns.

11

THE SHADOWS OF the trees this night are like stains someone couldn't quite clean up and the branches hold themselves up like they've just stopped screaming. I'm playing hide and go seek, I tell myself.

In the distance, a lit window, gold in the blue night. The bitter smell after rain, under the trees, like used tea bags left out. I approach the house with the lit window. What do I expect? I thought it was Bridey who'd left the note. A Christmas surprise. I ring the doorbell, a metallic ping, and wait for a response. There is none, and then I hear someone behind me. I turn.

Warden. His breath a blue apostrophe in the cold air. He smiles. Hey, he says. He pulls a key from his pocket and opens the door. This way, he says.

What are you doing here, I ask in the doorway. He stands there for a moment holding the turned knob of the door.

He turns to face me. Anger in his face? Bewilderment. I remember the day I caught him as he fell, fainting. His body surprisingly light. I was reminded of my biology, the lesson about the hollow bones of birds. His face, just then, much like it is now. We enter the house together.

Whose house is this? I ask, as we climb the stairs.

The Whites. I'm looking after it for them.

A picture of the twins on the wall at the top of the stairs confirms this. Cherubs.

In their bedroom, he falls across the enormous bed, facedown. Are you all right, I ask.

You should go home, he says.

I should, I say. But you have something to tell me. I realize then, until I saw him on the bed I'd no intentions. Really. He was a child to me, he didn't exist. But his confusion was making him more than a child, as if that was what an adult was. And now he is sitting up to face me. He hands me the photograph. His bravery oscillates wildly. How did you get the picture, I say. I know what it is immediately.

How did you, he says.

A long time ago, I say, deciding to tell the truth, I was in love. I was in love with someone, and I knew he'd never love me, so I took the picture. Instead of trying to tell him how it was I loved him.

Me too, he says.

The silence between us eats me. I can't go away again, can I? I can't. His lips taste like wet grass, cold at first. That was the first kiss. I sit there and he moves about me as if I am a statue. As if I were something he's made. I will be, soon: his kiss, this silence, they make me into someone else. Someone I don't know. All of the ways I have of judging remove themselves from me like offended friends.

He tastes clean. Or empty.

What happens next goes by like a blow.

I get up, pull his clothes off. His eyes are wide, like something is trying to fit into them that can't. I put my hands on him and it seems like as my mouth moves across the hollows of his neck, as I put my tongue across his open mouth, as I hear him choke and go quiet, and I am dizzy, as if the world is spinning faster with each thing we do, faster and faster, so that by the time I leave, by the time my foot spreads to set itself down on the ground outside, this world should be spinning so fast no one could stand on it. No one could stand it.

12

TELL ME WHAT I did. If this then that.

Warden, even in front of me, still a memory of green eyes on fire, of gold melting, a memory not of fire but of what the fire burned. A boy who reminded you of something that constantly eluded you. Do you remember the way you caught Warden that day. See the gold flesh, so familiar from a hundred practices, the gold hair, flax but not tow, the gold that was everywhere on him, the one who burned first, the one you chased as far even as this. Remember the times you walked with him in sunlight and caught yourself looking at the way the sun caught on the gold hairs of his body, the tiny hairs shorter than eyelashes. Remember that you knew from first introductions how it was with him, how he wanted you. You.

Walk the stairs to the back of Warden's dorm. What had eluded you for so long was there literally on the tip of you, gold on you everywhere as if he could gild you. Him on you as if he could turn into light and cover and color you completely, so that he was a million times a million particles of altered color tossed into someone else's eye to show you, to take you out of the awful realm of being alone, in your body, to the realm of a shared thing, something seen. This journey that has always defeated you.

For a few short weeks, it goes like this. You at the dorm. On the roof at night. He is cold as the wind every time it starts, warm like a tear when you are done. Every time you feel less, every time you are more of a stone thing. And you go back every time hoping to feel again.

13

WARDEN SLEEPS ON the front seat. I put a blanket over him. He's a student of yours, my mother had asked, as he went into the bathroom, when we were at her house earlier this evening.

Yes, I'd said.

How do I feel, I ask myself now, in the car.

You feel great, he says, appearing suddenly by the window, a wind with green eyes made this time from dark leaves. *Yowu*. You feel like you know what you have to do. I nod at him, and he is gone again. Warden struggles with a dream, does not wake up. I lean my face against the car door and it warms slowly under my cheek.

Metal is like love, it takes its temperature from touch. How did we get here?

This way.

Open me, the day says to me that morning. Go ahead. Sunlight on the lawn, the gold stitches of the needle of light coming through our trees. I go outside with my coffee and dew steams off on my bare feet, until they are cold, and then I return to the house. The phone rings and I glance down to my caller ID, and I see the name, in block letters, flash there under the number: GORENDT, ERIC, and I freeze, watching it flash, letting it go to the machine, and then go, as the caller hangs up.

What happens next, is the phone rings again, and I pick it up, even as the name flashes back across the screen.

Hello, Warden says, even as I know who it is. Even as I know now who he really is. Fee.

Yes, I say.

He's crying then, and then he coughs and clears his throat, and he says, I need you to come here.

I can't, I say.

No, I really, really need you to come here. I'm not going to make it. I may not make it even if you come, but please.

And inside the cold space in me, still cold like my feet, I hear myself say, Not one more. Not even one more. And I say, Okay. I am coming. Where are you. As I say it, knowing and yet, really not knowing, where that man lived in this world.

I thought he had killed a woman, at first.

His legs stick out from behind a chair, like the way it is in monster movies. I know it isn't him anymore, that he's not there in the body, but I say his name. Eric, I say. I see the pale legs, rounded calves, the pale, pale feet. And I turn to see Warden come toward me. His pale face. Angel, I say. Why. I say it and the word fills up with my fear.

And he comes toward me, wraps his arms around me. Fee, he says. And then he lets go.

Love's not Time's fool, Shakespeare writes. No, Love's not. He's still right. Love buys time like we used to buy ice, cold pieces of it brought home to keep what's loved preserved from every day's heat. In a box in the basement are the pictures. Here, he says to me, hands me a sheaf of pictures, programs, clippings. Here, you're right there. Aphias Zhe. First soprano.

Ways to kill a fox-demon:
Burning. Trap it in a house. Set the house on fire.

He knows who you are now, and then you know now, too: he was Baby Eddie, the big-headed baby who peed down his mother's leg, the boy who bounced like a toy strung on a sun-beam, standing there with these pictures of you, transmissions from oh-so-far away, of Little Eric and you side by side in a sleep-ing bag, your hands slanting over your eyes as you hold your hands out to stop, as if you could stop, the light from landing on the film to color the negative, to make the space that burns the sil-ver into place on the contact sheet, that makes the photograph. I did this for you, he tells you. After he does it. This is what you don't see: he has all the pictures, he is burning all the pictures, he is scattering fire, and then the house is burning, and he leaves, and you leave, and there is nothing and everything between you and him. There is a way he was meant to be with you more than

Bridey, except that what you had for each other you have given each other and if there is more for you and Bridey it has nothing to do with what is meant by gods but what is chosen, in the most mortal way. Which one wins? The Fates rocked my cradle, Oscar Wilde once said, and you remember this saying right then, thinking that perhaps that is what this wild swinging of the earth is.

We decide that he has to go to the police and confess. I wait in the car for him. When Warden comes out finally, he's smiling.

What, I say.

Nothing, he says. Just happy to see you.

We drive in silence, or rather, you do. You drive him. You don't know what's going through his head and you don't ask. His happiness seems unlikely to the far extreme, it seems a product of insanity, but it's really, you find out, for some other reason altogether, when, as you near the exit sign for the highway, he looks at you and says, Take it.

What, you ask.

Take the exit. The house is burning now.

What?

Fee, he says. We have to go somewhere else now. I couldn't go to the police. And he curls up in the seat. He rolls the window down and produces a cigarette from his pockets, which he lights with the lighter. Smoke from his mouth. I set the fire, he says, and it's as if the fire is inside him. The house burning but the smoke coming out of him instead.

Jesus, you say, and you really are calling for him when you say it. For you see, Warden's happiness is from him thinking that he has you now.

And so in the car as you drive you realize that Eric is dead, and to the sky in front of your eyes, receding as you approach it, you address yourself to him, you say, I knew it from the beginning, always something you wanted, always, that there was something in you you wanted to have seen: that you were like us somehow, that inside the heavy body of you was something small and heavy, fear tidied up in muscle and skin. I wanted you dead and now you are dead and now I run from what I know, now I see what you always wanted us to see, the part of you that was just like us burns free now somewhere behind me. Zeus is you is the sky is dead. Ganymede getaway car. Escapes nothing.

You want to tell this boy next to you, how his father isn't dead. Not the part he wanted to kill. Not as long as you are there. He's hiding inside us now, you want to say, but you drive him away from the fire instead.

14

I GO TO my parents' house. I let Warden and myself in the back door, leave a note to my mother that I am napping on the sun-porch, and then do so, lie down on the beat-up couch under a sunbeam as thick and warm as a blanket and there in the bird-chirped quiet of the afternoon abandon myself. Warden sleeps on the floor below me.

I wake sometime after the sun had started setting. The sky deep blue above me leaves me nothing but a cold night's rest, waiting for me to resume it. For a moment I forget everything of why I am there. My mother, in the doorway, watches me as I raise my head. I was expecting you, she said.

I screwed up big, Mom, I said. She smiles.

Bridey called here, she says. We spoke. He'll be all right, I think. He said you'd had a fight, but he didn't say what and I don't want to know unless you want to tell me. He certainly didn't.

I laugh. It's not a fight. Not exactly.

Your father won't be home tonight, by the way, she says. He's got a conference down in Boston so he stayed in Portsmouth. Did you and your student want something to eat?

He spoke to you, I say.

You know he's my outlet buddy. He's my boy. Oh Fee. Come have some coffee.

In the kitchen, I drink her coffee. Warden walks around the yard, smoking, and I watch him through the windows. Did he tell you where he'd gone to, I ask.

He went to New York, she says.

Who's he staying with?

I think he's staying with John Mark, she says. It looked like his number when I wrote it down.

Did he mention anything else?

Fee, why don't you call him yourself.

I dial the number. It was indeed John Mark's, my friend, whom Bridey had gotten along with better than I had. John Mark, I think, had loved me in secret for some time, and then scorned me underneath that love, and so when Bridey arrived, he could welcome him. They'd become friends quickly. Bridey picks up the phone. Caller ID, he says. Hello Mister. Or is it Mom?

How's John Mark, I say.

He's okay. He's been busy. He put a bid in on an apartment, and so we're sitting here planning the garden.

What does he want, I ask.

What everyone wants. Low-maintenance greens, regular appearances by flowers. This isn't what I want to talk about, though, he says, and I hear the scrape of something closing. It isn't even what you've called about, unless I really don't know you.

I need help, I say.

You're crazy. I used to think it was charming but now it's just dangerous. You call it love but it's just humoring you, that I do.

There's something you need to know, I say. I can't say it over the phone.

I need to know, he says. You know what I need to know?

What, I say, afraid.

I need to know, he says. I need to know what that was.

Come here to believe me. Come back.

That day, he says. When I met you. I thought you were beyond belief. My diaries are full of entries about you, before I knew you. Me guessing this or that, talking about the things I'd heard about you. I loved you even then. But now it feels like I was set up.

I watch the insides of my mother's house. All of this furniture, all of these boxes. All of this life. No, Bridey. You never said this, I say. But, more importantly. You were set up, just not by me.

He's a boy, Fee, he says. He's a child, even if he's a beautiful child, or a mature child. He's a child. I look at him and I wonder what he'll look like when he grows up. I want you to think about that, he says. I'll call you tomorrow. And then he hangs up. I look up to see Warden in the door, looking at me.

16

FROM THE OBITUARY page the following day:

> Eric Gorendt, of Lincoln Falls, died sometime early in the morning the night before, at the age of 52. He had recently been released on parole, electronically monitored, to finish serving a sentence of twenty years in prison for sexually molesting twelve boys in his charge as their choir master for the popular singing group the Pine State Boys Chorus. An accomplished director at an early age, he is survived by his parents and a son, Edward. The cause of death was listed as burning.

In the dark morning, still roofed in blue and stars, Warden nibbles a doughnut, wanders the doughnut shop. We've gone out to get the paper and I am thinking now of how we should leave. Never come back. I shuffle the paper shut and look around. No one else here, except the counterperson.

You think no one is going to suspect us, I say.
No, he says. I think no one is going to find us.

17

I LEAVE HIM in a hotel room near the turnpike that night.

I check in, and he sneaks in once I've got the room open, so the clerk doesn't see. He's exhausted and so am I, and he falls back across the bed, arms over his head, in surrender, falling asleep almost at once. I look at him in the cheap yellow light of the room and take in the smell, of old smoke from the thousand cigarettes that must have gone out here. It's not us, I want to say. I want to wake him and tell him, that we need to escape this, that what he's done has trapped us and not freed us, but the planes of his sleeping face rebuke me, which is when I see myself in the mirror above the bed: tired, lonely, him stretched out below me, looking for all the world like I've knocked him out or worse.

You did this, I tell myself. Not him.

I don't want to be the one to turn him in to the police. I want him to do that or not. I want him to have the choice, to say he did it or not, but I want him to choose what happens next even as I do, as I walk toward the door and, leaving the key inside on the carpet, close it. From a pay phone I call the hospital and say I need an ambulance for room 322, that my friend has closed the door and won't answer and I think it's an emergency.

He's unconscious, the operator asks.

He won't wake when I call him, I say. I am lying only a little. What he needs to hear he'll never hear if I say it.

I roll the car down the drive to turn the engine over in the street. Drive off without headlights for the first two minutes, and then, when the headlights pick the night's hem up off the road, I head for Cape Elizabeth, for Fort Williams. There are empty houses over there, perfect to hide for a little while. A night.

I park the car at the edge of the beach and I begin walking out on the sand. I stopped it, I tell myself, not sure where I am walking. I stopped it. He didn't die. It is low tide. Dawn will be up soon and here on the beach there are scattered pools of water, shallow as a plate. The three streetlights along the beach's edge fret me a shadow three ways around me, so that I look like a walking crowd when I look down. Walking, I see the reflections of stars in the pools, my shadows across them. And I stop at the sight of one shadow that takes a pool of night for a face, two stars where the eyes should be.

Hello, he says.

I say nothing. I want him gone, even as I know, my standing here is the only way he can speak to me.

You know who I am now, don't you, he says.

I do, I say. The two shadows to the side of this one seem suddenly shadow wings, ready to take him away and take me with him. The night turns over us like a stile.

You know who I am now too, I say. So stay.

I wake up the next morning in the charred room of a ruined mansion that burned partly to the ground here in Fort Williams Park some time ago. No one rebuilt it. Supposedly the house is haunted, or cursed. The other houses in the historic neighborhood park, kept empty of residents to preserve them, were locked against me when I tried them, the good people of the town thinking no doubt of someone like me.

There's a blanket over me that I didn't put there. I get up, checking it, and then go to the window.

Bridey sits on the hood of my car, looking off to the sea. He blows on a cup of coffee, squinting. There's a car beside him I don't recognize, looking suspiciously like a rental.

Why did Lady Tammamo take her life instead of living forever? Love ruins monsters. She didn't need the spell of a thousand livers to become human. She just had to love one man. Feel the change come over her: the fur recedes across her brow, the fangs flatten to a smile. The paws turn to feet and say good-bye to flight. The danger of her hides itself in shame. I wrap myself in the blanket and walk down, and then I run down the stairs set in the hill, stopping only when I am in front of him. He doesn't move, just looks at me. It's not the time just yet for questions, not just yet.

Hi, Bridey says.

Hi, I say. Hi.

Acknowledgments

FOR THEIR EXCELLENT readings that helped me to shape this novel, thank you to Sarah Sheffield, Shauna Seliy, Patrick Merla, Kirsten Bakis, Emily Barton, Patrick Nolan, Karl Soehnlein, Julie Regan, Sandell Morse, Betty Rogers, Caleb Crain, my brother, Christopher, my sister, Stephanie, and my brother-in-law, Adam Barea. For her unalloyed support for this novel and for her advice, thank you to Hanya Yanagihara. Thank you to Quang Bao, for his support for the novel and his efforts on my behalf. For their beautiful example in persistence, thank you to my mother, Jane Chee, and to my departed father, Choung Tai Chee. For their assistance, without which this book could not have appeared, thank you to Frank Conroy and Connie Brothers, to the Iowa Writers' Workshop and the Michener/Copernicus Society, the Virginia Center for the Creative Arts, the Asian American Writers' Workshop, and to Donna Brodie and the Writers' Room of New York City. Special thanks to my aunt and uncle, Priscilla and Brian St. Louis, for the use of their barn, and to Katie Mac-Nichol, for her long friendship to me and to this effort. Thank you to my teachers, especially Kit Reed, Annie Dillard, Beatrix Gates, Mary Robison, James Alan McPherson, Marilynne Robinson, Elizabeth Benedict, Denis Johnson, and Deborah Eisenberg. Thank you to Elaine Kim, Tricia Juhn, Mina Park, and all the members of the dinner workshop. Thank you to Rebecca Kurson of Liza Dawson Associates, my agent, and to Chuck Kim, my editor, for having the vision to publish this book. Thanks also to

John Weber, Karyn Slutsky, Michele Rubin, Caroline Dennehy, Fritz Metsch, Christian Dierig, and Laura Jorstad, for their excellent work on the novel's behalf. And for my website, thank you to D.J. Paris.

This novel is a work of fiction, invented and imagined. A resemblance of the characters to people living or dead, and to situations from history, if it happens, will be largely a function of a synchronicity between the imagination of the writer and the life of the reader. I would acknowledge there is a boy I did not know, who did set himself on fire in my hometown when I was too young to remember fully, and the faint memory of which haunted me until I wrote this. His story is inviolate, and not here.